Snowbound
Fairy
Christmas

Moonstone Magic Series

Book 1

Brenda Hunt

Text copyrighted 2015 by Brenda Hunt

Cover Design by Fionajademedia.com

ISBN:099094591X

ISBN13:9780990945918

Library of Congress Control Number:

Brenda Hunt, Houma, LA

Dedication

My grand daughter

Alexis Kiley

Who insisted one afternoon, during Christmas vacation,

we needed to take a nap.

It was awakening from this nap, this story and these
characters

came to me.

I am not sure whether it was a dream or

just a thought that popped into my head and grew.

I often wonder, if Alexis had not insisted we nap

would this story have ever come to life.

Thank you, Alexis.

Snowbound Fairy Christmas

Acknowledgments:

To my YA YA sisters, Barbara Barker and Ruth Babin for their support and willingness to read and edit and critique for me. We have known each other since grade school/junior high. You are the best.

To Barbara Ortego Arcement and Joyce Graham my two other friends who read, edit and critique for me. Thank you for your input and undying support. It means the world to me.

To my family, my daughters and their families, my son and his family. You have taught me what family is all about. I always wanted a big family. Thank you for giving it to me. I love each and every one of you.

Last but not least to my husband who has encouraged me every step of the way on this new journey I have undertaken. Just your sitting in your recliner next to me while I write has been the greatest support I could ever have. You listen as I bounce ideas off of you. You read and critique. You answer my history questions. You taught me how to love again through good times, bad times, in between times. Love you!

Just a note for those who don't believe in ESP, clairvoyance, precognition and the like, there is a saying:

Faith consists in believing

It is the power of reason to believe.

To one who has faith

No explanation is necessary

To one without faith,

No explanation is possible.

Voltaire

I have faith and believe in these things for I have experienced them time and time again, where no explanation is possible except to believe.

Snowbound Fairy Christmas

Chapter 1

Deep within the winter forest
Among the snowdrift wide
You can find a magic place
Where all the fairies hide….

Author Unknown

Quietly, one small foot followed the next and approached the small stand of trees that stood like silent sentinels in this world of white. The snow had been slowly falling since just before noon but from the looks of the gray clouds in the sky above, it was just a prelude of what was to come. Dulcey glanced up knowing it was only going to get worse and get worse soon. She was glad she had gathered her holly boughs, ivy and mistletoe earlier to decorate her small cottage for Christmas. Now, she was concentrating on getting food for the table. She already had two partridges in her bag. She wanted another one, for if she was right about the weather, she would not be able to hunt again for days.

As it was, she was afraid her hunting days would soon be limited, if not done away with all together. Who knew who the new Baron might be or when he would be taking up residence? Would he allow her to hunt as Lord James had? If Lord James could have had his way, she would have moved into the manor house when Grammy Digby died. They had argued time and time again. In the end, he had allowed her to have her way and stay on at the cottage. But now that Lord James had died, things would more than likely change. Dulcey hated change. Oh, how she missed Grammy and now Lord James. They had been her rock in the strange world she lived in. If the new Baron did not let her hunt, she had no idea how she would survive.

Slowly, quietly, she approached the small thicket, hopefully hiding at least one partridge. Her bow was drawn as she carefully surveyed the fields, listening, watching, becoming one with the world around her. Out the corner of her eye, she saw a slight movement. She turned and let her arrow fly. Quickly, she followed her arrow. Her arrow was true, not the she had any doubt. The partridge lay dead. A small amount of crimson blood stained the white snow. She pulled her arrow out and cleaned it in the snow before placing it back in her quiver. She took the partridge in both her hands and raised it slightly.

"Thank you, Mother Earth for your most generous offering. Your humble servant is most appreciative." Dulcey gave thanks as her grandmother had taught her. Gently, she placed the dead partridge in her bag at her waist along with the other two from earlier. She would have food for the next few days. Maybe, the snowstorm would not be as bad as she believed.

She turned, every intent of hurrying home, for the sky appeared to be growing heavier by the minute. Soon, it would be snowing hard. She stopped. She heard something, a whimper. Dulcey shook her head. No, it was just the wind in the tress. Often, the wind made sounds that were strange and human like. She shook her head to dispel her thoughts but the feeling that something was amiss with the world around her only got stronger. She paused, listening, before she made another step. The sound came again, only louder. No, this was human.

Dulcey moved cautiously in direction of the sound. It was just over there by that small stand of trees. There was a large bolder at the base of one of the trees. The sound came again, only this time louder as she got closer.

Dulcey peered around the boulder. A small child sat huddled on the ground, softly whimpering.

"Hello there," said Dulcey softly, not wanting to frighten the poor child.

Beautiful big blue eyes, glistening with huge tears, stared back at her. Her small mouth quivered. Dulcey's heart went out to the child. "Have you lost your way, little one?"

The small head of dark blonde curls covered by a soft blue velvet bonnet that matched her eyes nodded. "I was chasing the bunny and then I was lost and I couldn't find the bunny and I couldn't find Uncle Nate." She explained between soft sobs.

"You must be very scared, but don't worry, I have found you," comforted Dulcey as she knelt down beside the little girl. Dulcey wasn't sure where this child had come from but she had no time to look. The snow was about to start coming down heavily. It was imperative they get into shelter soon. "How about I take you home with me until the snow stops and then we can find your Uncle Nate?"

The little girl nodded, still taking sobbing breaths.

"My name is Dulcey. What is yours, little one?" asked Dulcey. Maybe, it would give her a better idea of who she was. She knew just about everyone in the country side here but this child was new to the area. The most important thing, at the moment, was to get them back to the cottage before the storm hit. They would have to hurry.

"Abigail Beckham. Uncle Nate calls me Abby."

Dulcey nodded. "Pleasure to meet you, Abigail. We need to hurry Abby. Can you walk?"

Abigail nodded. Dulcey helped her up. With her small hand in hers, Dulcey hurried her through the field. All Dulcey could think about was getting to the cottage as soon as possible. Already, the wind had picked up and the snow was falling heavily. Soon, it would be hard to see out in front of ones face. It was slow going with Abigail in tow. Dulcey stopped and stooped to Abigail's level.

"Sweetie, I need you to climb on my back and let me carry you." She needed to make better time.

Abigail nodded. With Dulcey's help, she climbed on Dulcey's back and wrapped her little arms around Dulcey's neck and held on.

Once Abigail was secure, Dulcey began a slow trot covering the ground much faster now. She kept a watchful eye for all her familiar landmarks. Already, some of them were beginning to blur. Desperate, Dulcey picked up her pace and soon the cottage came into view. Never had she been so glad to see her small cottage. Her breathing was hard and heavy. She didn't know how much longer she could have kept up the pace. She could feel the cold air cutting into her breath.

Opening the door, she and Abigail stepped into the warmth of the small cottage. Dulcey allowed Abigail to slide off her back on to the floor.

Abigail stood and looked around. It was warm in here. The snow and the dark couldn't get to her, she thought. Her new friend, Dulcey, would take care of her until Uncle Nate found her.

Dulcey hastened to the fireplace, added more peat to the fire and stoked it till she had a good blaze going. She turned to Abigail, "Little one, I think we need to get some of those wet clothes off. You need to get warm."

Dulcey began taking off Abby's velvet coat that matched her bonnet. Her clothes were soaked. She needed to get Abby dry and warm. She did not want the child to get sick. She would give Abby a tonic later to make certain.

"Is Uncle Nate looking for me?" asked Abigail, as she allowed Dulcey to undress her.

"I'm sure he is but with the storm outside, he may have to wait. We will wait for him here, where it is nice and warm. And if he doesn't find us, then when this storm is over, we will go looking for him. How about that?"

Abby nodded. Uncle Nate would come and rescue her. Uncle Nate always did. He would come. Now that she was with Dulcey, she would just wait for Uncle Nate. Dulcey was nice. She liked her.

Dulcey got Abby down to her under shift which appeared to be dry. She wrapped her in Grammy's quilt from off the top of the bed in the corner and sat her in the rocker in front of the fireplace.

"Better?"

Abigail nodded.

Dulcey smiled. "You've been a very brave little girl. Your uncle will be very proud of you. Now, I have to tend to some things. You just rest there in the rocker and warm up and I'll see about fixing us something to eat. Are you hungry?" asked Dulcey as she removed her own long coat and put the bag of partridges on the floor by the back door. She hung her bow and quiver on its hook by the back door as well. She took off her boots and put them by the hearth to dry. Her woolen stockings were damp. She pulled them off and replaced them with some dry ones and slipped on her other pair of dry shoes. She hung up all their wet clothes about the room to dry.

"I am going to go through that door right there. It just goes to where I keep my animals. I need to check on Albert and Sally and Lizzie and Chickie and McDougal."

Dulcey smiled at Abby's quizzical look. Good, she was getting her to think about something other than being caught in the snowstorm. "Albert and Sally are my goats and Lizzie, Chickie and McDougal are my chickens. I need to make sure they are warm too. I will be but just a moment."

Abigail smiled and nodded.

Dulcey went through the back door to the room attached to her cottage where she kept her animals.

11

Grammy did not believe in having her barn away from her house. A quick look around showed Dulcey they were fine, huddled next to the outside of her fireplace. She would milk Sally in the morning. She would need some more milk by then with her little visitor,

Back in the cottage, Dulcey noticed, Abby had nodded off in the rocker all safely wrapped in Grammy's quilt. Poor thing had gotten herself exhausted getting lost.

Dulcey went about cleaning the three partridges. In short time, they were cleaned and on the spit on the fire cooking. The rabbit stew was slowly simmering as well. They would have more than enough food to last for several days.

Abigail was sound asleep, all warmly wrapped up. Dulcey was hesitant to wake the sleeping child. Poor thing, she had had a rough time of it. Dulcey decided to let her sleep and feed her when she awakened. She just wondered who Uncle Nate was and how and when had they come to the district. She fervently hoped he was not in this storm looking for Abby.

The wind outside had increased. She could hear the wind whistling and howling as it swept around the eaves. She could never in her life remember a storm this bad. She was ever so grateful she had found Abigail when she did. She couldn't bear to think of her out in that weather. She would have never survived. She sent up a silent prayer to Mother earth in thanksgiving for putting her in the right place, at the right time, for being able to find her. Yet, still there was that same nagging feeling that all was not right. It had to be the storm.

Dulcey went about the room checking on the clothes hanging to dry. Soon, they would be completely dry. She was afraid this was going to be their world for the next few days by the sound of what was going on outside. Dulcey felt this storm was disturbing her world. Ever since yesterday, she had felt the change around her. It left her uneasy. She was afraid of this change because she couldn't tell whether it was for the good or the bad and that was very unusual.

She heard something strange outside. She couldn't sense what it was. This storm was really playing havoc with her senses. Her senses were all befuddled. It was distracting as though she could not trust her powers. It was almost as though they weren't working correctly. She felt all jumbled. She went to window but could see nothing but the swirling of the snow. It was bad outside. The swirling snow obliterated everything. Dulcey could not even see the rose bushes or the small yew that stood just outside her door.

A sudden loud banging shook the door. Dulcey jumped and cried out. Abby woke up and screamed in fright. Dulcey went to the frightened child and tried to calm her. The banging began again only stronger and louder. Abby clung to Dulcey, terrified.

Dulcey reassured Abby. "Stay right here, little one. I have to check and see, what is going on. It might be someone lost, like you were."

Abby nodded, but was reluctant to let Dulcey go. Dulcey walked back to the door just as the banging started again, harder. Quickly, she unlocked the latch and opened the door. A huge man stood on her stoop. There were icicles hanging from his hat. His face was covered with snow. He looked like he was ready to collapse, frozen on the spot.

"Please, help me," the voice croaked.

Dulcey grabbed his arm and aided him into the small room. He seemed to take up all the extra room. She escorted him to the chair at her table and aided him as he collapsed into the chair. He closed his eyes. For a moment, Dulcey was afraid he had passed out.

Suddenly, she was staring at the brightest blue eyes. They shone with a fever she was certain he had.

"Uncle Nate," yelled Abby as she ran to him and hugged him snow and all.

Dulcey watched the tension evaporate from him. He just sagged in the chair as he hugged the little bundle of energy that threw herself in his arms.

"Oh, Poppet, I have been looking all over for you."

"I'm not lost anymore. I've been here with Dulcey. She found me. I chased after the bunny but I couldn't catch him," explained Abby, as though he should have known all this time.

Nate looked over Abby's blond curls to the woman who had helped him. He was still so cold but he seemed to be warming up. "Poppet, you're going to get snow all over you." He said as he put her gently away from him. He tried to stand up but his legs were too weak to hold him. "Nathaniel Beckham, m'lady," he made a half-hearted motion with his hand. He closed his eyes for a second, then tried to rise again but could not. "My horse, I need to put him up."

"You just sit there. I will see to your horse. Abby, look after your uncle," Dulcey grabbed her boots and stomped into them. She grabbed her heavy coat from the door and with one quick glance at the two at her table, she walked out her door.

The wind whipped about her, nearly knocking her over. Her visitor's horse just stood there. She grabbed his reins and struggled to lead him around the corner to her lean-to. She struggled with the door and finally got it open. She led his horse in, closing the door behind her with the winds help. Her chickens clucked their annoyance at being disturbed, Albert moved over as though knowing the horse needed more room. She took the saddle off. She draped it over a pile of hay she had in the corner and quickly rubbed him down. At least, the lean-to had him out of the elements.

Dulcey walked in through the back door to find her guest draped across the table, his head on his arms. Abby looked up at her frightened and quiet.

"I think Uncle Nate went to sleep," she whispered.

Dulcey nodded. She removed her coat and boots. They would need to dry out again. Her guest would need to get out of his wet clothes. She just wondered how much help he would be. Very little, she thought. Together, she and Abby would have to manage.

She placed her hand on his shoulder. His eyes opened slowly. A feverish shine was still in them. She needed to get him dry and warm soon. "Sir, you need to get out of these wet clothes. They are making you sick. I'm going to need your help. "

"A beautiful woman wants me to take my clothes off. I shall be happy to oblige such a request," he said with a smirk on his face.

Dulcey sighed. She may live out here by herself but she was aware of what went on between a man and a woman. Her friend, Mary, had enlightened her on those facts.

He tried and managed to stand but he was weaving all over. "Abby stand up next to him so he has something to hold on to," instructed Dulcey as she tried to remove his greatcoat. Finally, with all three of them working on it, Dulcey was able to get it off. He sat down immediately. She could tell he was exhausted. She hung his coat on the peg near the door to dry.

She looked him over and decided to start with his boots next. He would be able to sit down while she did that. "Let's try his boots next, Abby. I think it's going to take both of us to get them off."

Abby nodded. Between the two of them and much struggling with very little help from Nate, they were able to finally get his boots off. Abby sat on the floor, looked up and giggled. Dulcey smiled. With Abby's help, she helped him remove his jacket and cravat until he was down to his shirt and pants. His shirt appeared to be dry but his pants were soaked and definitely needed to come off. His pants proved to be even more of a problem that his boots, but finally Dulcey was able to get them off along with his stockings.

Those long hard legs of his filled his underpants much to her discomfort. His shirt was open showing a chiseled chest with a light covering of soft light brown hair. With him in his shirt and under pants and Abby's help, she was able to walk him the few feet to her bed. He collapsed, barely aware that he was even being helped.

For a moment, he grabbed her arm and pulled her down on top of him. She felt as if a bolt of lightning had shot straight through her. Her whole body felt alive with the strangest sensations. As quickly as he had grabbed her, he let her go.

Dulcey rose quickly. Abby started laughing. "Uncle Nate made you fall down."

"Yes, darling he did," she replied trying desperately to make sense of all these new feelings she had just experienced. It was just the storm and the off balance feelings she had been experiencing all day, she told herself.

Dulcey pulled one of the quilts up and tucked it in around him. She felt his forehead. It was hot to her touch. He grabbed her hand and kissed her palm sending sensations like liquid fire cascading through her body again. "Ah, my lady, come join me."

Dulcey removed her hand from his grip and gently tucked it back under the covers. "You need some rest, sir." She watched him close is eyes with a smile on his face. Dulcey shook her head.

"Uncle Nate is funny."

Dulcey smiled and nodded. "Your uncle is sick, my darling. We're going to have to take care of him. Do you think you can help me with that?"

Abby nodded, suddenly being very serious. "Is Uncle Nate going to die?" she asked.

Dulcey could see the fear in her face.

"Not, if I can help it. I need you to sit by him while I mix up some special medicine for him and after that, we shall see about eating."

Abby sat down beside her uncle and watched intently, as Dulcey went to the cupboard on the far wall. Dulcey took out several vials, looked at them, then carefully measured each ingredient until she was satisfied she had what she wanted. She brought the cup to the bedside. With Abby's help, she raised his head and got him to drink the medicine. Abby watched everything Dulcey did with wide eyed wonder.

"Are you a witch?" asked Abby, a little uncertain. "Miss Franny read a story about a witch who made special potions."

Dulcey smiled tolerantly. She had heard her grandmother called that many times. She smiled and knelt down beside Abby. "Can you keep a secret?"

Abby nodded very seriously and watched the cup Dulcey held in her hands. "I know a fairy and she showed me how to make these medicines so I could help people."

Abby eyes grew big and round, as she looked at Dulcey.

"A fairy? Fairies are good." She replied in childlike innocence.

"Yes, and she is a very special fairy." Dulcey knew most people believed fairies to be good and witches to be bad. Grammy had taught her that fact, as well. People would better tolerate a fairy than a witch.

"Can I meet her? Will you become a fairy, too?"

"I don't know, I don't think so. I just do the medicine part to help people get better and I think this should help him get better," said Dulcey trying to reassure Abby. "How about you, little one? How are you feeling?"

as she felt Abby's forehead and neck area. It was cool to her touch, much to her relief.

"Good."

Dulcey nodded. "All right, let's see what we can have for supper. We have roasted partridge and rabbit stew. How about we have a little of each?" asked Dulcey, as she set about fixing their bowls. It was simple fair but good and filled their belly. After supper, Dulcey went through the back door to the lean-to and checked on the animals. They appeared to be doing fine. There was an old horse blanket from when Grammy owned a donkey. She placed it across the horse's withers.

Moments later, she was back inside. Abby was sitting in the rocker keeping careful watch of her uncle.

Dulcey pulled out the bottom trundle bed, pulled the mattress out and placed it on the floor near the hearth. She and Abby would sleep on it. "This is where we will sleep. We will let your uncle have the bed."

Dulcey sat in the rocker and Abby crawled in her lap. Dulcey wrapped the quilt around them. "How about you and I get to know each other? You live with your Uncle Nate?"

"Un hunh. Momma and Papa died. He was Uncle Nate brother. I live with Uncle Nate and Grandmother."

"And where is that.?"

"Uncle Nate wanted us to spend Christmas here. I wanted to play in the snow."

Dulcey smiled. "I think you got your snow."

"Is it still snowing Dulcey?"

"Yes, and I think it will all night. But we are safe here, so don't you worry about that." Trying to get her mind off the storm, Dulcey asked, "I thought heard your uncle call you by a special name.''

"Un hunh. Uncle Nate calls me Poppet."

"May I call you Poppet?"

"Un hunh."

Dulcey nodded. "Where are you staying?" She was afraid she knew the answer. Uncle Nate's clothes were much too nice not to be of elite gentry or nobility. She had her suspicions.

"A big house."

"Did you hear them call it Brandanlyn Manor?" She was afraid to ask, but knew she had to. Afraid that Uncle Nate was the new Baron or at least related to him.

"Un hunh. Grandmother did not want to come but Uncle Nate said she had to."

"Well, one good thing we are not very far from the manor house. So once it stops snowing, you and Uncle Nate will be home quickly. How about we get ready for bed?"

Dulcey half listened as Abby chatted away as she changed into a nightdress. Abby wore one of Dulcey's winter wool chemises. She banked the fire to make certain it would last through the night. She checked on her patient. He was resting quietly. Dulcey blew out the candle on the table and lay down on the pallet on the floor next to Abby. She pulled Abby close and covered them both with a quilt.

"How about I tell you a story, Abby?"

"Yes, please. Tell me about the fairy that showed you how to make the potions, medicines."

Dulcey sighed and began telling her story about a beautiful fairy that lived in the woods. She only came out when the moon was full and danced in the moonlight. Dulcey elaborated on her story, making it up as she went along. It wasn't long before Dulcey heard the soft even breathing of Abby sleeping.

Dulcey stared up at the ceiling watching the shadows and the flames do an intricate dance. She sighed and turned to her side, snuggled Abby close to her. It wouldn't do her any good to worry. It was out of her hands. It had always been out of her hands. She knew outside forces were at work. The future was hazy, like the moors on a misty morning. It was hard to tell what was real. Until the mist receded, Dulcey felt she must tread very carefully, until the future was revealed to her. She had never felt like this before. It was a disconcerted feeling she had never experienced before. It left her unsettled.

Chapter 2

"A gentleman is someone who
DOES NOT what he wants to do,
But what he SHOULD do."
                    Haruki Murakami

Dulcey woke with a start and for a brief moment wondered why she was asleep on the floor. It only took her a moment to remember. She heard a mumbling coming for her bed. It had to be what had awakened her. Dulcey eased herself from Abby's side and softly approached her bed. Abby's Uncle Nate was mumbling. Dulcey laid her hand on his brow. It was hot. She went to the medicine cupboard and mixed another dose of her medicine. This time she added something else for his fever.

She sat at his bedside. For a moment, she was at a loss as to what to call him. Was he the new baron? Was he Lord Beckham or was he Mr. Beckham? She sighed.

"Nate," she said softly. He didn't respond. "Nathaniel?" she waited a moment. "Nathaniel, please, I need you to take this. Please, wake up for a moment."

She waited and then suddenly his eyes opened. She raised his head enough for him to take the medicine she had for him. She sat for a moment staring at the handsome face lying there in her bed. His nose was a little on the long side but it fit his angular face, the square jaw that gave the hint of stubbornness. His brown hair, he wore long and had a tendency to curl at the nape. She had seen his bright blue eyes earlier. Looking at Abby and then at Uncle Nate, she could see the family resemblance. She sat there studying him. Was he the force that was disturbing her balance?

Suddenly, he grabbed her and pulled her down on top of him holding her tight as he kissed her. She tasted the medicine on his lips but something else as well. She tasted him and he tasted good. He turned till she lay under him. One of his hands immediately went to her breast massaging it till his fingers found her nipple and teased it till it hardened. He trailed kisses down her neck.

Dulcey felt like she was on fire. Her body arched into him with almost a will of its own. She could feel the entire length of him, the hard muscles of his chest, the legs that held her pinned down under him. She could feel his manhood enlarged against her thigh. Her body was alive and tingling in places she did not know existed.

"Oh, my sweetness," he whispered in her ear.

Just as suddenly, he collapsed on top of her and unquestionably passed out once again. He was heavy on her now, but the feelings he had stirred within her were not so easily dismissed. With difficulty, squirming, feeling more of his body against her, she removed herself from his embrace. He murmured when she finally managed to remove herself out from under him.

She stood at a safe distance watching him again, trying desperately to get control of her chaotic heartbeat and breathing but most of all her chaotic thoughts, no, feelings. What had just happened?

Dulcey sat down in the rocker and stared at her bed and the man in it. This was a definite shift in her world as she knew it. She was at a lost at how to deal with it. She could blame it all on the storm and the fact Abby's uncle was delirious. It had to be the storm. No, this was best forgotten. She was almost assured Nathaniel Beckham would not remember it in the morning due to his fever. She just hoped she would not remember it but she knew that was an impossible feat. How was she to forget that aching need he had brought from her in just that short period of time? Aching need for what, she knew not. But it was there. Her body still tingled, especially her breast where he had touched her so.

With a deep sigh of resignation, Dulcey laid down at Abby's side again. The child snuggled closer, but sleep would not come to Dulcey. Were these the feelings Mary talked about when she talked about her gentlemen callers? She knew about the physical act but she had not realized these strange intense feeling were a part of it as well. What was that feeling deep within her that ached for more? Maybe when she next talked to Mary she would ask her. Maybe Mary could explain it to her.

She must have fallen asleep, because she awakened to Abby sitting up.

"Good morning, Dulcey."

"Good morning, Poppet," replied Dulcey as she rose from their bed on the floor. She immediately went to the fire added more peat and banked it till it roared back to life, quickly dispelling the chill that had crept in from the outside. She put a pitcher of water on the hearth to heat. "Give me a moment to check on the animals and then I will come back and we will fix breakfast." She slipped her light green wool dress over her head. It was her warmest.

Dulcey checked on the animals. It was cold in the lean to but the animals were doing fine. Quickly, she milked Sally and checked Chickie and Lizzie for their eggs. She couldn't remember ever having done her chores with the animals as quickly as she did. Back in the cottage, Dulcey smiled at Abby sitting in the rocker wrapped in the quilt.

"Let me get our porridge cooking, while I get you washed up. If you want you can stay in my woolens for I don't think we will be going out today."

"Is it still snowing?" asked Abby with a frown.

"I'm afraid so, not as much as yesterday. We will just have to stay here where we are warm until it stops."

Abby nodded in understanding, but Dulcey wondered how much did she truly understand.

The weather outside still warranted they stay inside. The wind had died down but an occasional gust could still be felt and heard. The snow was not falling as hard as yesterday but it was still lightly falling.

"I thought after breakfast we could work on the Christmas decorations. I have some red ribbon we can use to tie our greenery and we can decide where we want to put it," suggested Dulcey knowing she needed to keep Abby occupied. Christmas was still three days away. If the weather continued, they would still be here at Christmas.

Dulcey approached her bed warily remembering what had happened during the night. She laid her hand on his brow. She was glad to find it cool to her touch. His breathing was even and not labored as though he was sleeping.

"Is Uncle Nate getting better?" asked Abby. Dulcey could see the worry frown on her face.

"I think so. He doesn't have a fever this morning so I think he's on the mend. We will just have to wait and see. I suggest we eat our breakfast and get our decorations done."

Abby nodded, sat down and watched as Dulcey prepared breakfast. Abby kept up a steady stream of conversation. Dulcey answered her questions, many were about the decorations they were about to put up around her small home.

For several years now she had not been here at her home for Christmas. She had helped Lord James at Brandanlyn. Lord James always insisted she spent time there until after twelfth night the very least. So much had changed in her life the past couple of years since Grammy's death. And now, since Lord James's death last August, it was even more so.

Sometimes, she felt adrift on a sea of uncertainty. Even her dreams and premonitions were muddled, not giving her directions as they had in the past. She felt vulnerable to outside influences, influences she did not truly trust nor understand.

After breakfast, Dulcey with Abby's help began tying her green boughs with the red ribbon she had used year after year. She had collected holly and ivy, several long branches of evergreen and of course several sprigs of mistletoe. Together they put them on the window sills. Dulcey stood up on the chair and placed two of the larger boughs atop the door frame. Of course, Abby had some definite opinions on how it should look. Dulcey smiled but she did everything Abby instructed. She sighed with yearning. She would love to have a child of her own but she knew that was impossible. Grammy had told her so time and time again.

~~~~~~~~~~~~~~~

Nathaniel woke to the sounds of voices. He immediately recognized Abby. For a moment, he was confused as to why he was lying in this bed, this strange bed. Memories came flooding back, the fear of having Abby lost in the snow, of looking and not being able to find her. That fear had clutched his heart the likes he had never known. He remembered riding through the snow, snow that had become blinding and a temperature that had been dropping dangerously low. His fear for Abby had been intense, knowing there was no way she could survive the snow storm. He remembered finding a cottage at least he thought he had. Only things after that had become very blurred and confusing.

Nathaniel opened his eyes and looked around. He was in a cottage, a one room cottage. Abby was chatting with a young woman. They were discussing where to hang the mistletoe. The young woman turned and Nathaniel found himself gazing at what he would have considered a wood fairy. Her face had that pixie look of big beautiful eyes, small little nose, pink rosebud mouth, and her long hair of curls, the color of dark honey hung in a braid all the way down her back to just above her buttocks. Her dress of soft green was outdated and hugged her hips. He watched as she walked across the room, her hips swaying gently.

A memory surfaced or was it a dream that this fairy waif had laid beside him, no under him. He shook his head, no it had to be a dream, but the feeling was so strong. The memory of that soft body under him felt so real. He could feel himself responding. Careful, he told himself. It was but a dream.

He raised himself on his arms.

Abby noticed immediately and ran to his bedside. "Uncle Nate, you're awake."

Nate smiled at Abby, glad to see she was indeed fine. He looked past her head and found himself looking in the brightest green eyes that belonged to his fairy waif. He watched the blush that stained her full checks and wondered why.

"Well Poppet, it seems I have found you."

Abby looked down and bit her bottom lip. "I am sorry, Uncle Nate. I chased the bunny and I got lost. But Dulcey found me."

Nathaniel sighed but with Abby safe, he was not about to bicker or chastise her. She was safe and that was the most important thing. Looking over Abby's head he mouthed, "Thank you."

Dulcey smiled softly and nodded. She could see how much he was concerned about Abby's welfare but she could not get the memory of him kissing her and pulling her under him out of her mind. She turned away from him afraid he could read her mind and remember what had happened in the dark of the night.

"Are you hungry?" she asked as she turned back to him. What was she to call him?

"Yes, but I need the privy first."

Dulcey nodded and pointed to the screen near the door to the lean to.

Nathaniel swung his legs over the side of the bed and realized he was only in his underpants. Wrapping the quilt about him, he walked gingerly to the screen. He was a little more wobbly than he first thought. Having relieved himself, he joined Abby and Dulcey at the table that sat in the middle of the room.

He looked around him noticing it was just one large room with the fireplace against one wall, a large cooking fireplace, the door to the lean to at the corner of that wall. The bed he had just vacated lay on the wall across from the entrance door. In the far corner stood a spinning wheel and loom and in the other corner stood a cupboard of sorts. An old trunk stood at the foot of the bed. There were only two windows in the cottage, one on each side of the door. The table he sat at stood in the middle of the room with only two chairs. A large rocker stood before the fireplace. So this was his woodland fairy's home.

Dulcey put a bowl of porridge in front of him, "My lord, I also have rabbit stew if you would like."

"I think we have gotten past the "my lord" thing. I am Nathaniel Beckham. Nate, to most of my friends." He held out his hand to her.

Dulcey took his hand in hers and she immediately felt warmth flow up her arm like liquid fire. For a moment, she almost dropped his hand like it was a hot rock, too hot to touch. But she didn't. She smiled nervously.

"I am Dulcey, Dulcey Langely," she made a small curtsey.

Nathaniel smiled. Here they were snowbound in this small cottage of hers and she was trying to observe proper etiquette. Proper etiquette was out there in the snow storm. In this small cottage of his woodland fairy, proper etiquette had no place, for here he sat at her table in his underpants wrapped in a quilt. Proper etiquette indeed.

"This porridge will be just fine." He took a bite and realized he was indeed hungry. He finished it in short time and felt much better having food in his stomach.

Abby silently watched her uncle eat.

"Well, ladies, I do think I need to observe some semblance of decorum."

Abby frown and asked, "What is decorum?"

"Decorum, Poppet. It means proper manners, behavior. It means I need to put my pants back on."

Abby giggled. "It was funny taking them off."

Nate looked up and met Dulcey's eyes. They twinkled even though a blush stained her cheeks.

"Abby, how about you and I look at the spinning wheel while your uncle puts his pants on?" Dulcey guided her to the spinning wheel in the corner. She had her looking at the yarn so their backs were to him.

Nathaniel made quick work of putting his pants on. They were stiff and dirty in places. His tailor would be screaming and having a severe case of the vapors if he saw the condition of his jacket and pants. Desperate times called for desperate measures.

"Very well ladies, you may turn around now."

Abby turned around and smiled. "You've got your decorum on, Uncle Nate."

"Yes, it seems I do. Now tell me Poppet, have you been helping Dulcey since she was nice enough to find you and bring you to her home." He sat in the rocker and Abby crawled into his lap.

"I helped her decorate for Christmas Uncle Nate. Look," Abby said as she pointed to all the decorations they had put up earlier. "Will we be here for Christmas?"

Nathaniel shrugged, "I don't know. As long as it continues to snow, we shall have to stay here, if Dulcey will let us. I would not want us to get lost in the storm again."

Abby looked at Dulcey.

"Of course, you can both stay as long as you need to. I do not want either of you out in the snow. We are safe and warm in here and here is where we will stay until this storm is over."

"Good, cause I like it here," said Abby.

Nate looked at Dulcey. "Me, too."

Dulcey blushed and looked away. She wanted to say me, too, as well, but she didn't. Instead, she took the quilt from the bed and folded it. But looking at the bed brought last night to mind and the memory of his body against her. She had never experienced such feelings and now, she must spend possibly the next few days in his company within the walls of her tiny cottage. She convinced herself, he was ill at the time and did not remember any of what had happened. She needed desperately to believe it.

Nate watched her intently and wondered why she was suddenly so skittish, like a young colt bolting from a sudden sound. She intrigued him. What was she doing living here all alone? He was ever so grateful she had found Abby. He did not even want to contemplate any other possibility.

"Uncle Nate will you tell me a story. Dulcey told me a story about fairies. Dulcey knows fairies. They teached her how to make the medicine to make you better." Abby looked at Dulcey then remembered, "I'm sorry, I told your secret, but Uncle Nate can keep a secret, can't you, Uncle Nate?"

Nate looked from Abby to Dulcey. "Of course, I can keep a secret especially one about fairies and Poppet it is taught her not teached." Nate watched Dulcey and wondered why she looked relieved. What was this talk of secrets and fairies?

"Well, I don't know stories about fairies so I'll leave Dulcey tell you those stories since she knows all about them. How about I tell you a story about a prince knight in shining armor who rescues the beautiful princess?"

Abby nodded and relaxed against his chest.

"Let's see, there was this very handsome prince. He got lost in the woods but he found this most beautiful princess living in a little cottage all by herself," said Nate as he looked at Dulcey.

"No, Uncle Nate, she lived with some very special fairies," added Abby. She was determined to have fairies in her story.

Nate smiled. Dulcey returned his smile.

"Yes, there were some very special fairies with very special powers."

"What kind of special powers?" asked Abby, looking at Dulcey.

Nate looked at Dulcey. "I'm not familiar with fairies and their powers. Dulcey can you help us? What kind of special powers do fairies have?"

Dulcey relaxed and realized Nate was making up the story as entertainment for Abby. She would play along. "Special powers, of course they have special powers. Let's see, they loved roses so there were roses everywhere."

Nate smiled. "Yes, and they do not like snow. So, it never snows."

"But what about the prince and the princess, Uncle Nate?"

"Ahh, the prince got lost in the woods."

"You said that already, Uncle Nate."

Dulcey turned to hide her smile.

"Yes, as I was saying. The prince got lost in the woods but the fairies took pity on him and showed him the way to the princess's cottage. There were roses everywhere and no snow. When the prince saw the princess, he fell madly in love with her. The fairies had put a spell on him so he would fall in love with the princess.

For you see, the fairies knew the princess needed someone to protect and love her."

Abby nodded slowly, her eyes closed and she sighed.

"The prince took the princess to his home and they lived happily ever after." Nate looked down at the sleeping child in his lap and then up at Dulcey. Was he wishing he was the prince and Dulcey was the princess? He was aware he had only known this young woman before him only a few hours but there was something about her that touched him.

Had the fairies Dulcey told Abby about, put a spell on him? It almost felt like it. He had never in his entire life been so attuned to a woman. It wasn't like he hadn't had a woman in some time. Actually, he and Yvette had a last fling before he left for Brandanlyn. Then they had gone their separate ways. But there was something about Dulcey that touched him in so many ways. It was strange but a good strange.

Dulcey stared into those bright blue eyes of his, mesmerized. She felt with certainty, a disturbance in her life force. A strange intense disturbance, the likes she had never experienced before. She looked away afraid he could read what she was thinking.

"I'm going to check on the animals," said Dulcey feeling the need to put some distance between them. It was the only thing she could think of.

"Shall I go?" asked Nate.

"No, I'll be but a moment. You should not disturb Abby." Dulcey grabbed her coat and was out the door before he could say more. She took her time checking on his horse making sure he and the goats had enough hay. She would need to muck out the lean to in the next couple of days. Hopefully the snow would stop by then. She had milked Lizzie earlier so she had no need to do it again. She looked around again and knew she had stayed in here more than long enough. She could no longer delay going back into the cottage.

She entered the cottage quietly, careful not to awaken Abby. She smiled when she saw Nate had his eyes closed and a soft snore could be heard. He was asleep, too. He sat in Grammy's rocker with Abby in his lap both wrapped in one of the quilts. It was a special man who could be so kind and concerned with a child. Her senses did tell her, he had a kind heart.

Dulcey went quietly about her cottage, putting things back in order not that there was much to do. She added more peat to the fire to make sure it stayed warm. She would see about making bread when Abby woke up. She would let Abby help. She would enjoy that.

Dulcey sat at her loom and worked. It always quieted her chaotic thoughts. Her hands deftly plied her shuttle through the threads continuing the pattern she had begun weeks ago. Slowly her thoughts quieten and the familiar feel of the thread and shuttle in her hands brought balance back into perspective. She lost herself in her weaving and the rhythm.

Chapter 3

Her lips were frosted with sugar and faeriedust.

Allyse Near

Nathaniel woke slowly. The nap had helped him. He felt stronger. Abby was safe in his arms of which he was so very grateful. It sounded quiet outside. No wailing of the wind as before, just the sound of the crackling of the fire in the hearth and the soft humming coming from the far corner. He shifted ever so slightly and watched as Dulcey rocked slightly as she worked her loom. She looked so content, like she was one with the loom.

He wondered exactly who she was? Why was she living here all alone? Surely, Lord Fergers knew of her. She was residing in a cottage on his land and she admitted to hunting on the land. Yes, who was this Dulcey Langley? He had several questions she needed to answer but he couldn't ask her with Abby in ear shot. No, Abby did not need to be privy to these questions. She had become attached to Dulcey. He did not want to upset her. She was of no threat to anyone by living here.

Abby stirred in his lap and looked up to him with her big blue eyes. He had taken over her care a little over a year ago when his older brother and his wife died. So much had changed for him at that time. He had inherited the title and all the responsibilities that went with it. Abby had wrapped herself around his heart like a clinging vine he welcomed gladly. He could not think of not having her in his life. Thanks to Dulcey, he would not have to even think along those lines. He would be forever in her debt.

"Hi, Uncle Nate. Are we still lost in the snow?"

"Yes, Poppet, we are still with Dulcey in her cottage."

Dulcey heard their exchange and immediately got up from her loom. "Hello, you two. Did you have a good nap?"

Abby popped off her uncle's lap. "Uncle Nate says it's still snowing."

"It is still snowing but not as hard as it has been. I think it may stop soon."

Abby looked to Nate.

"Just because it stops snowing does not mean we will be able to leave. I'm going to have to go outside and check to see how deep the snow is." Nate explained.

Abby nodded. It did not matter to her that they would be forced to stay here longer. She liked it here. She liked Dulcey.

"I need to make some bread. I thought maybe you could help me. Have you ever made bread before?" asked Dulcey. She thought this would keep Abby occupied. Besides, they needed bread to eat.

Abby looked to her uncle. "Of course, Poppet. Dulcey needs your help. Do you need mine as well?"

Dulcey looked at Nathaniel with skepticism. She could not imagine him making bread, getting his hands full of flour.

"I want to help. What do we do first?" asked Abby.

Dulcey set up all the ingredients on the table and patiently instructed Abby how to mix the flour mixture. By the time Abby was finished, there was flour everywhere. Several times, Nate chuckled at their antics for which he received several narrowed eyed looks from Abby. Nate tried to be serious but was not very successful.

The bread was near the hearth rising. "Since you've been such a big help to me making our bread, how about we make some gingerbread planks? Grammy always made them for Christmas."

Abby nodded eagerly. "Gingerbread, yes."

"Very well then, let me get what we need." Dulcey went to her cupboard and got the extra ingredients they would need. She would be sharing a tradition Grammy had shared with her. It made it seem all the better.

She helped Abby in mixing it all together and then rolling it out. She took out the cookie boards Grammy always used and with Abby's help stamped them. Even Nate got involved taking a knife and making designs for them. Dulcey soon had them baking and the sweet aroma of gingerbread filled the cottage.

Abby talked non-stop about everything, the house they lived in, her nanny governess, her dolls, how much she wanted a puppy. Sometimes Dulcey answered her, sometimes Nate did.

Dulcey removed them from the oven and put them to cool. When she let Nate and Abby eat one, she watched their faces.

Nate closed his eyes, savoring the taste. These were good. These were very good. "Umm! Heaven!"

"I like these Uncle Nate," said Abby with a mouthful and took another big bite.

"I like these too, Abby girl." He looked to Dulcey with a look of total pleasure on his face.

Dulcey smiled. Grammy's gingerbread planks were the best. She was glad to share it with them. She had decided after Grammy died, she would be alone for the rest of her life. But the last couple of days with Abby and Nate, she realized exactly what she was giving up.

There was a strange tightness in her chest and tears came to her eyes. Till this moment, she had not realized how much, how very much she wanted this. She turned away from them before they saw the longing in her. This kind of life was not meant for her.

Nate had watched Dulcey closely and saw the happiness suddenly change to such a sadness, it made him hurt. He watched her turn away but not before he saw the tears in her eyes. He walked over to her and placed his hands on her shoulders and turned her toward him. Those big green eyes glistened with unshed tears. What had brought this on? He dropped his gaze to her lips, pink, soft and so very tempting.

Slowly, he lowered his head and claimed those lips. She tasted of gingerbread. His tongue licked her bottom lip. This was just a taste and oh, how, he wanted more. He wanted all of her. He could feel every part of him responding to her especially his manhood. It was bulging with need. Never had he felt such a connection with a woman like what he felt with this woman he held in his arms. The strength of passion that coursed through his veins was formidable.

When Dulcey felt his hands on her shoulders and he turned her around to face him, she knew she was lost. She wanted him to kiss her, to feel his lips on hers and when he did it was more than what she had experienced last night. So much more. And when his tongue licked her bottom lip and she felt it all the way down into that secret part of her. She clung to him knowing her legs would not hold her.

Last night had been a prelude. This time he was awake and he knew what he was doing. And she wanted more. She wasn't sure what more was, all she knew she wanted more. She sighed, her lips opened slightly, she felt his tongue penetrate her mouth and tease her tongue with his. Had he not had a tight hold on her, Dulcey was certain her legs would have completely given out.

"Uncle Nate what's the matter with Dulcey?"

Nate released her mouth reluctantly. "Dulcey has some flour in her eyes. I'm helping her get it out."

"Oh, can I have another gingerbread?"

"Yes, Poppet but just one. We don't want to ruin supper."

"Thank you."

Nate looked down at the woman he held in his arms. Dulcey had her forehead leaned against his chest. He couldn't see her eyes. With his fingers, he raised her chin until she looked him in the eyes. The passion he saw reflected in them thrilled him, yet frightened him at the same time. He knew he wanted her, but he also knew she was an innocent. Yet, something deep down inside of him told him he had to have her. There was something about her that made him whole. He didn't understand it, just knew it was there and obscured every rational thought about this situation.

"Dulcey," he needed to say something. He just didn't know what and that had never happened to him before.

She pushed away from him, but he refused to let her go. "This shouldn't have happened," she whispered.

"You feel this connection just as I do. It's bigger than both of us."

"No," she shook her head, refusing to look at him. "We come from two different worlds. I could never fit into yours. You are the new baron and I am the witch in the woods. No," she pushed harder and he let her slip reluctantly out of his arms.

Dulcey stood by her loom staring at it unseeing. Her emotions were so out of kilter. Never had she felt the forces around her so jumbled. Usually, they were crystal clear showing her the way to go. Even the deaths of Grammy and Lord James had not affected her as Nate did. She sighed deeply. She needed to get back to reality. Nate was a dream, an unattainable one.

Dulcey turned to Abby. The table was a mess from their cookie making. It would need to be cleaned for supper.

"Oh my, look at the mess we made," said Dulcey as she approached the table and began cleaning it up. She did not look at Nate. She could not.

"No more flour in your eye, Dulcey?" asked Abby, as she helped Dulcey, but she looked at her Uncle Nate.

"No, Poppet. My eye is fine. What shall we have for supper? Rabbit stew or partridges?" asked Dulcey knowing that was all they had.

"A little of both," answered Dulcey and Abby together. They both laughed.

Nate watched Dulcey closely. It was going to be torture to stay in this small cottage with her in such close proximity. "I think I will go outside and check on the snow." He grabbed his greatcoat off the wall, put it on and walked out the door. A blast of cold air entered as he walked out. Dulcey stared at the closed door. She knew that it was best they go back to Brandanlyn as soon as possible but she would miss Abby. If she was honest with herself, she would miss Nate, too.

They were putting the last of supper on the table when Nate came back in from the outside. Another blast of cold air accompanied him. He looked frozen. Dulcey went to him and helped him with his greatcoat. She helped him remove his gloves and took his cold hands in her warm ones and blew on them hoping her warm breath would help.

Nate eyes flared with passion, coming in from the cold, he wanted to warm up with her. The walk in the snow had not quenched his thirst for her. Her warm breath on his hands was torture.

Dulcey pulled her hands away and turned to the table. Her heart beat was chaotic. Why had she tried to warm his hands? She knew touching him was dangerous, but she could not help herself. "How is it outside?"

"Good news. It has stopped snowing. But the snow drifts are rather high and large. Hopefully, by tomorrow we can walk out of here. It will be slow but I think Max will be able to walk us to Brandanlyn."

"It's about an hour on a good day," suggested Dulcey. "Do you remember the way?"

"Not exactly, but since you are coming with us, I'm sure you can show us the way."

"But I am not coming with you," argued Dulcey. "I cannot leave my animals." She did not want to go back to Brandanlyn knowing it was his home now.

"We need you to show us the way. I will send one of the servants back for your animals, but you are coming to Brandanlyn."

Dulcey opened her mouth to argue with him but when she saw the hard determination in his eyes, she thought better. There would be time enough tomorrow, when they left.

Dulcey set supper on the table. If they did not leave tomorrow, she would have to use what was left of the ham hock that hung in the lean to. Maybe she could go hunting in the morning. Supper was a quiet affair, except for Abby who kept a steady stream of conversation. Often throughout the meal Dulcey looked up to find Nate studying her intensely. It was unnerving. As much as she loved their company, especially Abby's, she would be glad for the peace and quiet again. But then Dulcey wondered if she would ever be able to accept the aloneness again, after tasting what her heart truly dreamed of.

After supper and the table was cleared, Dulcey pulled the pallet out from under the bed. Nate took it from her and placed it on the floor by the hearth.

"Thank you," said Dulcey.

"Are we sleeping on the pallet again Dulcey?" asked Abby as she laid down on it once it was in place.

"No, Poppet. You and Dulcey will have the bed and I will sleep on the floor tonight."

Dulcey could not look at Nate. All she could think about was last night and how she felt when she lay under him and then his kiss again this afternoon.

"Let's get you washed up and I have another chemise you can change into." Dulcey poured some warm water in the bowl. She made quick work of the wash and donned her extra chemise on Abby. "Into bed, Poppet."

"Are you putting on your night clothes, Dulcey?"

"No, Poppet, I think I will sleep in my dress tonight." Dulcey threw a short glance in Nate's direction. He was watching her again.

"Are you going to tell me another story about fairies?" asked Abby.

"All right, move over and give me some room and I will tell you your story."

Dulcey watched as Nate went about and extinguished the candles. The only light came from the fireplace. She watched as he added more peat to the fire and banked it till it glowed brightly. He moved effortlessly like the big tom cat at Brandanlyn. She knew the feel of that body against hers.

"My story, Dulcey?" interrupted Abby.

Dulcey sighed and forced her thoughts back to Abby. She made herself comfortable and allowed Abby to snuggle up against her. With another deep sigh, she began, "There once was a beautiful fairy princess who lived deep in the woods, all alone, except for all the forest animals but she wanted to go to the fairy village and live."

"Why didn't she just go to the village?" asked Abby, as she turned to look at Dulcey.

"Because the other fairies in the village thought she was different because she could do things the other fairies could not do."

"Like what?"

"Shhh! Let me tell my story without all your questions."

Abby nodded.

"Where was I?"

"She could do things the other fairies couldn't do but you didn't tell me what she could do."

Dulcey heard Nate's smothered laugh and smiled.

"Yes, well she could make people feel better but most of all she could see things happen before they happened, especially when she touched them." She wondered why she made the fairy like her. Maybe, she was just trying to warn Nate about her life. If she gave him a hint of what her life included, when she told him in detail, he might understand. Maybe. She could hope.

"Wow!" Abby's eyes widened in wonder.

"But the fairies in the village were afraid of her because they didn't understand her. They believed she was making those things happen and not seeing them before it happened. So, she lived all by herself, because sometimes, she believed they were right about her. But she made friends with all the animals in the forest, the deer, the rabbit, and the fox. But it was the birds she loved most of all, especially when they came to visit her and sing to her their songs. La, la, la, la, la, la, la, la, la, la, la, la, la, la, la, la, la."

Dulcey continued to sing softly, until she was certain Abby was asleep. She turned on her side and Abby snuggled closer. She gazed toward the pallet. Nate lay on his back, his hands under his head staring up at the ceiling. She wondered what he was thinking of. Was she haunting his thoughts the way he was hers? No, they were from two completely different worlds. He was the new baron and she was the granddaughter of the witch who lived in the woods. And now that Grammy was dead, she had become the witch in the woods. No, it could never be.

With a deep sigh, she closed her eyes, but lying in the bed, the same bed that last night he had pulled her down and just for a moment had lain with her, she wanted to lay with him again, to feel his arms around her, his lips on hers. Slowly and quietly, she let the tears fall as she mourned the loss of what could never be.

Nate had listened to her story and the song she sung softly to Abby. He remembered her saying earlier, she was the witch in the woods. No, she was not the witch, she was the fairy in the story she told Abby. And this small fairy like creature had come to mean so much to him. No other woman had ever gotten under his skin, the way Dulcey had. Good God, he had only known her a little more than a day and he could not think of being without her. He wanted her so badly his loins hurt and begged for relief, but the relief he so desired was relief in her. It wasn't like he hadn't had a woman in a long time.

He and Yvette had had an amicable separation just before he left for Brandanlyn. Yvette knew how to please a man and he had been very pleased with her. But Yvette had not touched him emotionally in all those months, as this fairy woman did in just this short time. They had separated on amicable terms and he felt no remorse.

Then why was he aching for Dulcey and could not even contemplate being separated from her. There was a connection with her, a connection he had never felt with another woman. It was crazy to feel this strongly after so short a time. He could not explain it. He could only feel it and feel it he did. He turned his head to the bed and saw her lying on her side her arms wrapped around Abby. For a moment, he was jealous of Abby. He wanted those arms wrapped around him.

He closed his eyes willing himself to sleep. Tomorrow, if the weather remained good and no more snow fell, they would venture back to Brandanlyn. Dulcey would come with them. She would not live here alone. He needed to find out more about her. How did Dulcey fit into the picture? What was her relationship to the old baron?

Tomorrow, when he got back to Brandanlyn. Tomorrow, he would find the answers. Tomorrow.

Chapter 4

To convert someone to go
And take them by the hand and guide them.
                              Saint Thomas Aquinas

Nate stretched as he came awake. Sleeping on the pallet on the floor had not been the most comfortable but it had been a place to sleep. He had slept in worse. He rose quietly from his bed. Abby and Dulcey were still fast asleep. For a moment, he stood over the bed and gazed down at the two of them and smiled. Both of them needed his protection. He took his responsibilities seriously.

He splashed some water on his face, dried it then went into the lean to check on the animals. The goats were doing fine, so were the chickens, Max nuzzled him as Nate petted the side of his neck.

"Hopefully, boy, we can go home this morning, well to Brandanlyn, anyway. Let's hope the snow holds off, so we can leave." Max nickered. Nate pulled some hay from the corner for Max.

He went quietly back into the cottage. They were still sleeping. Good. He pulled his great coat on and quietly opened the door and stepped outside into a world of crystal white. The sun was topping the hill like a big orange ball in the sky. It was a clear crisp morning. The sky was a bright blue, not a snow cloud to be had. There were mounds of snow pushed around yesterday by the wind. But today, they stood there like silent white sentinels. It would be slow going. The snow drifts were deep. Dulcey and Abby would ride Max and he would walk. That would mean two maybe three hours. The sooner they got moving, the better. That way, they would be traveling through the warmest part of the day.

Nate walked back in the cottage. Dulcey immediately looked up from the fireplace. "What does it look like outside?"

"It has stopped snowing. The sky is clear but the snow drifts are high. We will need to go slow."

"Yes, you and Abby will need to be very careful. I will help you get started," explained Dulcey.

Nate looked at her for a moment. "No, I think it would be best if you come with us all the way to the house. I don't want Abby and I to get lost again. You know the way."

"Once I get you to the road," began Dulcey.

"No, you will be coming with us all the way." He was determined she was coming with him to Brandanlyn. She would be safe there. He was not about to leave her here alone.

"But my animals. I can't leave them. Besides---."

Nate interrupted. "I'll send one of the servants for them. You are coming with us. I will not take no for an answer."

Dulcey looked at Nate with the intent of arguing with him, but the stubborn look in his eyes and the tilt of his head, she thought the better of it. He was one used to giving orders and having those orders obeyed. She would go with them, get them safely to Brandanlyn and then she would come back home. It was not worth arguing with him now. Besides Nate was right, they could get lost again and she could get to Brandanlyn with her eyes closed.

"Is there anything you wish to bring with you? When I send someone for the animals, they can pick up the larger items."

Dulcey turned away from him so he would not see her smile. Little did he know, she would be coming back in a couple of days.

"Uncle Nate, Dulcey's coming home with us?" asked Abby sitting up in the bed.

45

"Yes, she is," Nate answered, waiting for Dulcey to argue again.

"Hooray!" said Abby, jumping up and down on the bed.

Nate smiled. She had gotten very attached to Dulcey. Abby needed someone like Dulcey. His mother had never been motherly material. Sometimes, he wondered how he and his brother had survived. Yes, he knew. His father had always been there for them.

"Well get dressed, Poppet, and as soon as we eat we shall be on our way."

He watched as she scrambled out of the bed. "Can you help me Dulcey?"

Dulcey smiled. "Yes, Poppet. Come we will wash first."

Nate watched as Abby and Dulcey got ready to leave. He was anxious to leave, now that he had made up his mind.

Dulcey watched as Nate put snow on the fire in the fireplace. It sizzled and the smoke swirled up the chimney. She felt strange, dizzy, the changes in the forces around her overwhelming. She felt like her life was swirling away just as the smoke from the fire. There was something new on the horizon and she could not make it out. It was cloudy and swirling encompassing her. She felt like everything around her was changing and for the first time she had no control over it, nor could she see the future. Never in all her years had her visions been so murky. She felt entangled in the murkiness.

Nate turned to Dulcey to ask if she was ready, but the question died on his lips. She stood holding on to the back of the chair, pale with a strange far-away look in her eyes, almost like she was somewhere else and not here in the cottage. He stepped toward her and grabbed her arm, "Dulcey?"

For a moment, she simply stared at him and then the light came back in her eyes and she smiled tentatively at him. The connection to the other world had been broken by his touch. Her life was about to change and she had been warned.

"I am ready," she said softly, though she wasn't quite sure whether she was or not.

Nate nodded, still gazing at her intently. "After I saddle my horse, I will bring him around to the front."

Dulcey nodded and watched him go to the door.

"Poppet, I think we should bring these quilts to wrap around us. It's still very cold out there." Abby helped her get two of the quilts and bring them to the front door.

Moments later, Nate was at the front door. Taking Abby easily in his arms, he went out of the door. From the porch, he placed Abby on the saddle. He turned to Dulcey. "Your turn."

"Where will you ride?" asked Dulcey.

"I plan on walking," replied Nate. He thought it was best that he lead the horse through the snow drifts. Besides, the thought of Dulcey sitting in front of him was more torture than he was willing to subject himself to.

With his hands on her waist, he easily helped Dulcey on his horse behind Abby. He handed her one of the quilts. She wrapped it around her and Abby. He turned and pulled her front door close. The other quilt he wrapped around himself, grabbed Max's reins and began slowly walking away from the cottage.

Slowly, carefully, they treaded through the snow drifts, many waist high. Occasionally, Dulcey gave him directions. Even Abby was quiet. The country side was white and pristine with the newly fallen snow. It was a world none of them had ever seen. The beauty of it was breathtaking. The trees glistened in the sunlight with thousands of icicles. It was almost too bright. Before too long, Abby leaned back against Dulcey, sound asleep. She tightened her grip on the child and hugged her closer wrapping the quilt closer about her.

Never had it taken so long to get Brandanlyn in Dulcey's memory. Several times, they had to go around a large snow drift which added more distance and more time. As they turned the corner, Brandanlyn came into sight in the distance. It was a beautiful sight, snow covered, like some painting she had seen in one of the books Lord James had often showed her. She truly had come to love the place. But what the future had in store for her and Brandanlyn was unknown to her and that troubled her

Nate looked up to her and smiled. "We are almost there."

Dulcey nodded, not trusting her voice. Would this be the last time she visited here, she wondered? She closed her eyes for a moment hoping something would be shown to her but nothing came. She sighed, concerned that the forces about her were quiet.

It seemed the closer they got, the further away Brandanlyn was. Slowly, carefully, the trio made their way through the gate and up to the main entrance. Just before they got there, Dulcey shook Abby gently.

"Abby, we are at Brandanlyn."

Abby looked up at her sleepily and then she looked out. She saw Brandanlyn just in front of them, sat up straighter and began fidgeting.

"Be still little one or you are going to slide right off this horse," whispered Dulcey.

Abby immediately stopped squirming. "We're back, Dulcey."

"Yes, Poppet."

Nate stopped at the bottom of the front steps and turned to help Abby down from the horse, then turned to assist Dulcey. His hands stayed longer at her waist than was necessary. Dulcey looked up. Nate was smiling down at her with a smug look. He had gotten her here to Brandanlyn. Now, she was in his home.

Abby ran up the steps to the open door. "We're back!"

Dulcey with shaking fingers took Nate's offered arm and walked up the steps following in Abby's wake.

Dulcey smiled at the gray haired butler that held the door open for them. "Hello, Evers."

Evers the staunch head butler smiled, "It is good to see you again, Miss Dulcey. It's been too long since you were last here. You have been missed."

Nate watched the exchange. So, Dulcey was a common visitor here. Why was he not surprised? She told him she knew Lord James. How well did she know him?

"Your lordship, I am glad you and the little girl survived the storm. We were all so worried." Nate had been impressed with Evers before, but the genuine concern he expressed at this moment added to his respect for the butler.

"Yes, Evers, thanks to Miss Dulcey here. She found Abby and then I found her."

Evers nodded.

"Nathaniel?" a loud feminine voice from the top of the stairs called out.

Dulcey watched as a woman with gray hair walked regally down the stairs. Every hair in place, the lavender gray dress, the latest fashionable style, no doubt. Dulcey could feel the haughtiness from the woman across the space that separated them. It was like a solid wall, impenetrable.

"Grandmother," called Abby as she ran to the woman.

The woman stopped several feet away and held out her hand to stop the charging child. The frown on her face was enough to stop anyone.

"Child, you are a dirty mess."

Abby stopped dead in her tracks, as though she was used to this type of behavior from the woman.

"I'm sorry, Grandmother but I got lost chasing the bunny and Dulcey found me and then Uncle Nate found us." explained Abby.

A young woman slightly older than Dulcey appeared behind the gray haired woman. Her dress, plain brown, her brown hair pulled back in a tight bun. She reminded Dulcey of a little brown wren.

"Thank God, you are here, Miss Bennett. Please take this child upstairs and see to it she is cleaned and properly dressed." The woman waved the child away.

Abby turned and ran back to Dulcey and hugged her tightly. "Thank you, Dulcey. I am so glad you came home with us."

Dulcey hugged her back and kissed the top of her head. "So am I, Poppet. Now go upstairs and get cleaned up. So will I, and then we can meet again."

Abby nodded and grabbed Miss Bennett's hand and bounded up the stairs.

"Nathaniel."

"Yes, mother." Nate raised an eyebrow. As much as he loved his mother, he was not blind to her faults. She was a snob, breeding and proper behavior were the only things she considered important.

"Where have you been? You are filthy. You had everyone worried, when you left as you did."

"I believe Abby explained it all to you just moments ago. Were you not listening?"

"Of course, I was, but children have such a perchance to exaggerate so greatly. You can't believe what they say," replied Nate's mother. She looked from Nate to Dulcey with disdain.

"Well, Abby was correct. She got lost chasing after a bunny. Dulcey found her and brought her to her home. I left to look for Abby, knowing the snow storm would be a bad one and I did not want her in it. I was lucky to find Dulcey's cottage, half frozen when I got there. So mother, had it not been for Dulcey and her cottage, your son and granddaughter would have most probably died in that snow storm. She saved our lives," explained Nate, irritated with his mother.

Nate turned to Dulcey, "Dulcey this is my mother, Lady Roberta Beckham, Dowager Countess of Shefley. Mother this Miss Dulcey Langely."

Dulcey dropped a small curtsey. She did not offer her hand knowing how dirty she must look. It appeared the Countess of Shefley was not in a receptive mood. She had the same blue eyes as Nate and Abby, but these eyes were cold and hard and regarded her like soiled baggage. She could feel the contempt like a battering ram against the forces around her.

"Forgive me, Countess. I would much rather continue this discussion, once I have bathed and changed." Dulcey needed to get away from her to breathe again.

"Yes, very much so," stated Nate, hoping to avoid one of mother's intense questionings. "Evers, can you see to it a room is prepared for Miss Dulcey."

"I've seen to it that her suite was ready, as soon as I saw, she had accompanied you, m'lord." To Dulcey, he said, "Peggy, I am certain is waiting upstairs for you, miss."

"Thank you, Evers," replied Dulcey, then turned to the Countess, nodded and walked up the stairs to her room. She could feel their eyes watching her, but she kept her shoulders straight, her head erect.

Nate looked at Evers for further explanation. "Miss Dulcey has had her own rooms at Brandanlyn for years, m'lord. She has spent much of her time here, while growing up."

Nate nodded. There was much more to Dulcey Langely than he was first led to believe. He watched her go up the stairs and turn down the hall like she knew this house very well.

"Nathaniel, I demand that you tell me who this woman is? The only saving grace is that Abby was with you. Not the best of chaperones but given the circumstances, it will have to be enough." Her son needed to explain this woman to her.

"Mother, I am cold. I am tired and dirty. And I am most definitely hungry. I am heading to my suite for a bath and a change of clothes and then Evers, I would like a large lunch set up in the small dining room. Once all of those have been dealt with, then I will be most pleased to answer all your questions. Until then, they will have to wait."

"Nathaniel William Hollins Beckham. You will not speak to your mother in that tone." She could not believe her son was speaking to her in such a manner. This was beyond tolerable.

"If you continue mother, I may not speak to you at all." With that said, he turned and walked up the stairs. He noticed the slight smile on Evers lips.

No doubt, his mother was wrecking her usual havoc. He could hear his mother muttering but at the moment all he wanted was a warm bath. He would deal with his mother later. His father had spoiled her immensely and she had taken advantage of it. Since his father's death, he and his brother had continued spoiling her. It had made it easier for all concerned, especially Grayson. He, Nate had avoided her for the most part, being the younger son had been able to. Well, it was time she realized, she could not control him. He was not Grayson.

~~~~~~~~~~~~

Dulcey entered her room. She had not been here since Lord James's death in August. She loved her rooms. The soft greens and golds of the bed hangings and drapes and the butter cream on the walls made this her ultimate sanctuary. Lord James had spared no expense when he set up this suite for her. It was at the end of the far hall. It had its own dressing room and its own sitting room. It allowed her the privacy, she always sought.

Peggy was there waiting for her as she stepped into the room. "I have a tub of hot water waiting for you. I have put out your favorite soap, Miss Dulcey. You look so tired. Shall I help you with your hair?"

Dulcey sighed. "I think, I would like that very much, Peggy." Dulcey allowed Peggy to help her remove her clothes and slip into the tub of hot water. Again she sighed, as she felt the stress of the last few days drain from her body. Peggy began washing her hair gently rubbing her hair, her fingers massaging her scalp. She had never wanted Peggy's help before. Now, she wondered why, because this felt like heaven. Dulcey felt the bucket of water pour over her head, rinsing her hair. Peggy held a large bath cloth as Dulcey stood up and stepped out of the tub and wrapped it around her. Peggy took another towel and wrapped it around Dulcey hair.

Dulcey sat down in the chair in front of the roaring fire. Peggy hand rubbed her hair. Slowly she brushed Dulcey's hair using the heat of the fireplace to dry the long tresses. It was the first time Miss Dulcey had let her assist her in this manner. She sensed Miss Dulcey did not want to talk. Peggy merely did what was needed without talking.

Dulcey sat for a moment savoring the peace. But she knew she could not hide here for forever. "Which dress should I wear Peggy?"

She turned to Peggy to find her holding a soft wool dress of deep rose. It was one of the dresses she had never won.

"This one would look lovely, miss." Peggy wanted Miss Dulcey to look her best. The master, the new baron was a handsome man. She wanted Miss Dulcey to be able to hold her own with the Countess, too.

Lord James had bought her a total wardrobe after Grammy died, when he believed she would move in here permanently. He had been so disappointed when she had refused. But she had compromised with him and stayed more often and for longer periods of time.

Dulcey nodded and dressed. Peggy did her hair very simply with a dark rose velvet ribbon. Dulcey looked at her reflection in the mirror. The soft wool clung to her body accentuating her every curve. She wondered, what would Nate think of this Dulcey? No, she was not of the same class as Nate. She had heard his mother comment, as she walked up the stairs.

"Thank you Peggy, for all your help."

"You know it's always a pleasure to help you, miss." Peggy smiled. Everyone loved Miss Dulcey and all only wanted what was best for her.

Knowing she could no longer delay going downstairs, Dulcey left her room to see what awaited her.

Chapter 5

Suspicion is the companion of mean souls
And the bane of all good society.
Thomas Paine

Upstairs in the master suite, Nate found his valet, Simmons waiting for him with a tub of hot water.

"Good gracious, m'lord, you look a sight worse for wear," said Simmons as he helped Nate off with his jacket. "But I am glad to see you have returned in one piece. Many of us worried about you and the little one. T'was a bad snow storm." Simmons had been with his lordship for years and though he had worried about him, he knew the earl could take care of himself and find the little miss, Abby.

"That it was Simmons. I was lucky this time to have come across the cottage and then to find Abby safely there, too, was a God send," replied Nate as he sank grateful in the tub of hot water. It was just the thing to get the chill out of his bones from walking through all that snow. He let out a deep sigh of relief for so many things.

"Aye, the staff believed you would stumble onto Miss Langely's cottage."

Nate looked at Simmons thoughtfully. "What does the staff say about Miss Langely?" Nate knew if anybody could find about Dulcey, it would be Simmons.

"She is very well liked by all here. It seems the baron doted on her. She visited often, sometimes, for several weeks at a time. The baron thought she would come to stay after the grandmother died, but she did not," explained Simmons as he laid out the earl's clothes.

"Do they know what her relationship was to the baron?" questioned Nate. Usually, the staff knew as much or more about the nobility they worked for. This whole situation was very curious to him.

"That's the strange part, m'lord. No one knows for sure. There are speculations, but no one is certain. But the one thing of certain, she is well loved here. They are worried you will send her packing and turn her out of her cottage. I've never seen you do such a thing and have said as much, but the Countess has made some rather odious remarks on the issue. "

Nate sighed in exasperation. "I take mother has been her usual charming self."

Simmons snorted. "Begging your pardon, m'lord, she has been exceptionally difficult. Nothing here has pleased her. I have had to reassure the staff that you are not -----."

"Like my mother. Thank you, Simmons. I knew I could count on you. I'm afraid it may get worse. I have brought Miss Langely back with me."

Simmons raised his eyebrows. This did not bode well. The Countess would not like this at all. He shook his head. The Countess could be a formidable foe and she was not in the best of moods having been coerced into coming here.

~~~~~~~~~~~~~~~

Nate made it downstairs in a better mood. A warm bath and clean clothes had made a big difference in how he now felt. He went to the sideboard and poured himself a liberal glass of whiskey. It burned as it went down but it tasted so good. He would need this to deal with his mother. He heard the door open, turned to find her striding purposely to his side. She must have been lying in wait somewhere close.

"Nathaniel, I am deeply upset by your very rude behavior earlier to me, your mother," she began through pursed lips. Nathaniel was being extremely condescending as far as she was concerned. He knew better than to speak to her in such a manner. She would simply not allow it.

"Mother I was not about to let you be rude to our guest." He took another sip of whiskey

"Humph! Your father would be rolling in his grave if he had heard how you spoke to me earlier, all because of that girl." She stood before him, intent on him answering all of her questions.

"You seem to forget that girl saved my life and Abby's." Couldn't his mother understand the importance of that fact. He took another sip of whiskey.

"Who is she, Nathaniel?" demanded the Countess staring him in the eye.

"She is a friend of the Baron," answered Nate and looked away. Actually, that is all he knew about her.

"The Baron's whore or by blow? I do know about these things." She was determined to find out which, especially if she had spent two nights under the same roof with her son.

Never had she seen the fire in her son's eyes as she did at this moment. It was like his eyes were ablaze with anger. It frightened her more than she cared to admit. But she would not show her fear to him.

"Never, I repeat, never put those two words in the same thought as Dulcey. Do I make myself clear? Father spoiled you and allowed you to get your way. Grayson allowed it to continue for the most part, until he married. I, for the most part have allowed it to continue as well, because it was easier for us. But rest assured mother, I will not hesitate to pack your bags myself, put you in the carriage and send you back to London." Nate tightened his hand on his glass. He was surprised he had not broken it. He was just that angry. She put his own suspicions into words.

Countess Shefley took a step back as though her son had physically hit her. Never in her entire life had she ever been talked to in that tone or manner. She was shocked and at a complete loss for words.

"Now, mother, I need to talk to Evers so that he may send someone upstairs to check on Dulcey. I am hungry and I would like her to join me for lunch. You are welcome to join us as well, as long as you behave yourself. Do I make myself clear?"

The countess nodded slightly. But she was not about to let this be. She would find out more about this woman.

"Good," replied Nate and walked out the door in search of Evers. He stopped at the stairs, for coming down the stairs was undoubtedly the fairy Dulcey described to Abby in her stories. The soft rose wool clung to her body temptingly. This was not some borrowed dress like he first believed she would find. No, this dress was made especially for her.

Her hair had a golden shine, the color of rich honey. The soft tendrils framed her face as the rest was tied to allow it to fall softly down her back in curls. His first thought was what would it feel like to have it wrapped around the both of them. He shook his head slightly to dispel that vision in his mind.

But it made him ask, what was Dulcey relationship to the Baron? His mother had put some rather ugly scenarios in his mind. No, he would not listen to his mother and her ugly innuendos. She always loved thinking the worse of people. She thrived on gossip and immensely enjoyed spreading it about. The more damaging, the better she liked it. Just not this time.

He held his hand out to Dulcey and assisted her down the last few stairs.

"I must say you look very charming." He smiled. He had realized in the cottage she was something special. But to see her dressed as she should be, was striking. There was a fresh clean smell about her. He couldn't place the fragrance, but it suited her to perfection, light and airy, fresh and clean. She fit in here like she was supposed to, like she had been here all of her life.

Dulcey laughed softly. "You're not so bad yourself, m'lord. You no longer look like a frozen icicle."

Nate laughed. "I am famished. I know you tried your best but you were not prepared for guests. Evers is luncheon served?" he asked, as he saw Evers coming toward them.

"Yes, my lord."

Nate safely tucked Dulcey hand through his arm. "Then let's eat."

"Nathaniel," called the countess, as she watched the exchange. No, this was not good, not good at all, she thought.

Nate looked over his shoulder and replied, "You are more than happy to join us, mother." He walked into the dining room with Dulcey on his arm, his mother followed, much to Nate's chagrin.

He escorted Dulcey to the chair at his right, pulled her chair out. He went to his mother's chair and held it out for her. He would need to placate his mother somewhat for now, in order to have some semblance of peace.

As the food was served, the Countess began her inquisition. She was determined to find out more about this girl that her son seemed to be so enamored with. This infatuation, he seemed to have developed for this nothing girl must be stopped, at all cost. She would not allow this whatever to disturb her life, especially her son's life. No, she was not going to allow that to happen.

"My dear, I understand you stay at a cottage on this land, yet, you know your way about the manor, as well."

"I grew up and lived with Grammy Digby at the cottage. She died two years ago. I have always come to Brandanlyn ever since I was a child. Grammy would bring me two, three times a week and Lord James tutored me," explained Dulcey.

"Tutored?" asked the Countess. Young ladies were not tutored by an elderly gentleman.

"Yes, I can read Latin, Greek, and French and a little Spanish and German though, not as well. Lord James also taught me writing, science, mathematics, geography, or whatever I showed an interest in. Lord James believed females should have the same opportunity to education as men." He had stressed that fact to her time and time again, until she firmly believed it.

"I heartily agree. That is what I want for Abby," answered Nate. He was impressed to know this about Dulcey. She continued to surprise him.

The countess was not impressed. She pursed her lips and narrowed her eyes. She firmly believed that women did not need to know all these things. Such things were useless and wasted. "But I still don't understand. Why?"

Dulcey shrugged and looked away from the cold blue eyes that stared at her. "I'm not exactly certain myself. I just know it was something he and Grammy Digby agreed upon." Dulcey herself had asked the same question many times. Grammy Digby would just say that was the way it was. Lord James had told her after Grammy Digby died, that one day soon she would understand.

"I take it that you lived with this Grammy of yours because you have no parents," continued the countess. She was not getting the information she needed. The girl was being obtuse, perhaps on purpose, thought the countess.

"My parents died when I was about two," explained Dulcey. There was not much of her past to tell.

"Who are your parents, my dear?" continued the countess. Surely, the child knew who her parents were.

Nate eyed his mother through narrowed eyes. He was suspicious. What was his mother up to?

"My mother's name was Anne and my father was George. I was told Lord James knew my father very well before he died. That is all I know." Dulcey wished she knew more.

Enough of the inquisition thought Nate and turned the conversation to Christmas preparations, now that he was back here at Brandanlyn. He wanted to make a memorable Christmas as this was Abby's first Christmas without her parents. To have gotten lost as well must have frightened her, too.

The food was good. Cook here was very good. He wanted to talk to her about what to serve for Christmas. He wanted it to be special. He would get Dulcey's help.

He was surprised. His mother was, far the most part, rather sociable after he changed the subject to Christmas. Still he did not trust her. She was up to something, of that, he had little doubt.

Dulcey turned to Nathaniel at the end of the meal and rose from her seat. "I'm going upstairs to check on Abby."

Evers was waiting in the grand hall. "My lord, several of the staff would like to go outside and cut the greens for the decorations. We know it should be done tomorrow on Christmas Eve but we thought to start the celebration early, especially since you and Miss Abby have returned safe. We will do a special yule log to bring in tomorrow."

"Yes, Evers, of course. Do you need my help?"

"No, your lordship. I think perhaps you have had enough of the snow," Evers said with a slight smile.

Nate chuckled. "I think you may be right, Evers. We will help once you bring it in."

He watched as Dulcey climbed the stairs. He liked watching the way her hips swayed. Oh, how he wanted her. In fact, the need was only getting stronger. There was that dream of her under him. He wanted it to be reality and not a dream.

The countess watched her son with pursed lips. She knew when a man wanted a woman and her son wanted this girl. Not if she had anything to do with it. She needed to find something about Dulcey that would change Nathaniel's mind. It shouldn't be hard to do. She was a nobody. There was bound to be something. She would not stop till she found that one thing that would bring her down.

"Mother, I shall be in the study. Lord James left several legal papers I need to go through. Please behave yourself."

"M'lord, there is a reply to your letter to Mr. Kinley, his lordships solicitor. I have placed it on your desk," said Evers.

"Thank you, Evers. Mother?"

Countess Shefley gazed at him with innocence. "I shall be on my best behavior."

Nate looked at her doubtfully. "See that you do," he said as he reminded her. As much as he loved his mother, he knew her too well. He did not trust her. She would try to destroy Dulcey just for the simple fact she was not of what his mother called noble birth.

He walked to the study at the back of the house with Dulcey very much on his mind.

~~~~~~~~~~~~~~~~

Dulcey walked to the nursery. She could remember using it as a child. The countess had brought back many questions to her mind concerning Lord James. Some she had asked him or Grammy but had never gotten any meaningful explanation. She had felt for a long time, they were hiding something from her but she had no clue to what it was. Even her visions had never showed anything to her.

Dulcey opened the door and Abby was sitting at a small table having tea with her governess, a bear, and a doll. "Hello, Poppet."

Abby ran to her. Dulcey bent down and hugged her. "Oh, Dulcey, you look like a fairy princess."

Dulcey smiled. "And you my little one, look very nice, too." Dulcey extended her hand, "I am Dulcey Langely."

"I am Franny Bennett, Miss Abbigail's nurse, governess. I am sorry Miss Abbigail got away from me and caused you so much trouble."

Dulcey looked at the young woman in front of her. She was sure Franny was but a few years older than she. She wore her brown hair in a soft bun. She had soft brown eyes. She was petite in statue. Her smile echoed in her eyes. As their hands met Dulcey felt a calmness about the young woman. This was a kind and gentle young lady. She was good for Abbigail.

"It was no trouble having Abby. I enjoyed her visit very much."

"Dulcey tells stories about fairies." Abby looked up the Dulcey and asked, "Can I tell her our secret? Please?"

Dulcey looked at those big blue eyes and realized Abby was not very good at keeping secrets. Dulcey nodded.

"Dulcey knows real fairies and they teached her how to make medicines."

Franny immediately corrected, "taught her."

"Yes, taught her. She knows fairies."

Franny looked up with a smile. "How lucky for you, Miss Dulcey. Fairies."

"You must keep it a secret, Miss Franny. Uncle Nate knows, too."

Franny nodded. "Lord Beckham knows the secret, as well. Well, if we tell too many people, the fairies may not tell Miss Dulcey any more of their secrets," she whispered to Abigail very seriously.

Abigail stood there very thoughtful and nodded. "You mustn't tell anyone, Miss Franny. The fairies have to talk to Dulcey. It's very important you keep her secret."

Dulcey and Franny looked at each other and smiled, knowingly. As long as it was Abby talking about fairies, everyone would think it was her childish imagination, thought Dulcey.

"May I join you for tea?" asked Dulcey.

Immediately, Abby started talking about her doll and tea. Dulcey and Franny sat at the table with her and pretended with her.

"Poppet, I need to go back to my room."

"Will you come tell me a story tonight?" begged Abigail.

"Now, Miss Abigail, Miss Dulcey has other obligations," answered Franny.

Dulcey took Abby's small hand in hers. "I promise Poppet, I will tell you a story for bedtime, every night I am here."

Abby looked at her still not sure. "You promise?"

"Yes, poppet, I promise. But you must listen to Miss Franny."

Abby nodded. "Yes, I promise."

"Good. Then I will see you tonight."

Chapter 6

Morality is the attitude we adopt
Toward people whom we personally dislike.
Oscar Wilde

Dulcey left the nursery. She walked down the hall
with the intent of going to her room to rest. She should
have known, it was not to be. The Countess was lying in
wait for her down the hall.

"My dear, I was just going to my sitting room.
Would you join me for tea? I think we need to talk," said
Countess Shefley.

"Yes, of course, my lady. I will be glad to join you
for tea," replied Dulcey. She could feel the hostility from
the countess likes waves against the forces around her. She
had felt it earlier when first introduced but now, it was
more pronounced. As jumbled as the forces were, she
could still feel intensity of this woman's animosity. She
would have to tread very carefully around her. This
woman was going to be a formidable adversary. This was
not going to be a pleasant tea. Dulcey followed the
Countess's to her private sitting room.

The tea tray was there awaiting them. "Please sit,
my dear." Dulcey choose the small rose brocade seatee
across from the Countess's rose brocade wing chair. She
watched as the Countess poured. "Sugar? Milk?"

"Yes, please," replied Dulcey, nervous about the
coming questioning. She didn't know what more she could
tell her than what she had said at lunch. Nate was not here
to keep her in check. She was about to know what the
inquisition felt like.

Countess Shefley smiled sweetly as she handed Dulcey her cup of tea, a smile that did not reflect in her eyes.

Dulcey smiled nervously. She was not accustomed to the social obligations, even though Lord James had made certain she was trained to attend such. She felt that she and the countess would always be at odds. She would always be considered an enemy to the Countess.

"Tell me about yourself, my dear. You seem to be very comfortable here."

Dulcey felt like she was one of those insects Lord James made her look at under the looking glass. "As I said earlier, I have been here many times."

"So you have said and that your parents died when you were about two?" the Countess asked. She needed to know more about this woman, no matter what her son said. It was because of him, she needed to find this information. It would simply not do for him to get involved with this young woman.

"My mother and father died when I was a baby. As I said earlier, Grammy Digby raised me." She didn't know what more she could add. She didn't know very much herself.

"Is this your grandmother on your mother or father's side? You did not say earlier."

"I am not certain. I never asked." Dulcey had often wondered but had never asked Grammy. There were many questions she had asked but Grammy had not wanted to answer them. She always said one day, she would understand. She had hoped after Grammy died, Lord James would tell her but he never did.

"How is it you don't know?" questioned the Countess. How could she not know about her family and her past? There was a secret here and she was determined to find out what it was. She needed more information from this young woman. Information, she could use to show her son, this woman was not right for him in the least. She was a nobody, way beneath his title and rank. She needed her son to realize it. This was not a good match for him. She should have argued with him more, when he suggested she come here.

Dulcey shrugged. "I have asked both Grammy Digby and Lord James many times but both refused to answer me and always said one day, I would understand. Now, they are both dead and I was never told anything." She did not know what more she could add. She simply did not know. She had never been told.

The countess eyed her sharply. "So, you have no idea who your parents are." Can this child woman truly be that ignorant about herself. She was hiding something, she had to be.

"Their names were Anne and George Langely. That is what I have been told." Dulcey did not know what more information to give her. "I was only two when they died. I don't remember them at all. I truly wished I knew more."

A knock sounded at the door just before Nate walked in. Evers had informed him his mother had ordered tea. Peggy had stopped him at the head of the stairs and informed him she had seen his mother escort Dulcey into her sitting room. Dulcey was not equipped to handle his mother when she decided to interrogate. He had seen his mother's frown of disapproval. That did not bode well.

He could feel the tension in the room when he walked in. "Ah, so this is where you both are. The staff has come back with the greens to decorate. I thought you would like to give your suggestions since you have done this here before. I was on my way to get Abby. She did have some definite suggestions at the cottage, didn't she, Dulcey?" He could see his mother's sour expression.

Dulcey smiled, grateful for Nate's rescue. She was certain his mother was just getting started with her questions.

Nate's heart skipped a beat when Dulcey turned her smile on him. Something in him stirred, that made him want to see that smile, every day from now on. It was something, he would need to work on.

"Are you coming downstairs, Mother, to help out?" Nate asked, as he offered his hand to Dulcey.

"Of course, I would not miss it," replied the Countess. She was not about to have her son alone with this young woman. He had already been too much in her company.

Nate looked surprised. His mother was never interested in Christmas decorations before. The staff always saw to it.

Dulcey followed Nate with his mother close behind them as they walked to Abby's room.

When they entered Abby's room, Franny was reading to Abby.

"Poppet, we are going downstairs to decorate. Would you and Miss Franny like to help us?" asked Nate.

"Like Dulcey's house?"

"Yes."

"Yea!" replied Abby, jumping up and down.

Immediately, the Countess admonished, "Young ladies do not act in that manner. Stop this display at once."

Abby stopped abruptly, her eyes wide with fear.

"Oh, mother, it's Christmas. Abby is excited. Come, Poppet, let's get downstairs and get started." He took Abby's hand in his and with Dulcey at his side, he escorted everyone downstairs.

A large bundle of evergreens stood in the entrance way, just to the side of the door. Evers stood nearby.

"I've brought down the rest of the decorations, Miss Dulcey" said Evers.

Dulcey smiled. "Thank you, Evers."

The countess eyes narrowed. This young woman was way too familiar in this house, with the servants and the running of it. She needed to be put back in her place. This all belonged to her son now. She had no right to be giving the servants orders like she was the lady of the house.

"We will not be putting up all the decorations, Evers," ordered the Countess.

Nate turned with a questioning glare. "And why ever not, Mother?"

"Why in observance of proper mourning for Lord Fergers, of course."

Dulcey nodded. The Countess was right. But it was Lord James most favorite time of year. He would not like the fact they were not celebrating Christmas as it should be. He was never one for following proper protocol.

"Evers, let's just put some greenery on all the mantles throughout the manor and above the front door. We must do something for Abigail," replied Dulcey.

"Yes." replied Nate. "Where shall we begin, Abby?"

Abby directed the placement of all the greenery throughout the manor. Dulcey made suggestions of how best to use them in the places Abby wanted them. Amid the laughter of all involved, except the Countess who looked on disapprovingly, the manor was decorated. Upon completion, Dulcey looked around and smiled. Lord James would have loved this. Had it not been for the Countess most sour disposition and constant complaints, it would have been perfect. Abby had the best time, especially after Nate took his mother aside and spoke to her and the complaints slackened.

Dulcey had told Abby the story of the mistletoe at the cottage. Abby was determined it was to be hung on top of the doorway to the green salon where guests were entertained. Dulcey stepped through the doorway in search of more ribbon when Abby called for her to stop. Little did she realize, she had stopped right under the mistletoe.

"Uncle Nate, you have to kiss Dulcey," chirped Abby.

Dulcey blushed and made as if to continue on, but Nate would have none of it.

"Tradition is tradition, my dear," said Nate as he grabbed her hand. He bent his head and lightly brushed her lips. It took every ounce of his willpower not to take her in his arms and give her the kiss he so desperately wanted. Problem was he wanted much more than a kiss, he wanted all of her.

Dulcey looked up and past Nate to find his mother staring daggers at her.

Abby stood clapping her hands. "Yea, it works."

Dulcey gently pulled away, turned and continued on her way for more ribbon. Her emotions were in turmoil, not just from her reaction to Nate, but from the looks of his mother. This had not been a good idea in coming here. She could feel the forces of change surrounding this house and the people in it. It was all so muddled. She could feel the force of change growing ever so strong. Soon, that was all she knew, soon. That change felt like it would affect her most of all. It frightened her, but she knew it was coming and there was nothing she could do to stop it. She would just have to let it play out. She sighed in resignation.

Nate had Abigail and her nanny join them for supper much to the Countess's displeasure. To all others, it was an enjoyable time. Dulcey followed Abby and Franny upstairs to tell her the bedtime story about fairies just as she promised.

Dulcey walked slowly down the hall to her rooms, deep in thought. She would stay until after Christmas for Abby's sake, but she would need to leave soon after that.

"Huh hum." Nate had watched for her, wanting to talk with her. Actually, he wanted to do more than talk, but he knew his mother was lurking about.

Dulcey looked up. "Nate?"

"I didn't get to tell you, but I received word from Lord James's solicitor here in the district. It seems he wishes to talk to both of us. Lord James it appears has some special bequests that concern us both, especially you."

Dulcey looked at him puzzled. "Why does he wish to speak to me? I thought it was all settled. That is why you are here."

"No, I was told I inherited the title because of lack of male heirs and though the relations were distant, it seems it traced back to my brother and since his death to me. Even Mother did not know of these relations. Whatever it is, Kinley will be here two days after Christmas to discuss it with us."

This meant she would have to remain here another few days. This was proving to be more difficult than she first imagined. Just being this close to Nate simply talking, Dulcey could feel the strange pull between them.

Dulcey slowly leaned toward him, but quickly pulled away, when she noticed the Countess behind Nate.

"I am on my way to retire for the night, I suggest we all do the same, as I am afraid tomorrow being Christmas Eve, will be quite busy," suggested the Countess.

Nate frowned. Mother again. "I suppose you are right, Mother."

"Yes. Will you walk me to my room? There is something I would like to discuss with you." She needed to separate her son from this young woman. There was something between them. She could feel it. It must not be allowed continue.

"Yes, I was heading toward my room myself." She nodded to each in turn. "Goodnight, Lady Shefley, good night, Nate." Dulcey turned and walked on down the hall.

"Good night, Dulcey." Nate watched her walk down the hall. Oh, how he liked to watch the sway of her hips. Taking a deep breath, he turned to his mother. "Well, Mother, what did you so desperately need to talk to me about?"

The countess pursed her lips, narrowed her eyes, "Don't use that tone of voice with me, Nathaniel."

Nate sighed. Sometimes dealing with his mother stretched his patience. She had been exceedingly difficult since he returned. She had taken an instant dislike to Dulcey and it did not bode well. She did not do well with what she considered common people.

"Yes, Mother," he placated for the time being. He was tired and did not wish to argue. It had been a long day.

"Have you gotten a present for Abigail for Christmas? I have a new dress for her, but she will be expecting something from you as well."

"I bought her that doll she liked before we left London. I had it packed and brought with us." Nate walked his mother to her room. He stopped at her door. "Rest assured, Abby will have a good Christmas."

The Countess stopped at her door her hand on the handle. "What is this meeting with this Mr. Kinley about?" Nathaniel was the heir to this place and the title, a very distant heir but the heir none the less. What did this meeting mean? She did not like it, especially since it also involved this Dulcey woman.

Nate shrugged. "I don't know, Mother, except that he must speak with myself and Dulcey. It could be

anything."

"I don't like it. No telling what that woman influenced Lord Fergers into doing."

Nate sighed deeply. "Mother, please." He was tired and he did not wish to speculate on the meaning of this meeting with his mother.

"Some women, even as young as this one knows how to get an old man to do things---"

Nate interrupted, "Mother I am tired of repeating myself about your disparaging remarks concerning Dulcey. They need to stop and they need to stop, now. I will not hear you talk in that manner again. Do I make myself understood?" This was becoming too much to be anywhere near acceptable even for his mother.

The Countess pursed her lips and squinted her eyes as she looked him calculatingly. She was not about to stop, no matter what her son threatened. She did not like this Dulcey woman. No, this was far from over.

"Good night, Nathaniel." She offered her cheek for him to kiss.

Nate barely touched her offered cheek and replied, "Good night, Mother." He walked on to his rooms, wondering if any of his words had gotten through to her. He seriously doubted it. This was not going to be an easy Christmas.

Chapter 7

This above all: to thine own self be true.
William Shakespeare

Christmas Eve morning was bright and sunny. The snow of the past few days was quickly beginning to melt. Nate woke up early, after a rather restless night. Dreams of Dulcey had plagued his rest all through the night. Something about her had gotten under his skin. Never in his life had a woman so affected him. He was truly beginning to maybe believe the stories she told Abby about being friends with the fairies. He wondered, if they had not given her some of their fairy dust.

Nate shook his head to dispel such thoughts. As he entered the dining room, he found Dulcey already sitting at the table eating. He smiled when he saw her there. He would have several hours with her this morning. Abby would be with her governess. His mother did not usually arise before noon. He planned on enjoying this time with her.

"Good morning. I hope you slept well," Nate said as he approached the side bar and began loading his plate. He sat down beside Dulcey as he had done the night before.

Dulcey smiled. "Good morning, Nate." She had risen early as she always did. She had hoped Nate would not. "Yes, thank you," she replied. She could not tell him she had tossed and turned most of the night due to dreams about him.

"Does your mother come down for breakfast?" asked Dulcey, hoping she did not. Hopefully, she would have several hours without the Countess hovering about. It was bad enough her forces were so jumbled but to add the Countess to the mix, made for a very disconcerting atmosphere. As much as she wanted peace, she knew that would not be possible.

"No, she does not. She has breakfast in her bed, sometime around noon usually," replied Nate as he took a bite of ham.

Good, she thought. "Have my animals been brought here?" asked Dulcey. Her routine had been interrupted by coming here. As soon as she finished eating, she would check on them.

"Yes, I was told Lil John went after them yesterday and they are safely in the barn." Nate watched her. What woman had he ever known would be worried about the animals, but Dulcey was. Today, she was dressed in a light brown straw colored wool dress. On most of the women in London, it would have looked drab, but on Dulcey it brought out the honey color of her hair and skin. She wore her hair again in a long braid that reached to the bottom of her back.

Again, Nate wondered what she would look like with her hair undone, the only thing covering her. He could feel himself responding to that vision in his mind. He shook his head to dispel those thoughts, but it was becoming more and more difficult.

"Tomorrow is Christmas day. How did you and Lord James celebrate it?"

Dulcey smiled, remembering past Christmases. Lord James had always enjoyed Christmas. She had always spent several weeks here at Brandanlyn. As a child, she always had several presents to open, a new doll, a new book, always new clothes. Most of her clothes remained here at the manor house then, just as they did now.

"We usually attended church in the morning but with still so much snow on the roads we might forgo that this year." Nate nodded in agreement. "We usually had a large breakfast when we returned home. Sometimes when we had several guests from around the area, we had a large late luncheon instead. When it was just us, after we ate, we would sit in the green drawing room and talk."

She still felt the pain of his loss. So much had changed since he died. And more change was coming. She just she wished she knew what. Just when she needed to be able to see what was coming her ability to see was murky and unclear. It made her uneasy. In the past, it had always meant it was something in her future, but it had never been this strange, this unreadable.

Nate nodded. It was what he had in mind. Because of the snow storm, he had decided not to invite some of his neighbors. Maybe, he would have a party of some sort later.

"Does Cook know what to prepare or shall I talk to her?" It would be better for him to talk to cook than his mother. From all reports, his mother had been up to her usual autocratic self and alienated the staff with her demands.

"I can talk to Cook for you. I did it for Lord James. Is there anything special, you or your mother would care for?" asked Dulcey. She had seen to it in the past. Lord James had insisted, saying she needed to know how to, when she ran a home of her own.

Nate gazed at her thoughtfully. She continued to surprise him. "Please do. I'm sure anything you plan will be fine. Please, tell Cook she is to take orders from you only, from now on."

"Certainly. But your mother will want to have some say in it."

"Mother does not always deal well with new servants. I would rather you handle it, if you don't mind?" Hopefully, he could avoid the havoc his mother was capable of causing.

Dulcey finished eating. She wanted to check on her animals and talk to Cook and said as much.

Nate nodded and watched her walk off to the kitchen. As much as he wanted to follow her, he decided for both of their sakes it was best, he let her go alone. But he was beginning to very much like watching her walk away, watching the way her hips swayed so temptingly. He let out a sigh of frustration. How his body wanted her.

He needed to find out more about Dulcey. Perhaps, Lord Fergers kept something in his study that would explain how Dulcey was enmeshed into all of this. There had to be a reason why Lord James had provided for Dulcey as he had. He refused to think along the lines his mother had suggested, yet he could not help but wonder if Dulcey was not his bastard child. Much that he hated to think along those lines, it did make sense. Yes, perhaps there was a clue in his study. He would look and he would find something.

~~~~~~~~~~~~~~~~~

Dulcey found her animals safe and very well taken care of. She knew she would. She knew Lil John would. After a short conversation with him, Dulcey went back into the house through the kitchen. She spoke with Cook and decided on the menu for Christmas, soup, roasted goose, smoked ham, cabbage, potatoes, carrots and of course plum pudding.

"Will ye be making yer gingerbread planks, miss? We all like them. It wouldn't be Christmas without them," said Cook.

Dulcey smiled. "I had planned on it. I was hoping to have Abby help me. We made some at the cottage and she enjoyed it so. That is, if we are not troubling you."

Cook smiled. "Not at all, Miss Dulcey. That little one needs some mothering." Cook then frowned. "That Countess ain't much of one."

Dulcey sighed in resignation. She was reluctant to disagree for she felt the same way but she would not say so in front of Cook, no matter how much she agreed.

"Would now be a good time? I'm not sure if Abby has lessons this morning."

"Now would be fine. I do believe Miss Franny said there were no lessons planned for the next few days being Christmas and all."

Dulcey nodded. "Good. I'll go upstairs and fetch her. Oh, and have you seen Lord Beckham?"

Cook smiled. "He went in Lord James study right after breakfast, he did. I don't believe he's come out."

Dulcey nodded again and left in search of Abby, thinking it would be good Nate was busy in Lord James study. Why she couldn't say but it would be easier for her, if he wasn't helping again. It only brought back memories of his kiss, something she was trying very hard to forget but with very little luck on that account.

Abby and Miss Franny were in the nursery just as Dulcey suspected. The moment she walked through the door, Abby ran to her and hugged her. "Dulcey!"

"Hello, Poppet. Good morning, Miss Franny." Dulcey smiled and hugged Abby back in return. "I have a surprise for you, if Miss Franny says it is all right."

"What? What?" asked Abby wiggling, unable to stand still.

"I have talked with Cook and she says it is fine with her, if we come down to the kitchen and make some more of the gingerbread planks. That is, if Miss Franny says it is all right."

Abby faced broke out in a big smile and she clapped her hands. "Oh, please, Miss Franny. We made them at Dulcey's house. They are so, so good. Can Miss Franny come too? Please?"

Dulcey smiled. "Of course Miss Franny can come, too. But maybe she has something she would like to do instead, since you will be with me." Dulcey looked at Franny who nodded her head.

"I would love to join you. It sounds like a wonderful adventure," agreed Franny. Gingerbread planks did sound delicious.

Dulcey took Abby's hand and said, "Well, then let us adventure on."

The three of them invaded Cooks domain. Cook had everything set up for them when they arrived. Several of the kitchen staff joined in with the making, much to everyone's delight. Soon the kitchen had the wonderful smell of gingerbread wafting through the house along with laughter from everyone involved.

Chapter 8

Love is that condition in which the happiness of
another person
Is essential to your own......
                    Robert A. Heinlein

Nate walked out of Lord James's study
disappointed, for he had not been able to find anything that
had given him any clue to his relationship with Dulcey.
Maybe, Mr. Kinley would have the answers. The sweet
smell of gingerbread met him in the hall as he walked out.
He looked at Evers who smiled, "I know that smell.
Dulcey must be in the kitchen."

Evers nodded. "Yes, my lord, and so is Miss Abby
and Miss Franny. Last time I peeked in, they were all
having a grand time."

Nate smiled, nodded and walked off toward the
kitchen with a spring in his step. Thoughts of finding out
about Dulcey's relationship to Lord James pushed to the far
recesses of his mind.

He pushed open the door to the kitchen. Abby had
flour in her hair and on her face, but then so did Dulcey and
Miss Franny. There was a pan of gingerbread planks
cooling on the table with several missing. From the looks
of things, the missing planks were being thoroughly
enjoyed by all in the kitchen.

"Now this is not fair. The lord of the manor not
invited to this party. Shame on all of you," stated Nate
trying to be stern but not being able to carry it off cause of
the smile on his face.

Cook and a couple of the servants were
momentarily startled, but then seeing his lordship's smile,
they relaxed.

"Oh, Uncle Nate, stop being silly. We saved one for you. We have some more in the oven, too."

Nate laughed. "Well on that invitation, don't mind if I do steal one." He took one and bit into the warm gingerbread. It was just as good as he remembered. He licked his lips and looked at Dulcey, remembering licking the crumbs off her lips just a couple of days ago. He watched her blush and look away, knowing she was remembering that kiss, too.

"Delicious," said Nate, meaning not only the gingerbread but the kiss as well.

"Indeed, my lord. It would not be Christmas without Miss Dulcey making her gingerbread," replied Cook. All the servants in the kitchen nodded.

"Then we must keep this tradition going Cook," replied Nate as he walked over to where Dulcey and Abby were. He flicked some flour off the end of Abby's nose. "What do you think Poppet? Shall we keep making gingerbread for Christmas?"

Abby thought about it and pouted. "But I don't want it just for Christmas. Can't we have it all the time?"

Nate laughed. "We will just have to see. After all, we can't keep Dulcey here making gingerbread all the time. Then we would get tired of the gingerbread and it wouldn't be a treat."

Abby looked at him and thought for a moment very seriously about it. "Maybe," she replied, "not all the time. Just some of the time, so we don't forget what it tastes like."

Nate laughed. He could hear some of the staff chuckling as well. Dulcey had a smile on her face. It came to Nate. "Well then, we will just have to keep Dulcey here." He looked at Dulcey with meaning.

Abby looked at him puzzled. "She is here."

"That she is Poppet."

The door suddenly opened and the countess walked in, a frown on her face. "What is going on here?" She took one look at Abby with flour all over her. "Abigail Beckham you are covered in flour. Who allowed this to happen? Miss Bennett, please take Abigail up to her room and get her cleaned up this instant. This child should not be in the kitchens. Nathaniel what are you thinking allowing this child to socialize with the servants."

The servants scattered. Abby's bottom lip began to quiver and tears came into her eyes. Miss Franny grabbed hold of Abby's hand. Dulcey came to stand in front of the Countess before Nate could say anything.

"My apologies, Countess Shefley. Abby helped me make some gingerbread planks in my home while we were stranded. I thought she would like to help again. It is tradition here at Brandanlyn." Dulcey stood in front of the Countess, shielding Abby.

"I should have known you were behind this. The daughter of an earl and my granddaughter will not associate with the servants," stated the Countess in no uncertain terms. She would simply not allow this! And how dare this woman stand there making excuses!

Nate came and stood at Dulcey's side. "Mother, if I remember right, who decides what Abby is allowed or not allowed to do is my decision, not yours. I see nothing wrong with Abby helping make gingerbread for Christmas. I think it is a nice tradition and I see no harm in it."

The Countess fumed with indignation. How dare her son redress her in front of the servants! It was all that, Dulcey woman's fault. Nathaniel had been fairly biddable before, but since his tarriance in the storm with that woman, he was acting defiant. She did not like the effect this woman was having on her son. No, this had to stop.

"Miss Bennett, take Abbigail upstairs as I have instructed and you and I, Nathaniel shall talk in my drawing room, now." She brushed passed Dulcey and totally ignored her.

Nate turned to Miss Bennett and Abby. "Go upstairs and get cleaned up, Poppet. I will talk to grandmother about this. Neither one of you are in any trouble." He looked at Miss Bennett to reassure her. Both nodded and slowly left the kitchen.

Dulcey stood motionless, dejected. This was not going well, not well at all. It seemed as though the Countess was forever finding fault with her. She had never met a woman such as her. The forces had warned her about the Countess but they had not been very specific.

Nate came and stood before Dulcey. He raised her chin with his fingers until she looked him into his eyes. "This was not your fault." Damn, he hated what his mother had just done. They all had been having a good time and she had come in and spoiled it all. Why was he surprised? Hadn't she done that kind of thing all of his life? He did not want that for Abby. He wanted her to enjoy things, even the simple things.

The tenderness she saw reflected in his eyes was nearly her undoing. "I just wanted to share with Abby some of the happy memories I have had here," explained Dulcey. She knew Abby had had a hard time not having a mother. She could relate to that. But she had people who cared about her, Grammy and Lord James. She wondered who cared for Abby. Nate did, but was it enough?

"I know. I am very grateful for that. I'm new at this parenting thing and I didn't exactly have the best of teachers," he replied, thinking of his mother.

Dulcey nodded. She turned to Cook. "Will you see to the rest of the gingerbread?"

"Of course, Miss Dulcey. I will see to it all." Cook shook her head in agreement. That Countess had caused a great deal of turmoil since she had arrived several weeks ago. Nothing was ever good enough for her. And that maid of hers, Leta. Always asking questions that were none of her business. Now, his lordship was completely different. It was all right to be nasty to the staff but to Miss Dulcey, that was something completely different. The servants here would not put up with it.

"I think I'll go to my rooms after I have checked on Abby."

"I'll check on Abby. You go upstairs, rest. Dealing with Mother can be exhausting."

"Well, it's you she wishes to talk to." Dulcey was glad it was not her. The more time she spent with the Countess, the more she realized she could never be in the Countess's company for any length of time. She drained the good energy of all its power. It exhausted her.

Nate frowned. "Mother can be rather demanding." He heard Cook make a snort and smiled. Perhaps, it was an understatement.

"Come let me escort you to you room." He offered Dulcey his arm.

Tentatively, she put her hand on his arm. Nate took it and placed in the crook of his arm and placed his free hand over hers.

Dulcey felt her heart beat begin to pound in her chest. She was afraid Nate could feel it, hear it. Why was she reacting in this way? She did not talk all the way to her room. At the door, Nate stopped. She made the mistake of looking up to him, to say something but it died on her lips when she looked into his eyes. She should have known better. She watched his eyes flare with passion and knew she had lost the battle within her.

Nate gazed at Dulcey. The need to protect her burned within him. The way his mother had treated her, enraged him. "Dulcey," he said softly. He could not deny himself. Slowly, he lowered his head, gently, tenderly, capturing her lips. Again, like the first time, she tasted of gingerbread. He pulled her closer, till her soft body molded against his. He wanted more.

Dulcey could not deny him, even if she wanted to. Here was the crux, she did not want to. She clung to him. Why did he make her feel this way? Where were her guiding forces? They seemed to have left her where Nate was concerned. She was adrift in these new feelings of want and need of what she did not know, only that it was there, demanding gratification.

Reluctantly, Nate raised his head and looked longingly at Dulcey. Why did this young woman make him feel things he thought he could - would never feel. He went to say something.

"Nathaniel, I thought I had summoned you. I want to talk to you now!"

Nathaniel tensed with growing exasperation that came very close to fury. He had to keep reminding himself, she was his mother, but she was getting very close to going beyond his endurance.

"Just a minute, Mother!" replied Nate. He looked at Dulcey with tenderness. "Get some rest while I deal with this."

Dulcey bit her bottom lip, nodded, and turned and walked into her room, but not before she had stolen a quick glance at the Countess down the hall. The contempt and scorn on her face made Dulcey shiver. She could feel the bombardment on her forces, of such contempt. The Countess could now be considered an enemy. The time for her to leave could not come soon enough.

Nate turned to his mother once Dulcey was safely in her room. Why had he thought of it in that manner but then one look at his mother's face, he knew why. He walked past her not offering his arm to escort. He knew it would infuriate her but at the moment he was too angry to care. He strode into her room and waited for her to join him.

The moment she walked into the room, she started, "Nathaniel, what were you thinking, having Abbigail downstairs in the kitchen with the staff. Such things are simply not done! She is being brought up to be a lady. Your brother was the earl."

"And I am now the earl, Mother," Nate interrupted. "I am Abby's guardian, remember, not you. So, I say what she can and cannot do. I found no harm in letting her partake of a tradition that occurs here at Brandanlyn at Christmas time. My God, Mother we were only making gingerbread." He ran a hand through his hair in exasperation. She was becoming more and more difficult.

"If she is to be brought up to take her rightful place in society as a Shefley, she must learn from an early age, that we simply do not socialize with the servants. As a man, you do not understand these things." Lady Shefley sat down on her chaise.

"Perhaps not, but Abby is still a child who is without her parents and I am trying to make her childhood have some semblance of happiness. Now, if you will excuse me, I have things that require my attention. And for further references, do not summon me again as though I was a young boy of Abby's age. I am the head of this household, the current Earl of Shefley. I beg you to remember that." Nate turned and strode out of the room with his mother's voice calling his name as he closed the door with considerable force.

He headed to the nursery to make certain Abby was not overly upset. He shook his head thinking about his mother. Why did she make things so difficult for all involved? He now understood how difficult it had been for Grayson and Caroline. He should have helped them more. That was one of the reasons why, he was determined that Abby not be raised by his mother. He believed heartily that This was what Grayson and Caroline wanted.

Brenda Hunt

A quick knock on the door, Nate entered the nursery. Abby was in a new dress and was playing with her dolls

She looked up smiled and said, "Uncle Nate!" She ran to him with open arms. No, Abby would not be raised under his mother's guidance. She looked like she had not been affected by his mother's rebuke. He was glad. He wanted this Christmas to be special for Abby. It had been a hard adjustment for her this past year. He had seen the change in her with just that short time in Dulcey's company. He would not let his mother crush her spirit.

"Hi, Poppet. Just checking to see if you are ready for Christmas," asked Nate. Abby nodded energetically. "Yes, Uncle Nate. Dulcey will be here for Christmas?"

"Yes, Poppet. Dulcey will be here. She is not going anywhere. I will make sure she stays." Nate reassured her.

Abby nodded again. "Miss Franny helped me paint a picture for Dulcey. Do you think she will like it?"

Nate looked at a picture of a child's drawing of a house.

"That Dulcey's house and that's the snow," explained Abby, "and that's me and that's you and that's Dulcey." She pointed to the three stick figures.

Nate smiled, touched by Abby's drawing. "Poppet, she will love it." Abby beamed. "Why don't you and Miss Franny wrap it up once it dries and give it to Dulcey in the morning for Christmas."

"That's what Miss Franny said, if it was all right with you."

"I think that will work out very well."

"Will you see to it, Miss Franny?" Nate looked over to Miss Franny.

She nodded. "Yes, my lord, of course."

"The plans for tomorrow are for a late breakfast. After, we will all go into the green drawing room and open presents," said Nate with a smile.

"Yea, presents. Did you get me a present Uncle Nate?" Abby clapped her hands.

"Of course."

"What did you get me? Please? Please?"

Nate tweeked her nose and laughed. "Not until tomorrow. It's a surprise."

Abby sighed. "Oh, all right. Will Dulcey still come to my room tonight and tell me a bedtime story about the fairies?"

Nate nodded. "I'm certain she will. She did promise you, did she not?"

Abby nodded.

"Well then. She will be here."

"And you too, Uncle Nate?"

"Yes, I will be here, too."

"Good."

Nate looked over to Miss Franny and smiled. "I have business to tend to Poppet. Listen to Miss Franny and be good."

Abby hugged him and nodded. Nate walked out of the nursery wondering how that child had wrapped herself around his heart in so short a period of time. He had barely known her before his brother died. Now, he could not imagine her not being a part of his life. How he had balked when he first learned Grayson had left him as Abby's guardian. Now, he was fighting his mother concerning her welfare.

Nate stopped at the head of the stairs and looked longingly down the hall that led to Dulcey's rooms. He shook his head and headed straight for the study. A bottle of whiskey awaited him there. Suddenly, he found himself in desperate need of a good stiff drink.

~~~~~~~~~~~~~~~

The supper meal turned out to be a quiet affair much to Dulcey solace. Nate was quiet. He seemed deep in his own thoughts. The Countess kept up a steady barrage concerning people she knew in London. Lady this was doing that and Lord something or other was in another scandal. Dulcey knew none of the people whom the Countess talked about. It truly made Dulcey glad she had never gone to London. It sounded like no one liked each other. All they were interested in gossiping about each other.

Lady Shefley turned to Dulcey. "It is a shame dear, you will never be able to be a part of London society. It can be so fascinating and rewarding."

Nate was about to say something but Dulcey beat him to it.

"From what you have said, it sounds like Londoners do not like each other very much. It seems their greatest joy is in destroying each other's happiness. If that is the case, as you have alluded to in your discussions just now, then I will be very pleased if I never set foot in London. I find no joy in hurting people nor do I find it amusing watching others do so." Dulcey rose from her seat. "Excuse me, my lord, but I promised Abby I would tell her a story before bedtime. I believe it is that time." Dulcey turned and walked away her head held high, glad to be gone from the table and the Countess's snobbery.

People here treated one another with respect. From the Countess's account, London did not. It was not something she would ever care to partake in. Another reason why, Nate's world could never be her world. She sighed with sadness.

Nate watched Dulcey walk away a smile on his face. A very astute observation for one who had never attended any of society's events. But then his mother did love spreading the dirt about, whether it was true or not. She often did not care. It was one of the reasons, why he did not care for London and London society.

"Well, I never. How dare she leave the table in such a manner? One can tell she was not brought up properly. Her in London society. Ha! She indeed would be the talk of the town with her crudeness. Yes, no manners at all." Lady Shefley shuddered at the thought of that woman amongst the *ton,* especially if she was any way associated with the Shefley's.

Nate had different ideas. Dulcey would be a diamond of the first water if presented to the *ton,* her beauty, her honesty, her knowledge. She would be a breath of fresh air, a beautiful wild rose amongst a hot house of perfectly groomed flowers.

"I beg to disagree, Mother. Dulcey would take the *ton* by storm." But then the thought of all those fobs hanging on her every word disturbed him. No, he did not want Dulcey in London, on second thought. There would be too many like his mother, who would want to destroy her, just because of her honesty. She would become miserable in a short time. No, he would not put her through that kind of nightmare.

Lady Shefley humphed. "Well, that will never happen. The place that woman would be welcome at is Covent Gardens with the rest of those type of ladies. Never, in the home of any of London's *ton,* for certain. I shudder at the thought."

Nate tightened his fist and clenched his jaw. He shook his head. "I beg to disagree." Nate rose from the table. He had had about enough of his mother. Maybe, he should follow through with his threat of sending her back to Shefley Hall. At least then, there would be some peace and quiet here. "We'll forgo our after dinner drinks. I think I'll go upstairs and say good night to Abby, as well." He tried to walk away.

"Nathaniel, I would like to speak with you some more about this." Lady Shefley called out after him.

At the door, Nate turned back for a moment and replied. "Not now, mother, another time." And walked through the door. He was beginning to truly understand why Grayson and Caroline spent so much of their time at Shefley Hall and their mother at the townhouse in London.

The door to Abby's room stood ajar. He stood just outside listening. Dulcey's voice was soft as she told her story of the fairy princess who loved the prince but could not marry him or go with him because she was of the fairy world and he was of the human world. But they promised to meet every time the moon was full and one day the fairy king would grant her wish to become human and marry her prince.

He watched as Dulcey rose from Abby's bed and kissed the top of her head and silently walked out. He stood in the door.

Dulcey looked up and gasped, momentarily surprised to find Nate in the door. Under usual circumstances, she would have felt his presence, felt his forces. But Nate disturbed her forces and she was unable to sense him until he was right beside her.

"Shh!" whispered Nate. "You'll wake Abby." He took her arm and led her away from Abby's room.

"Where are we going?"

"Somewhere quiet where I can be alone with you."

Dulcey shook her head and stopped. "As much as I want to, Nate, I simply cannot. We don't belong to the same worlds." She knew she could never be good enough to enter his world. His mother had reminded her of that fact at supper. Only sadness and heartbreak awaited her there if she tried. His mother would make certain of it.

"Are you comparing us to the story you are telling Abby?" asked Nate, knowing very well what she said was true. She was beneath him in the order of things. It should not matter but it did. He was head of the Shefley family and as much as he wanted it to be different, it was not.

"Perhaps. I was going to give my story a happy ending. But I do not see a happy ending for us. You are an Earl, a member of the realm. I am a nobody. Some even consider me a witch because of certain abilities I possess. I would only bring you disgrace and I could not bear it, if I hurt you or Abby." Dulcey looked up at him, pleading for him to understand.

Nate cupped her face in his hand. Dulcey leaned into it and closed her eyes. The urge to pick her up in his arms and carry her off down the hall to his room was strong within him. But then she looked up at him with those pixie green eyes of hers, pleading with him and he knew he could not. It took every bit of his self-control to simply stand there with her. Just as she did not want to hurt him or Abby, he could not bear the thought of hurting her.

Dulcey sighed deeply. Every particle of her being cried out to him but she believed she was not good for him. If she was a part of his future, the forces would have showed her but they had not. They had not told her anything, which in itself, was alarming. So much about all of this was so confusing. Never in all of her life had the forces about her been in such disarray. It left her exposed, susceptible, feelings she was not accustomed to.

Dulcey reluctantly pulled away. "Good night, my lord." She needed to think of him in that context now. It would make it easier for her to deal with all these feeling, if she thought of him as Lord Beckham, instead of Nate. She walked away and did not look back, even though everything within her screamed for her to turn around and run back to his arms. At the head of the stairs she met up with his mother. She had the feeling she had been lurking about.

"Good night, Lady Shefley," she said softly and continued on down the hall to her room.

Lady Shefley nodded and walked on toward her room.

Nate turned when he saw his mother and walked on toward his room. He did not wish to speak or deal with his mother and her opinions. In some manner, he was aware that much of what Dulcey had said, had some truth to it but never had he felt this way about any woman. These feelings were strong but so very new. He didn't know what to make of them. All the accusations his mother had voiced echoed in his head. Who was Dulcey and what was her relationship to the baron, his by-blow or his mistress? Just thinking of her as his mistress sent waves of jealousy through him.

Damn his mother for putting these thoughts into his head. No, he would not rest until he found out the truth about Dulcey's relationship with Lord James. Perhaps the solicitor, Mr. Kinley, could shed some light on the matter. Kinley did want to talk to both him and Dulcey. He would have to wait till then. Hopefully, Kinley could. It would be a long two days.

Chapter 9

The family is the key of Christmas.
                    Scott Hahn
In her hand was a necklace with a small oval
pendant, ...
                    Cassie McCown

        The dawn did not come soon enough for Dulcey.
She had spent a restless night.   She had hardly slept and
when she did, she dreamed of Nate. His lips, the feel of his
body against hers. All of it haunted her dreams, leaving her
wanting more but what that more was, she did not know.
These feelings left her achy, jittery.   She was already
dressed when Peggy came up with her hot chocolate.
        "You're up early, miss."
        Dulcey smiled. "I couldn't sleep any longer."
        "Aye, miss. T'is Christmas morning. Will you be
going to church?" asked Peggy, as she began brushing
Dulcey's hair.
        "No, I talked with Lord Beckham last evening. He
thought there was still too much snow on the roads."
        "Charlie went to the village yesterday. Took him
all afternoon, it did. The snow is melting but there are still
hills of snow. He said maybe in a couple of days the
carriage could travel."
        "Yes, Lord Beckham said possibly having a get
together for the neighbors.   I thought I might suggest
Twelfth Night depending on the weather. He would like to
meet the neighbors."
        "The folks about are very curious about him, they
are. He seems to be fair. Now, the little Miss Abby, we've
all come to love her. But that mother of his, the Countess,
now, she is making everyone's work here very hard. And

that maid of hers always snooping about, asking questions she has no business asking," explained Peggy.

Dulcey was not surprised by the information Peggy stated. She was curious. "What is her maid asking about?"

"Mainly now about you. Wants to know everything we know about you and Lord James. Some of the things she be asking, suggesting, they aren't very nice, miss." Peggy looked away.

"Like what Peggy?" asked Dulcey, yet, she knew what she was looking for.

"Now, miss Dulcey, them too ugly to even say again." Peggy did not want to repeat the questions that were asked. She would not upset Miss Dulcey with that ugliness. Everyone who worked here at Brandanlyn knew what that maid said was not true.

"Besides Mr. Evers set her straight, he did. Told her if she ever said anything of the sort again, she was not welcome in the servants' quarters and when she asked about her meals, he told her he didn't care if she ever ate again. And he told her if she went complaining to the Countess, he'd be telling his lordship. His lordship has threatened to ship the Countess back to Shefley Hall," explained Peggy.

Dulcey closed her eyes in pain. No wonder, the Countess did not like her, if Nate was threatening all of this. She must try to get along with Lady Shefley, at least for the next few days. After her meeting with Mr. Kinley, she would go back home. It was too difficult being this close to Nate. Once back at the cottage, her life would go back to normal, to what it was like before Nate and Abby wondered into her life. Why was it, her heart did not believe a word her head was telling her? Nothing would be normal ever again.

"We must be nice to the Countess. I feel she is a very unhappy person," said Dulcey.

"Humph!" replied Peggy. "Tis no reason to make everyone else's life miserable."

"It's Christmas, Peggy. Let's try."

Peggy nodded. "Yes, Miss Dulcey. For you, I will do this."

"Thank you."

Dulcey looked at her reflection in the mirror. Peggy had done an exceptional job with her hair. She had braided it then wrapped it around her head like a coronet. Her dress of soft dark blood red velvet was trimmed in gold braid about the hem and end of her long sleeves. It hugged her body. The gold ribbon tied under her waist hung mid-way down the front of her dress. She wore red kid leather slippers on her feet. Peggy handed her the gold and red shawl to wrap about her shoulders.

She wondered why she had dressed as she had. Could it be the conversation of Lady Shefley last evening, criticizing her inability to be presentable to London society? Lord James had always told her, she would be acceptable wherever she went. No, it was Christmas, she wanted to be at her best.

"You look lovely. We miss him, too. Merry Christmas, miss."

Dulcey smiled with tears in her eyes. "Yes. Merry Christmas, Peggy."

Dulcey walked down the hall. She met Abby and Miss Franny at the head of the stairs.

"Merry Christmas, Dulcey!" She skipped to Dulcey's side and grabbed her hand.

Dulcey smiled. "Merry Christmas, Abby. Merry Christmas, Miss Franny."

"Merry Christmas, Miss Dulcey."

"I have a present for you, Dulcey," said Abby as she tugged Dulcey by the hand, down the stairs.

"You do?" asked Dulcey. "I'll let you in on a

secret, Poppet. I have one for you, too."

Abby eyes widened and a huge smile crossed her face. "Can I open it now?"

Nate stood at the bottom of the stairs and watched the trio come down the stairs. Dulcey took his breath away. The red of her dress brought out the green in her eyes, the gold trim, the gold of her hair. He could feel his body responding to her. He was grateful the pants he wore today were not tight. Otherwise, everyone would know how he lusted after her. Damn, she stirred his blood. Last night's restless sleep did not help. How many times had he awakened with dreams of Dulcey? With dreams of her body under his.

Reining in the direction of his thoughts, he turned to Abby. "No, Poppet, presents will be opened after breakfast. After your grandmother comes down."

Abby frowned. "She takes forever."

Nate smiled. "We shall see, Poppet." He turned, "Merry Christmas, Miss Franny. Merry Christmas, Dulcey."

"Merry Christmas, Lord Beckham," replied Miss Franny and smiled.

Dulcey felt Nate's eyes devour her. She looked away and replied softly. "Good morning, my lord. Merry Christmas."

Nate raised an eyebrow in question. When had she changed and stopped calling him by his name? He remembered she had called him such last night as well. He offered Dulcey his arm.

Dulcey hesitated for a moment, then placed her arm through his. When his hand covered hers, she felt the sensation deep within her. Why did he make her feel so?

Nate felt her hand tremble against his arm. He smiled. He was not going to let the fact that she was beneath his social status ruin this day. This was Christmas and he planned on enjoying every minute of it. Tomorrow, he would deal with all that, just not today. Today, he wanted Abby and Dulcey to have a good Christmas.

Miss Franny helped Abby at the sideboard load her plate and sit at the table.

Dulcey followed after she put some ham, eggs and toasted bread on her plate. She was not very hungry this morning. She watched as Nate sat down at the head of the table his plate piled high with food.

Nate looked at Abby. "Take your time eating, Poppet."

"But Uncle Nate, you said we could open presents after breakfast."

Nate chuckled, glad to see Abby was being anxious to open presents as any child would. He worried about her. "I know Poppet, but the waiting is the most fun."

Abby looked at him through narrowed eyes and shook her head. She didn't understand what Uncle Nate was talking about. Unwrapping the presents was the best part.

"I promise you, we will open presents."

Abby sighed and ate slower.

"Dulcey says she has a present for me, too"

Nate raised his eyebrow. Dulcey had not been able to leave the house due to the snow so where had she gotten a present?

"I'll explain later," she replied with a smile.

Nate nodded. "How did you spend your Christmases here, Dulcey?"

Dulcey smiled as she remembered past Christmases. She entertained them with stories of times she had spent here, of some of the gifts Lord James had given her

Nate listened and saw the love in her eyes when she talked about Lord James. A knot of jealousy grew in his stomach. What was their relationship? All the innuendoes his mother had instilled in his head reared their ugly head to make him question Dulcey's relationship. But something didn't make any sense. From the information Simmons had supplied to him, Dulcey lived here from a small child. That could only mean she was his illegitimate daughter. How would that affect him?

Could he marry a baron's bastard child? Where had that thought come from? Marriage? He looked at Dulcey differently.

"We've finished eating, Uncle Nate. Can we go open presents now?" interrupted Abby.

"We'll see, Poppet. Let's all of us go to the green room and I will send someone upstairs to check on your Grandmother."

Abby grabbed hold of Miss Franny's hand and pulled her out of the dining room.

Nate rose and offered his arm once again to Dulcey. The touch of her hand on his arm felt right. If he stayed at Brandanlyn, what would it matter who Dulcey was related to? According to Simmons, Dulcey was well liked here. It would not matter to them.

Dulcey walked to green drawing room in silence. She felt Nate, no, Lord Beckham, she told herself, was deep in thought. At the open doorway, he stopped for a moment.

Abby giggled. "Look up Uncle Nate."

Nate looked up to see the mistletoe they had hung yesterday. Here he was again with Dulcey at his side, standing under the mistletoe.

"You have to kiss her again," encouraged Abby.

Dulcey looked up to Nate and saw the raw passion in his eyes. She felt like she was drowning in a sea of emotions. The forces that always surrounded her, protected her were as tangled as the wool before she combed it. She wanted to, no, needed to take her time and sort through all these feelings but Nate's nearness seemed to be cause of all those tangles.

"You have to kiss her Uncle Nate," said Abby impatiently.

"Yes I do, don't I?" replied Nate. He could see the confusion but he could also see the desire flare in her eyes. He lowered his lips and claimed Dulcey's slowly, drinking in the sweet taste of her. Marriage to Dulcey meant he could have her, every sweet part of her. Being Lord James bastard child should not interfere with marrying her. Reluctantly he released her lips realizing, he could have her after all.

Dulcey looked up mesmerized by the look in his eyes. Her breathing was shallow, her heart wanting to beat out of her chest. She felt hot and cold all at the same time. She was so glad he had a strong hold of her because she had little doubt she could have stood on her own.

"Nathaniel, what is going on here?" demanded the Countess as she walked up.

Nathaniel raised his eyes in frustration.

Abby giggled. "Uncle Nate kissed Dulcey. He had to. They walked under the mistletoe, Grandmother. It's tadditon."

"Tradition," corrected the Countess automatically. She clenched her fist at her side in vexation. This relationship was developing much too fast. It needed to stop. It needed to stop now. She needed to get that woman out of this house. "Yes, well, Nathaniel, tradition or not, there is Abbigail in the room. You need to think about the decorum of the situation," admonished the Countess.

"But Grandmother, Uncle Nate has his decorum. He has his pants on."

Nathaniel tried desperately not to laugh, but the laughter could not be held in as he looked first at Dulcey, then at Abby.

Dulcey placed her hand over her mouth to stop the laughter that tried to bubble out. The Countess walked over to Abby and looked from Dulcey to Nate in confusion.

"What is Abbigail talking about?" questioned Lady Shefley curtly.

Nate turned to his mother with a smile still on his face. "A misunderstanding, mother."

"I would like an explanation, a detailed explanation."

"Not now, Mother. It's Christmas and Abby has been waiting patiently to open presents."

Lady Shefley looked from one to the other through narrowed eyes. Something had happened at that cottage and she was determined to find out what. What was this about Nathaniel having his pants on?

Nate watched as his mother walked into the room and sat down in the large dark green winged chair like a queen sitting on her throne. Nate shook his head. She would never change and that frightened him. But this was Christmas day and not the time to deal with it. "Ah, Evers shall I light the yule log. Do you have a bit of last year's one?"

"Of course, my lord. I've prepared it so you have but to light it."

"Good," replied Nate. He made a big production with the lighting of the yule log, getting Abby to assist him.

"Can we open presents now, Uncle Nate?"

Nate rubbed his chin, deep in thought, then turned to Abby with a big smile, "Yes, Poppet. I think you have waited long enough."

Abby clapped her hands. "Where are them?"

"Abigail I suggest you calm down," corrected the Countess from her chair.

Nate eyes narrowed. How could one person take the joy out of so many things? "Mother we are about to open presents. Allow Abby some excitement." He turned to Abby. "That one with the red ribbon over there, I believe it has your name on it. Why don't you get it and bring it here."

Abby ran to where Nate pointed and carried the gift back to where she sat her eyes wide with anticipation.

"Go on, Poppet, open it," said Nate.

Abby tore the paper apart and squealed with delight when the doll became visible to her. "It's the one in the window." She hugged it tight. She ran to Nate and hugged him tight. "I love her! I love her!"

Nate hugged her back. Watching her, filled his heart with joy. He was truly beginning to like this family life. It had is moments. "I thought you would."

"What do you say when you get a gift, Abigail?" admonished the Countess.

Abby looked at her grandmother, then turned to her uncle, and gave him the biggest smile, "Thank you, Uncle Nate."

"You are very welcome, Poppet."

Leta, the countess's maid walked in with a present and gave it to the countess. She nodded to the countess as she handed the gift to her.

So this was Leta, thought Dulcey. She was thin, dressed all in black, her gray hair pulled tight in a bun at the back of her head making her hawkish nose more pronounced.

Dulcey met Leta's dark beady eyes when she looked at her. She felt a shiver, a disturbance in the force, but it was gone so quickly Dulcey shook her heard in perplexity. So many things lately with her force were muddled. This was another time when she couldn't trust herself. These feelings were new and strange to her, not being able to trust the forces about her.

"Abigail, come to your grandmother."

Abigail walked slowly to her grandmother her new doll held tightly in her arms.

Nate came to her side. "Give me your new doll to hold."

"Here is my gift."

Abby took the package from the Countess and open it slowly. Abby pulled out a new dress of light pink and pair of shoes to match. Abby smiled. "Thank you Grandmother."

Lady Shefley nodded.

"That's a lovely dress, Abby," said Dulcey. "I think that's a big girl's dress and such a pretty color. You will need a special occasion to wear it."

"Yes, indeed and you will need to save me a dance on your dance card," teased Nate.

Abby giggled. "I can't dance, Uncle Nate."

"Oh well, then I will just have to wait until you grow up."

"Nonsense. That is a long time from now. There is no need to talk about that now. Well, now that gifts have been opened, you may go upstairs with Miss Bennett and play with your new doll," dismissed Lady Shefley.

"But Uncle Nate, I haven't given Dulcey her Christmas present," cried Abby looking from Nate to Dulcey.

Nate turned to his mother. "We are not finished opening gifts, mother. If you do not wish to stay then you are free to go back up to your suite. Abby has something for Dulcey."

Lady Shefley shuddered in distaste. "Nathaniel, boxing day is tomorrow. Do not confuse the child."

Nate blew a long breath out in suppressed anger. He had to remind himself this was Christmas Day. "Dulcey is a guest in this house and not a servant. Please remember that fact, Mother. "

"So you say."

She looked at Dulcey with a look that Dulcey interpreted as the Countess considered one of the servants.

"Yes, I so say." Nate looked at her through narrowed eyes till she dropped her gaze in surrender. He turned to Abby with a smile, "Get your gift for Dulcey, Poppet. I am sure she is dying to know what you have for her."

Abby looked at her grandmother who was looking at Dulcey.

"Go on now, Abby. Get your gift for Dulcey," encouraged Nate. He gave her a wink and a nod.

Abby smiled and moved to Miss Franny's side. She took the package handed her and presented it to Dulcey like it was something of great value.

Dulcey took Abby's gift tenderly in her hands. The smile of pride on her face touched Dulcey's heart. If she could have a wish for Christmas, then she, Dulcey, would wish to make Abby her little girl. But it was not to be.

Carefully, Dulcey unwrapped her gift. It was a hand drawn picture. Immediately, she recognized three stick people, a cottage and snow. She smiled at Abby. "Oh, Abby, I love it."

Abby grinned. "It me and you and Uncle Nate at your house in the snow," said Abby as she pointed to each and every thing she had drawn.

"Yes, I can see it all. You did such a good job. I could see right away what it was," complimented Dulcey. She would treasure it always as a reminder of this time. She felt the tears gather in her eyes.

"What's the fuss all about? It's just a child's drawing," stated the Countess.

Nate threw his mother a look of disdain. Must she always be so condescending.

Dulcey gave her a look of annoyance. The countess could say anything she wanted about her, but to berate Abby was unpardonable. Dulcey hugged Abby tightly. "Darling, I shall treasure it always. I know exactly where I will put it."

"Where?" asked Abby.

"On my mantle, so I can see it every day. Now, it is my turn to give you my gift." Dulcey rose and walked over to behind the brown chair near the window. She removed a small package and handed it to Dulcey.

Abby slowly unwrapped the gift. She looked up in wonder with a large smile on her face as she pulled the pendant from the velvet lined box. "For me?"

Dulcey smiled. "Yes, darling. It's a moonstone. It was given to me when I was a little girl. It will protect you and bring you luck," explained Dulcey. She knew Abby would be the closest thing to a child she would ever have.

"By the fairies?" asked Abby, her eyes wide with awe.

Dulcey had not thought of it being from the fairies but it had come from Grammy.

"Fairies aren't real, Abigail. And I'm afraid Abigail can't accept the gift. It is too much for a child. Frankly, I don't see how you can afford something this costly," said Lady Shefley vexed that this young woman constantly instilled herself into her family. How dare she!

Abby looked to Nate, crestfallen. She did not want to give Dulcey's present back. It came from Dulcey and her fairies. It was special.

"Mother," admonished Nate.

Dulcey interrupted. She was not going to allow the Countess to ruin this for her or Abby. "It is something given to me by my Grammy. It is my decision to give it to who I want to. I chose to give it to Abby." She looked from the Countess to Nate. She was adamant about this.

Nate nodded. "Mother, Dulcey is right. I see nothing wrong with giving Abby this pendant, if she so wishes. It is very thoughtful of her."

"I want to keep my fairy necklace," cried Abby.

"There are no such things as fairies," snapped Lady Shefley. She was not about to argue with this child and this woman. How dare they disagree with her!

Dulcey looked at Abby who had tears in her eyes. What kind of woman destroyed a little girl's beliefs, especially on Christmas Day? She had never met a woman as heartless as this one. Her heart ached for Abby, to be constantly subjected to this woman.

"Mother, enough of this! It is Christmas, after all. Please allow Abby her beliefs. She is still a child." He was so frustrated his mother was ruining another holiday. Why did she have to make everyone lives so miserable?

Lady Shefley narrowed her eyes as she looked from Nate then on to Dulcey. Yes, this woman needed to be dealt with and soon.

"Come, Abby," said Dulcey, "let me put it on you. Do you know why they say the moonstone is good luck? Someone went out on the full moon and caught the moon beams and put them in the moonstone," explained Dulcey, wanting to put some magic back into the day.

Nate gave his mother a narrowed look and shook his head in warning.

Abby looked at Dulcey, then to her grandmother and finally to her Uncle Nate. When he nodded, she went slowly to Dulcey's side.

Dulcey took the pendant from Abby's hand and placed it around her neck. Abby looked down at the pendant, then up to Abby. "Do you think it was the fairies that catched the moon?"

Dulcey smiled. "Grammy never said who caught the moon beams but I think you may be right. Fairies and moonbeams. Yes, I think you are right." She looked up to Nate who had walked over.

"Fairies are real, Dulcey, aren't they? They teached you about the medicines." Abby asked, but looked over to her grandmother.

"If you believe they are real, then they are. I believe," answered Dulcey.

Abby looked to her Uncle Nate, who stood beside her. "Do you believe in fairies, Uncle Nate?" If Uncle

Nate and Dulcey believed, then that meant they were real, no matter what Grandmother said.

Nate looked at Abby and saw the wistfulness in her eyes. He was not about to destroy her childish beliefs. Besides, maybe fairies did exist. Didn't Dulcey say so?

"Poppet, I think you and Dulcey are right. I have never seen one, but then I have never looked for one. I think you can't see them, unless you believe. So now that I know for sure they exist, I think I might just get the chance to see one. What do you think?" explained Nate, hoping this satisfied Abby.

Abby nodded. She lifted up the pendant to show Uncle Nate.

Nate looked at the pendant Dulcey had given her. It was a small tear drop moonstone attached to a silver chain by a simple wrap at the point of the teardrop. Very simple, but he was certain it meant a lot to Dulcey. For her to give it to Abby, meant she truly cared for Abby.

"Very pretty, Poppet. Dulcey must truly like you." He looked to Dulcey. This also meant a lot to him, that she would give Abby a part of herself.

Abby turned and hugged Dulcey tightly. "Thank you, Dulcey. I love you."

Dulcey was looking at Nate when Abby said those words. The pain that followed, knowing she had come to love Abby, too, was almost unbearable. She closed her eyes and hugged Abby back, committing the feeling to her memory. Years from now, she would want to remember once upon a time, she was loved by a child. It would have to last her a lifetime.

Nate watched the pain cross Dulcey's face before she closed her eyes and buried her face in Abby's hair. He didn't understand why this would hurt her.

"Well, I for one have had enough talk of fairies. Now, that all the presents are opened, I think it's time Abigail went back to the nursery," said Lady Shefley. She had had enough of all this. Abby, it seemed brought the two of them together. She did not like the way this was all progressing. It was all so frustrating. No matter what she tried to do to separate Nate and that woman, none of it was working.

"I want to stay down here," cried Abby.

Nate looked at his mother. There was no reason for Abby to go back to the nursery. It was Christmas Day. Did his mother ever consider someone else, beside her own selfish needs? When he had insisted she accompany him here, he had thought maybe, they would be able to tolerate each other. Well, he had hoped, but it had not worked out. All his past memories of dealing with his mother were now back in focus. Every day in her company, reminded him why he had had such little contact with her once he had reached of age and later over the past several years. With each day, he better understood the complaints Grayson had made. But he was not Grayson.

"Yes, Poppet you will be staying down stairs with us. I have other celebrations for us planned," he assured Abby. To his mother, he added, "Mother, if this is too much for you, we will understand your need to go back to your room." He was hoping she would take his suggestions. She did manage to put a damper on all of this.

Through pursed lips and narrowed eyes, Lady Shefley replied, "I was just thinking of Abigail."

Nate doubted it. He sighed in frustration. It appeared his mother did not take the hint. Well, she had better behave herself, otherwise, next time it would be more than a hint. It would be a command.

"Miss Franny, I do believe I remembered when I hired you, you did say you were able to play the pianoforte?" questioned Nate.

"Yes, my lord, I can play," she answered.

"Good. Dulcey can you play?" he asked.

Dulcey shook her head and laughed. "I was taught, but I seem to hit more bad notes than good."

"Well, Miss Franny, it appears as though you are the chosen one. Shall we go to the music room and sing Christmas carols," suggested Nate. Hopefully, this would occupy their time without his mother starting one of her tirades.

Miss Franny played the pianoforte and everyone but the countess sang carols. She sat on the chair and watched like a hawk watching her prey. Nate had hoped she wouldn't follow but she did.

No longer able to tolerate the strain in the room, Nate began making up words to the songs, silly words, till he had Abby giggling and Dulcey and Miss Franny shaking their heads. It had been worth it, to dispel the tension his mother brought into the room. He could see her disapproving frown without turning to look at her. He refused to let her put a damper on their festivities.

When Evers announced dinner, Nate offered his arm to Dulcey and Abby and escorted them to the dining room, still singing silly Christmas carols. He left Miss Franny to walk with his mother. Dinner proved to be amusing. Nate kept them all laughing with stories. Several times, he gave his mother a look to remind her not to ruin this for Abby.

As soon as everyone had finished their plum pudding, Abby asked, "Dulcey will you still tell me a story tonight? Maybe, it can be about the Christmas fairy?" She liked Dulcey stories about the fairies. Now, she had Dulcey's moonstone necklace, maybe, she would get to meet one of the fairies. She touched the stone about her neck.

Dulcey smiled. "Of course, Abby. I did promise you. A Christmas fairy, I think I can think of one."

Dulcey, Abby and Miss Franny all rose from the table as did Nate.

"Mother, I think I will forego drinks and escort these lovely ladies upstairs. So, I'll say good night, Mother." Again he offered Dulcey and Abby his arm.

"Good night Grandmother. Thank you for the dress," said Abby as she walked passed her grandmother.

"Good night, Abigail, Nathaniel," she replied.

Nate raised his eyebrows, then narrowed his eyes. It was a deliberate shun by his mother. He looked at Dulcey to see how it affected her.

Dulcey was very much aware the Countess had snubbed her. She met Nate's questioning look with a slight shake of her head. The more she encountered the Countess, the more aware she became of the spiteful forces about her. Forces that were as visible to Dulcey as the light shining from the candles on the table, a dark light filled with venom. It hit her like hundreds of tiny pin pricks against the forces that surrounded her. It felt good to walk away from her.

Abby kept up a steady strain of conversation about the moonstone necklace and fairies. Dulcey tried to answer her questions but Abby had some very definite ideas about fairies. In Abby's room, Miss Franny had her change to her night dress.

Nate came to Dulcey, but Dulcey shook her head. She did not wish to talk about his mother in front of Abby. She knew Nate was very displeased with his mother. She just didn't know what to tell him. Out of the Countess's sight, she felt more relaxed.

Abby jumped into her bed. Nate placed a chair at her bedside. Dulcey sat down.

"Goodnight, Miss Franny," said Abby. Nate and Dulcey echoed her words. Nate went about extinguishing the candle all except the one by the door.

"Good night, Miss Abby. Good night, Miss Dulcey and Lord Beckham," she replied and walked into the adjourning room and closed the door.

"A story about a Christmas fairy, please, Dulcey."

Abby still wore the moonstone about her neck. Dulcey noticed Nate leaned one shoulder against the door jam. She knew he was listening.

She began. "There once was a fairy princess who was in love with a fairy prince. But the man in the moon also loved the fairy princess."

Abby looked at Dulcey skeptical. "A man in the moon?"

"Yes, don't you know that story?" asked Dulcey.

Abby shook her head.

"Well, it is said, that this old man was banished to the moon because he had stolen something very valuable from the fairy king."

"What did he steal?" asked Abby with a yawn.

"What did he steal?" Dulcey looked up to Nate for help.

"He stole the king's watch. He had hoped he could get the fairy king to stop time so he could woo the princess," added Nate. He wanted to stop time.

"Like I said earlier, he was banished to the moon by the fairy king. He loved the fairy princess but now, he had to watch her from the moon. He watched as the fairy prince courted the fairy princess. But when the moon was dark he couldn't see them. He wanted to keep watch over them. So the man in the moon sent moon beams down to earth and his sister captured them and put them in a stone."

"Like my moonstone," said Abby, sleepily.

"Yes, like your moonstone," answered Dulcey. She watched Abby close her eyes her fingers holding the moonstone. "His sister gave the fairy princess the moonstone as a Christmas present. The sister did not tell the fairy princess, the man in the moon had sent it down for her. The fairy princess put it around her neck. Little did she know the moon beams captured in moonstone allowed him to see the fairy princess, even when the moon was dark."

Dulcey watched for a moment. Abby was asleep. Christmas had been a busy day. She smiled and then a sadness enveloped her. Telling fairy stories to Abby would end in a few days. She would not think about that. After all, it was Christmas. She would be grateful to have had this time with her.

Dulcey looked up to Nate at the door. She envied him this kinship he had with Abby. She would never have that. It left an empty place in her heart.

"She's asleep," said Dulcey, as she met Nate at the door. He nodded and blew the candle out. He softly closed the door behind them. Outside the closed door, Dulcey turned and said, "Good night, my lord."

"You were calling me, Nate." He watched her closely. He had noticed the sadness in her eyes, the glisten of unshed tears. Something within him wanted to wipe away that sadness, only he did not know what caused the sadness.

"Here, you are the lord of the manner," replied Dulcey softly, staring at his chest. She couldn't look him in the eyes. She knew if she did, she would drown in those crystal blue eyes of his. They would pull her in. She was as certain of that fact as she was of breathing.

He offered her his arm. "Let me walk you to your room."

Dulcey shook her head. No doubt, the Countess was lurking somewhere in the shadows. She could feel the pins again shooting at her.

"Please," she pleaded and looked up into his eyes. The tenderness, she saw reflected in him, tested her resolve greatly. She must get to her room, to the safety of her room.

Nate softly touched her cheek. The ache he felt for her was unbearable. Never, no never had he felt this way about a woman.   Hadn't the thought about marriage to her crossed his mind earlier? Yes, he could consider marriage to Dulcey. The plea he saw in her eyes made him realize, though she felt something for him, she felt she was beneath him. His mother and all her contemptuous barbs had done this to her.

Reluctantly, he said, "Merry Christmas, Dulcey. Good night."

She smiled, relieved he did not ask for more from her because she firmly believed, she could not have resisted no matter how resolved, she thought she was.

"Merry Christmas, Nate," she whispered, turned and walked away. It was the hardest thing she had ever done. She felt so vulnerable here. How she longed for his arms around her to keep her safe.   Safe from what, her forces would not tell, show her. But she knew, there was something here, trying to change her.

Nate watched her walk away. It appeared he was watching her walk away from him more than he cared to. He liked watching the way her hips swayed when she walked away, but the fact she was walking away disturbed him. Nate shook his head, turned and walked to his room. As he passed his mother's room, he noticed the door being softly closed. She had been watching. He sighed deeply with frustration. Mother, what was he to do with her?

~~~~~~~~~~~~~~~

Boxing Day proved to be uneventful. With Dulcey's help, Nathaniel was able give all who worked at the Manor their monetary gifts. For Miss Franny, Dulcey had a beautiful light green scarf she had woven months ago. Miss Franny was very moved to receive it.

The countess had stayed upstairs in her rooms claiming a migraine. No one had missed her. Miss Franny and Abby spent the entire day with Dulcey and Nate. The atmosphere in the manor was so much easier without the countess lurking about, ready to put a constraint on any and all activities.

Dulcey was appreciative that Miss Franny and Abby kept them company. She did not think she could have spent the day alone with Nate. Even with the two of them as company, there were times when she felt Nate's eyes on her. She would look away but not before she saw the longing in his eyes.

As much as she enjoyed the day, she was glad to retire to her rooms. She told the story again about the man in the moon. Abby did not go straight off to sleep. Nate stayed and talked with her. It warmed her heart, to see how much he cared for Abby.

As Dulcey got ready for bed, the feelings that had plagued her all day were more intense. She could feel the forces of change swirling, fluctuating about her, never giving her a clear picture. It made her feel anxious about the meeting with Mr. Kinley.

She sat on the edge of her bed and placed her hands together in prayer. "Grammy, please give me a vision of what tomorrow will hold for me. I know it will change me, I just do not know how. I am frightened. I have never had the forces so cloudy, yet at the same time, so strong. Why?"

Dulcey closed her eyes and waited. No visions came. Still she sat and waited. All she could see was swirling mists of colors, shades of gray with a swirl of bright red that changed to blue almost indigo and then back to shades of gray that turned to black. She opened her eyes quickly and the colors disappeared. Her heartbeat quickened. She took a deep breath to calm her breathing and heart.

Why could she not see clearer? It troubled her greatly. With a deep sigh, she laid down and closed her eyes, knowing sleep would elude her till the morning's light. Tomorrow, she would know. Tomorrow!

Chapter 10

There are two kinds of fools:
Those who can't change their opinions
And those who won't.
                              Josh Billings

Percival Kinley entered Brandanlyn as he had done dozens of times in the past. He and Lord Fergers had been friends, as well as solicitor and client. They had argued several times about the handling of this matter, but in the end, the ultimate decision had been Lord Fergers.

Evers escorted him into the study. It was a room he was very familiar with.

Lord Shefley met him at the door. He could see Dulcey sitting in a chair in front of the desk. An older woman dressed in the latest of the London fashion, sat in the chair near the fireplace. An empty chair stood between them. He assumed his lordship had occupied it.

"Mr. Kinley, welcome," stated Nate, shaking Mr. Kinley hand. "I have cleared the desk for you."

"Thank you, Lord Shefley" replied Mr. Kinley.

"I am aware, Lord Shefley is my official title now, but in my mind Shefley will always be my brother. I rather go by Beckham. Dulcey is here as you can see. This is my mother, Lady Roberta Beckham, Countess of Shefley."

Percival bowed, "Countess Shefley," and then turned to Dulcey, "Miss Dulcey."

The countess merely nodded as though this was of great inconvenience to her.

Dulcey smiled. She had met Mr. Kinley many times here, talking with Lord James. "It is very good to see you again, Mr. Kinley." She was slightly nervous about this meeting because as much as she tried, she could not see what was coming. So much had been cloudy these last several days. She did not know what to make of it. Never had she ever felt, so isolated. Her visions were always so clear in the past, showing her the way to go. But now, she was at a loss, waiting to see how it all developed. This was scarier than the visions, this not knowing. She sat her heart beating in trepidation of what was to come.

Percival Kinley sat at the desk and pulled several papers out of his satchel. Two of them appeared to be two sealed letters, one thin, one thick. For a moment, he looked searchingly at Dulcey. He sighed and realized he could delay, no longer.

"As you know Miss Dulcey, I have been Lord Fergers' solicitor for many, many years. I have been aware of all of this from the beginning."

"The beginning of what?" asked Lady Shefley. "How does all of this involve my son? We were told he is the heir."

"Mother, please allow Mr. Kinley to continue," Nate demanded with some irritation. He had hoped his mother would not attend this meeting but she had been adamant.

"Countess Shefley, please allow me to continue," replied Mr. Kinley. "It has nothing to do with the heir ship."

Lady Shefley humphed. She did not like any of this. This had something to do with that Dulcey woman. But then perhaps, it was the missing part to this situation that she could use against Dulcey. Yes, this would be the answer she was looking for. By the end of this meeting, this Dulcey would be on her way. She smiled with anticipation of finally being able to put this nothing in her proper place.

Nate nodded to Mr. Kinley.

Percival sighed. He was beginning to develop a dislike for the Countess. He began again.

"Lord Fergers left two letters, one addressed to your Lord Shefley, Lord Beckham and the other to Miss Dulcey. I am to read yours first, Lord Beckham. It is the shortest. After, I am to read the one Lord Fergers has addressed to Miss Dulcey next. I believe once they have been read, both of you will understand why Lord Fergers has done it this way."

He looked to Lord Beckham, who nodded, and then to Miss Dulcey, who nodded, as well. He took the first letter and opened the seal. He began to read:

Dear Lord Nathaniel Beckham, Fifth Earl of Shefley

After much searching, I have found your brother to be my heir, a very distant cousin, it appears. Upon my investigation, I have had reports that say your family is an honorable one. When I learned of his death, you then became my heir. I have this very serious request to ask of you. When I learned your brother had made his daughter your ward, it proved to me I could ask this of you. It is on your honor that I make this request. Once the letter I have written to my Dulcey is read, you will understand my request. As the new Baron of Chesterton, I request that you continue to provide protection for Dulcey, as I have done these past many years. My solicitor, Percival Kinley has assured me, I can depend upon you in this matter. If you cannot or refuse to, I have left other instructions with Percival concerning this. I leave this life with the belief that I can depend on you and know my Dulcey will be protected.

With kindest regards,
Lord James Fergers, Fourth Baron of Chesterton

Percival looked up and straight at Lord Beckham.

"I understand what he is asking of me, I just don't understand why?" questioned Nate. He was confused. He looked to Dulcey, but she shook her head and shrugged.

Dulcey was just as confused as Nate. Why did Lord James say she needed protection? Protection from what, from whom? All this left her anxious and confused. She was now frightened of what was to come. She could feel her heartbeat pounding in her chest. She heard that same beat loudly echoing in her ears. She clasped her hands together so tightly, she was certain that if she held something in them, she would have broken it to pieces. Oh, how she feared what was to come.

"I believe the letter Lord Fergers wrote to Miss Dulcey will explain it all for the both of you. Please, understand Miss Dulcey, I tried to get him to explain all of this to you when Mrs. Digby died but he thought he had time. When he became ill, he decided to do it this way," explained Percival.

Dulcey sat in her chair, biting her bottom lip in worry. Everything about her was cloudy. There were no clear pictures for her to see. She felt like she was looking into a swirling mass of colors. It frightened her. Her visions had never been this cloudy, this uncertain. All of her life, they had been there guiding her. Now, when she needed them the most, they were confused and as such, she was confused, lacking direction.

Nate watched Dulcey with concern. She looked frightened. Lord Fergers was asking him to protect her but protect her from what. Of course, he would protect her. He would not consider anything less. He wanted to reach out to her, to assure her, he would be here for her, always. He did not need the request of Lord Fergers.

"Please continue, Mr. Kinley," stated Nate, anxious to learn what this was all about.

Percival nodded and broke the seal to the second letter and began:

My dearest Dulcey,

Please know everything I have done, I have done to protect you, to keep you safe. I have loved you ever since I first saw you.

"I told you she was his by blow, his bastard child," stated the Countess with disdain as though Dulcey dirtied the air about her. She now had the proof she needed to get this woman out of her son's life. A baron's bastard daughter was not good enough for her son, for their family.

Percival looked up, startled by the Countess outbursts. "Countess?"

Nate turned in anger. "Mother! I will not hear you utter another word or I shall send you to your room to pack your bags. Do I make myself understood?" Nate was livid with his mother. How dare she continue to say such vile things about Dulcey! This was beyond enough.

"I just----." stated the Countess.

Nate interrupted before she could continue. "I am deadly serious about what I just said, Mother. I will send you packing back to Shefley Hall. Make no mistake about it. I have had enough of your remarks. Now sit quietly in your chair or I will call Evers and have you escorted out."

The Countess sat back in her chair and huffed. How dare her son talk to her in such a manner! He never used to. That is, until he met that Dulcey woman. She must do something about it and soon, before she got her hooks into her son.

Nate looked at Dulcey. She sat very still in her chair looking down at her folded hands in her lap. How he wanted to take her in his arms and tell her his mother's words were just that and not to let them hurt her so. But he knew they had.

Dulcey sat their unable to move while everything in her screamed, run from this place. Run till she was safely back at her home. But she did not. Her legs refused to move, so she sat their listening to them talk about her.

Percival looked at the Countess with displeasure. He was glad to see Lord Beckham was not like his mother. "It is not what you seem to imply, Countess, far from it, as you will soon know. May I continue, m'lord?"

"Yes, please do. I don't believe my mother shall make any further comments." He looked at his mother, daring her to say something more. He wanted any excuse to send her packing.

Mr. Kinley began again.

I have loved you ever since I first saw you in your mother's arms. So did your father, my younger brother Philip. He fell in love with your mother. Her name was Owena. She was the daughter of the Earl of Sayer of Wye Wales.

The Countess gasped. She was of noble birth. No, this could not be so.

Percival looked up and smiled smugly at her.

Your mother was very special. She had special abilities, to be able to see and know things about other people. To know of things before they happened. So did your grandmother. Everyone near your grandfather's estate knew and loved your grandmother and your mother. You have inherited some of their abilities, as well.

They were so happy the day you were born. We all were. Your mother, your father, your grandfather and grandmother. They lived near your mothers parents in Wales. And for four years all was well.

The vicar was old and left to live with his daughter in his old age. A new vicar was hired. Then on one of their visits, your mother could see the vicar's wife was very ill though she did not look ill. Your mother tried to tell her, explain to her but she and the vicar would not listen, would not believe her.

When she became ill, the vicar blamed your mother, saying and believing your mother had cursed her. When she died, he went crazy, calling your mother a witch. As a witch, she needed to burn. He tried to get many of the people of the area to believe your mother was a witch but they would not. That infuriated him even more.

Since he could not get help from anyone in the village, he set fire to the house himself. Your father was able to get you out to Grammy Digby who lived nearby, but by the time he returned back for your mother, the fire had spread throughout the house. The house collapsed before he could get your mother out, killing both of them.

The Vicar was heard screaming all must burn in hell for doing the devil's work, as he ran away from the house.

When he escaped and disappeared, your grandfather sent you to me with Grammy Digby, for your protection, afraid the vicar would come after you, as well. I gave you my mother's maiden name of Langely and had you live with Grammy Digby.

It was the hardest thing I have ever done, watching you live in the cottage, knowing you belonged here at the manor house. That is why I tutored you for this day, when you are to take your rightful place as Lady Fergers. That day, appears to be now.

Your grandfather and I searched for years for the Reverend Eandine. But he disappeared that night and we never heard of him again. But we were always afraid he would find you somehow and show up for you one day.

I promised your grandfather before he died, as he did your grandmother, I would always protect you. He left you five thousand pounds. I have invested it for you, along with money from your father and myself. The money has done well. There is a bank in London that has over twenty thousand pounds for you in your true name of Dulcey

Elizabeth Fergers. You are to be very well taken care of. Percival will instruct you on how you can draw from it.

I would like you to have your season in London. This money will see to it. Also, I have left the cottage and some of the surrounding land to you.

Lord Shefley, this is where my request comes in. I need you to protect my Dulcey from the possibility that the vicar is still alive and looking for her. I also need you to see to her coming out in London society and as such, I need you to also protect her from anyone taking advantage of her for her money.

My darling Dulcey, you have no idea how many times, I have wanted to tell you this, but I was afraid. Please forgive us, if we have hurt you in any way, for that was never our intent. We only wanted to protect you. After losing Philip and Owena we, your grandfather and I, were so afraid of losing you.

My one regret is that I have not lived long enough to see the beautiful woman you have become. Please know you have always been loved. Your father, your mother, your grandfather and grandmother and me your uncle. You were never alone.

Do not allow your special abilities to frighten you, especially knowing what happened to your parents. Your mother always said it was a blessing she was given. It is a blessing you have been given as well.

I wish you a happy life, my sweet Dulcey. You have been the joy of my life. I wish I would have told you all of this a long time ago, but I promised your grandfather and, I too, always feared for your safety. Please forgive me. It was never my intention to hurt you. Know all this time you have been loved by your family.

With all my love, I can now sign as your uncle.
Uncle James

The silence in the room was deafening as they all sat letting the words of the letter sink in.

Tears rolled slowly down Dulcey's cheeks. This letter answered so many of the questions, so many of the doubts, she had lived with all her life. She didn't know how to react to all of this. She felt numb, numb to her core. Never had she ever considered this was even as possibility. She was not prepared for this information. This was all so much, too much to take in and comprehend.

Percival broke the silence. "I will need you, Lord Beckham to sign some of these papers as well as Miss Dulcey or should I say Lady Dulcey."

Nate looked at Dulcey. She sat there like a statue staring into space. He so wanted to take her in his arms and tell her, it would all be alright. That he wanted to protect her, even before Lord Fergers asked him to in that letter.

"Lady Dulcey, I need your signature on these papers," requested Percival as he put a paper in front of her along with the pot of ink and pen.

"What are they?" asked Nate.

"Just acknowledging that she understands all that I have read to her and papers for her moneys at the bank," replied Percival. "Lady Dulcey?"

Dulcey stared at Mr. Kinley and took the quill he offered her.

"Lady Dulcey, I suggest that you sign Lady Dulcey Langely Fergers."

Dulcey nodded slightly and took the pen he handed her. Her hand shook. She needed to concentrate. She must sign her name correctly. Her correct name. Her new name. Lady Dulcey Langely Fergers. Slowly, she signed the paper and the second one he presented to her as well. She handed the pen back to Mr. Kinley.

She rose with the sudden need to get out of the room. The room was closing in on her. She couldn't breathe. If she didn't get out, she was afraid she would start screaming and seriously wondered, if once she started would she be able to stop.

Nate rose and stood in front of Dulcey to block her path. Everything in him wanted to gather her up in his arms and assure her this was good.

"Please let me by, Nate. I need some time alone to absorb all of this. Please, Nate!" she begged. Dulcey looked up and pleaded with him desperately for him to let her pass. She needed to get out of this room. She felt like she was suffocating. She could not breathe. She could not breathe.

Nate nodded and stepped aside. It took every fiber of his being not to follow her. To hold her, to comfort her as he knew she needed. But he respected her need for some time alone. This was a momentous disclosure for Dulcey. Anyone would have been shaken by it.

"Nathaniel, her mother was a witch and burned because of it. It claims she is one, too. You have her living here, putting us all in danger. You need to do something about this," stated the Countess, emphatically. This was the secret she would use to get rid of Dulcey. But she must tread carefully now. Soon, it will be known, she is a descendant of an earl and a baron. None the less, she was not the woman for her son. No, a witch, no matter the noble lineage, was not going to marry into this, her family.

Nate passed his hands through his hair in frustration. He turned to his mother. "Mother, I am so tired of listening to your pompous opinions. Can you not see how distressful this is for Dulcey?"

"What is distressing to me is that she is a witch and her mother has been burned as such. You have put us all in danger by bringing her here. Is not my distress important, Nathaniel? It's enough to give me the vapors." The countess laid her head back in the chair and began waving her hand in front of her face to fan her. She would use this information to her advantage. She would make her son see the folly of this association with this woman.

Nate exhaled strongly and looked upward. He was very much aware of his mother machinations at feigning illness when she did not get her way. He walked to the door and opened it. Evers was just outside.

"Evers, please have my mother's maid come down to assist my mother back to her rooms." He turned and walked back in.

"Nathaniel-----."

Nate interrupted. "Mother, I need to speak with Mr. Kinley. There are several things I need clarification on. I will check on you later."

"We need to discuss this further, now" whined his mother. She needed to get him alone to convince him. He needed to be shown the folly of his ways. Surely, now he could see how completely impossible a situation this is.

"After I have talked with Mr. Kinley, mother." Nate noticed Leta, his mother's maid at the door. "Leta, please escort my mother to her room. It seems she needs to rest." He went to his mother's side and offered her his arm.

"Nathaniel---."

He interrupted her again. "I promise you, mother, as soon as I have finished talking with Mr. Kinley, I will come to your room so that we may discuss this. Please, go upstairs with Leta and I will be upstairs shortly."

Lady Shefley sighed in disgust and rose easily to her feet. With lips pursed in annoyance, she eyed Nate with what Nate remembered as a child, he and his brother called the evil eye.

Nate turned away to talk to Mr. Kinley. He heard the door close behind her and immediately dismissed her from his thoughts. Dulcey was his primary concern now.

"I wanted to talk to you alone Lord Beckham, as well."

Nate went to the side bar and poured himself a glass of whiskey and raised the bottle in Mr. Kinley direction. When he nodded, Nate poured another glass. He brought the glass to Mr. Kinley and sat down in the chair he had occupied earlier. Percival sat in the chair Dulcey had sat in previously.

Each took a long drink.

"Lord Beckham, may I be frank with you?"

"Yes, please do." He was curious as to what the solicitor had to say. He seemed to have been close to Lord Fergers to have been entrusted with this mission.

Percival studied the earl for a moment. He had noticed the concern he had showed Miss Dulcey.

"Miss,-- Lady Dulcey is very well liked here. I did not always agree with Lord James but I do know he loved her dearly and what he did, he did to protect her. I sincerely hope you will honor Lord James request to see to her protection."

Nate nodded and looked Percival directly in the eye. "That is a promise I make readily. The last thing I want to see happen is for Dulcey to get hurt. This news actually makes it easier for what I have planned. I have plans on marrying Dulcey. In truth, only this morning, I have sent a missive to a good friend in London to petition the Archbishop for a special license. I had hopes of marrying Dulcey even before I knew of all this."

Percival smiled and nodded. He had noticed how Lord Beckham looked at Miss Dulcey. "An excellent idea, my lord." Then he frowned, remembering. "Your mother, the countess?"

Nate smiled tolerantly. "I am very much aware of my mother and her rude opinions, but she is about to realize, her only other choice is to accept this or live at the dowager house at Shefley Hall. It would mean sharing it with my grandmother, her mother in law. That is something she will avoid at all cost."

Percival smiled. He drank the last of his whiskey and stood up. "Then I will take my leave, for I do believe you have it all well in hand, my lord."

Nate stood up as well and offered Percival his hand. "Thank you, Percival. May I count on you for any legal issues I may have?"

"Of course, my lord. Will you be staying at Brandanlyn?" he asked.

Nate smiled. "Yes, for a time. I found I have liked it here."

"Good. I will be glad to assist with the arrangements with our rector here, Reverend Treadwell," offered Percival.

"Thank you. I may need that help. Does he know Dulcey?" He would make all this easier for Dulcey.

Percival smiled. "Yes, very well. In fact, he has told Dulcey countless of times, her special gift comes from God."

"Does she believe him?" Nate hoped so.

"I believe so. But it is hard to know for sure with Lady Dulcey," Percival answered.

Nate nodded. "Thank you, Percival."

Evers was at the door and escorted Percival Kinley out.

~~~~~~~~~~~~~~~~

Nate climbed the stairs and headed towards his mother's rooms. He would have rather gone to Dulcey, but he needed to make certain his mother accepted his plans. She would balk at the idea and probably throw one of her temper tantrums, then pretend to get ill. She had done it so many times in order to get her way but this time, it was not going to work.

He knocked, without waiting for her to bid enter, walked in. He found his mother reclining on her chaise.

Not a good sign. Well, let the battle begin. He was armed and ready.

"Mother, we need to talk," he started.

She looked at him through narrowed eyes. "Yes, indeed we do."

"Before you begin your tirade, Mother let me inform you that if you disagree with any of the plans I have made, you are welcome to pack your bags and go back to Shefley Hall, pack your belongings there and move in with Grandmother at the Dowager House." Nate watched his mother's eyes grow wide and the color drain from her face. He had had enough of her interference, first in his brother's life and now his.

"What did you say?" she asked in disbelief. No, there was no way he had just said what she thought she heard. He would not.

"I believe you heard every word I said, Mother. I stood by and watched as you made Grayson and Caroline's life miserable. Grayson always told me he had you under control, but I watched as you took pleasure in upsetting Caroline. I will not allow you do that again," stated Nathaniel emphatically.

"I never did any such thing," argued the Countess. "I cared for Caroline."

"No, you did not. You never cared for Caroline. Poor Caroline was afraid of you. Grayson did not want to hurt you for fear of you retaliating against Caroline. I will not be so malleable." He was determined, she would not interfere.

Lady Shefley pursed her lips together. Nathaniel was just being stubborn. She would bid her time.. He would not go through with his threats. She must handle him differently. He had always been the more stubborn of her two sons, even as a child.

"First thing this morning, I sent a missive to Worth requesting he procure a special license from the Archbishop for me."

Lady Shefley's eyes widened in disbelief and sat up from her reclining position with a start. No, he did not. No, she would not allow it. The Duke of Worthingston of all people. Caroline's brother. No, this must not be allowed to happen.

"Nathaniel, she is a witch," she argued. "My God, the gossip mongers will have a field day. We will be shunned by everyone, especially when it is known her mother was burned because of it. Nathaniel you simply cannot do this. I forbid you to. Think of our good name." How had this gotten so far?

Nate narrowed his eyes. He wanted to shake her but he knew he couldn't. But it was so tempting. "Mother, listen to me, as I am only going to say this once. I have already told you what will happen if you hurt Dulcey in any way what so ever. I am determined to marry Dulcey. I have set the process in motion. Nothing you say or do will dissuade me. Please, realize I set this all in motion before I knew of Dulcey's true relationship to Lord Fergers. "

Lady Shefley stood up and faced her son. "I forbid you put this family in danger by marrying that witch. This marriage you speak of will not take place. I forbid it," she demanded.

"Then I suggest you have Leta begin packing. I can have the carriage ready to go in an hour." He was tired of arguing with her. He needed to tend to Dulcey, to make certain she was all right.

Lady Shefley's eyes narrowed in anger. He could not be serious. She was his mother. He would never do what he threatened. "I will not be leaving."

"Then I take it you have accepted my decision." Nate did not trust his mother. She was up to something.

But he was adamant. He was not Grayson and would not tolerate his mother's interference.

"This decision will bring you, all of us, nothing but harm. It will be the ruination of this family. Think of Abigail. How will she be accepted by the *ton* if you marry this witch woman?" Maybe if she brought Abigail's welfare into the discussion, it would change his mind.

Nate raised his hand. "Enough, Mother. Call her a witch one more time and I will pack your bags myself and put you bodily into the carriage. One more word Mother. I mean it. If you stay, you will abide by my decision. The choice is yours and I need to know your decision now." He had had enough of dealing with his mother. He needed to be talking to Dulcey, yet here he was dealing with his mother. But for Dulcey's sake, his mother had to be dealt with first before she did irreparable harm. He could see her plotting.

"I am waiting for your answer, Mother."

Lady Shefley turned and walked to the window of her room and looked out. She knew Nathaniel had always been the difficult one but this was beyond her understanding. How could he put their good family name in such jeopardy? Oh, what a field day the gossip mongers in London would have. She had to be a witch. She had put some sort of spell on Nathaniel. Somehow she must see to it, this wedding would never take place. That meant she must stay, in order to accomplish that.

So, for the time being. "Very well, Nathaniel. I will abide with your decision." She turned back to face her son.

Nate nodded. "I will hold you to this, Mother. I will not think twice about sending you to Shefley Hall and the dowager house if you do anything to hurt Dulcey. This is not an empty threat." He did not trust her but he would give her the benefit of the doubt, at the moment. Perhaps, she realized how serious he was about this decision.

131

Lady Shefley nodded.

"Good. Now I need to see to Dulcey." Nate strode out of his mother's room into the hall with one purpose on his mind. He turned to go down the hall to Dulcey's suite.

"Uncle Nate," whispered Abby.

Nate looked around and found Abby hiding under a table near the staircase. Nate knelt down to her level. "Poppet, why are you hiding here?"

Abby looked toward her grandmother's rooms. "Dulcey is gone. She gave me a hug and said she had to go back to her house." There were tears in Abby's eyes. "I heard grandmother tell Leta, Dulcey needed to go away and never come back. She said she would make her. I want Dulcey to come back." Her bottom lip trembled.

Nate pulled her out from under table and held her close to him. "Shh, Poppet. When did she leave?"

"I don't know."

"Shh, dry your tears. I promise, I will bring Dulcey back here. I plan on going to the cottage to bring her back. Now, I don't want you to worry. It may take me a couple of days before I get back. But I promise you, I will not come back until she comes back with me." He wiped her tears from her cheeks.

While talking with his mother, Dulcey had left. He should have gone to Dulcey first. But he thought making certain his mother did not make things worse was more important. Damn, mother had interfered again. He should have realized how difficult all of this for Dulcey. He was not surprised she had gone back to the cottage.

"You promise?" Abby asked in a trembling voice.

Nate smiled at her. "Yes, I promise. Now I want you to smile," he looked up and saw Miss Franny. "Go with Miss Franny."

He turned to Miss Franny, "Would you take Abby back to the nursery? I have just explained to her I am going after Dulcey, to bring her back to Brandanlyn.

Please try to avoid contact with my mother as much as possible while I am gone."

Miss Franny took Abby's hand in hers. "Of course, my lord."

Several steps away, Abby turned, "Promise, Uncle Nate?"

"I promise," replied Nate, crossing his heart with his finger.

Abby nodded and followed Miss Franny to her room.

Nate turned and walked back to his rooms. Simmons was waiting there.

"I've heard, my lord. I've pack you a small valise," said Simmons.

Nate chuckled, shaking his head. "Thank you Simmons."

Simmons handed him the valise. "Good luck, my lord. I know my opinion doesn't matter, but she belongs here."

Nate smiled. "No, Simmons, it doesn't matter, but I still like to hear it. And you are right. She does belong here. Hope you like it here, for I don't plan on going back to Shefley Hall any time soon. In fact, I've sent word to Worth to procure a special license. Think you can deal with me as a married man?"

Simmons grinned. "I think I'll have no problems, my lord. And by the way, I'm beginning to like this country life very much myself."

Nate grinned back. It meant a great deal to him that Simmons approved. Simmons had been with him for the past ten years. Of all the people on the earth, Simmons knew him best of all. He took his valise and said, "Keep an eye on mother. I know she would never listen to you but------------"

Simmons nodded. "Of course, my lord. I have learned to maneuver around the Countess when need be. And I will watch out for little Abby, as well."

"Good. I shouldn't be more than a couple of days," said Nate as he walked out of the door.

Downstairs, he met with Evers in the hall. "She left about an hour ago. She went out the back stairs thinking none of us had seen her."

Nate nodded. "Have my horse saddled and brought around for me Evers while I talk with Cook."

Evers raised an eyebrow in question.

"Seems we ate all of Dulcey's food when we were snow bound," he continued. "It may take a couple of days to convince her, she belongs here at Brandanlyn. I would not want either one of us to starve to death."

Evers returned his lordship's smile. It appeared Lord Beckham was not very concerned that Miss Dulcey, no Lady Dulcey, he must remember that, had left. He was bringing her back to Brandanlyn. That was good. "I'll see to your horse immediately, my lord."

Nate walked off to kitchen to talk to Cook. When he emerged several long minutes later, he carried a sack of food Cook had packed for him and Dulcey. From the feel of the sack, it was more like for a couple of weeks than a couple of days.

Max awaited him outside. Nate gave his sack to the groom who tied onto his saddle, his satchel already there. He turned to Evers. "I should return tomorrow or the day after. Keep an eye on things Evers, while I am gone."

"Of course, my lord. We will all be waiting for you and Lady Dulcey's return."

Nate nodded and rode off at a gentle cantor. He would be with Dulcey soon.

Chapter 11

Love is when he gives you a piece of your soul,
That you never knew was missing.
                    Torquato Tasso

Dulcey sat in the rocker wrapped in one of Grammy's quilts in front of the fire. The fire was finally beginning to chase the chill from the cottage. She had not realized how cold she had gotten on her walk from the manor house to the cottage. She had been too engrossed in her thoughts to notice. Perhaps, it was not just from the chill of the weather but the chill that surrounded her heart that made it feel so cold.

She had cried, gotten angry, and cried again, only to come to realize, there was nothing she could do about it. When she entered the cottage, she realized there was no warmth here awaiting her. It made her realize, she was a changed woman from the one who had left here several days ago. Her life would never be the same again.

She was Lord James' niece. He was her uncle. How she wished, she would have known that all along. Would it have truly made a difference, she wondered. Now, she would never know. She mourned the loss of that relationship. Yet, she had known all along, there was a special bond between them. The forces had always showed her, he was important to her. Now, she knew how and why.

Sitting staring into the flames, she had to come to several decisions. She now knew who she was. But what exactly did that mean? Who was she and how had all of this changed her? She was not a nobody, as she had always believed, been led to believe. She was the niece of Lord

Fergers. Her mother was the daughter of a Welch earl and as such made her the granddaughter. But she was also the daughter of what many called a witch. Now, she understood why Grammy Digby would get so agitated when someone talked about witches.

This gift her mother had passed on to her, this ability to see into the future. It seemed hers was not as pronounced as her mothers. But it was there none the less. From an early age, it had frightened her. She did not understand it. She had tried, finally she had come to tolerate it, accept it as part of who she was.

Now, to learn it was the reason her mother and father had lost their lives, it frightened her more. Could something like that happen to her? Lord James said he had protected her identity all this time, but what if that madman was still out there, waiting for her. She mustn't think that way. After all these years, nothing had ever been found of him. Surely, after all these years, she was safe and he was no longer a threat. Surely.

But what if someone like him came to believe as he did, she was a witch because she could see into the future. Would that someone want to kill her, as well? No, she had to believe she was safe. She had to believe it to be so. For if it was not, then she would be putting all those close to her in danger.

All of these thoughts and more ran rampant through her mind during the long walk to the cottage. It had taken her a little under an hour. Once she had started walking, her emotions had set the pace. Her feet had moved quickly, covering the familiar path to the cottage. She hoped they hadn't missed her, yet. She didn't know why, when she thought of they, she meant Nate.

She knew Nate would follow her. It was one of the things she had seen. She just hadn't seen why. With Nate, it was all hazy. She never got a true picture. Now was the time she needed to see the future, to see Nate's future. Why, oh, why could she not?

Nate confused her. No, it was more than that. There was a connection between the two of them. A connection that was stronger than any she had ever felt. He made her feel things she did not understand and that frightened her. All she knew was that she wanted him with an ache she knew was all consuming. She couldn't think straight when around him. All she could do was feel.

Yet, with everything he made her feel, she still felt incomplete, wanting more from him. The more was what frightened her, for she had no clue to what the more was. She just knew it was there, pulling at her with a force she did not know.

She heard a noise in the lean to. All her animals had been taken to the Manor days ago. She knew it was him. She didn't think he would have been here so soon. She thought she would have more time to deal with and understand these feelings of hers. She sat huddled in a ball in the rocker staring at the door, awaiting his entrance. She had no idea what she would say to him.

~~~~~~~~~~~~~~~

Nate walked through the door of the lean to. He carried the large sack and his valise and placed them on the table. His eyes never left Dulcey's. He had not been surprised to find she had left the manor house. Just as he knew, she would come here. There were many things they needed to discuss. Here would be the best place to discuss such things.

She sat all wrapped in a quilt in the rocking chair in front of the fireplace. She did not look as devastated as she had in his study. She just looked lost. He was not surprised.

He pulled a chair next to her rocker. "How are you?" He studied her face. He could tell she had been crying. Her eyes were red and they still glistened with unshed tears. His heart ached for her. It had been a shock this afternoon, learning who she truly was, what had happened to her parents. So much to take in, to deal with. He wanted to take her in his arms and hold her but he hesitated just as he had earlier.

Dulcey nodded. "I am all right." She looked to the bag on the table. "What's in the bag?"

Nate smiled. "I remembered we ate nearly all your food. I had Cook prepare some food for us for a couple of days. I think she misunderstood. I think there is enough food here for a couple of weeks."

She smiled softly. Cook would have done that. It appeared as though Nate was not leaving any time soon.

"We need to talk," said Nate never taking his eyes off her face, watching her intently, hoping to see some sort of reaction out of her.

Dulcey shrugged slightly. "I believe everything that needed to be said was said earlier." She was thinking of the Countess's words. She kept hearing them, repeating in her mind, over and over again. It was bad enough to learn she was not who she thought she was, but she knew everyone would think as the Countess did. They would never remember she was the granddaughter of an earl or the niece of a baron. She would always be the daughter of a witch.

"I most heartily disagree," argued Nate.

Dulcey sighed and looked away. She knew if she continued to stare into those blue eyes of his she would be lost. "What good will it do? It will not change things."

Nate took her hands from her lap and brought them to his lips. He kissed one palm and then the other, never taking his eyes off of her. He watched her reaction closely.

Her abrupt intake of breath made him smile. She was not immune to him. She had not pulled away.

"You are right. Some things have not changed. Others have. These feelings between us have not. No, that is not truly correct. If anything they have gotten stronger. You feel it, just as I do. This connection between us."

Dulcey shook her head slightly. When he kissed her palms, it sent shivers all the way down to her toes. "There is too much against us. No, please let me finish. You are an Earl, and I am---------"

Nate put his fingers across her lips to stop her. "You are the granddaughter of an earl, the niece of a baron, your blood line is as acceptable as any."

"But I am also a witch. Should that come out, it would hurt you," she argued. At first, it had been the fact she was beneath him that had discouraged her. But now, that was no longer the problem. She needed to make him understand about her being called a witch. Hadn't that been the ultimate reason her parents were killed. That would put him in danger.

"You are not a witch. No, listen to me," replied Nate when she tried to interrupt. "Having the gift that you have does not make you a witch. It makes you special."

Dulcey shook her head. "You heard your mother. Others will think just like her."

Nate sighed, his mother. She had to have her say and in the process made things worse. He hoped his talk to her had made an impression. She knew his ultimatum. She knew exactly how serious he was. "Mother has been set straight about this. She will not repeat such words again. She knows this. She also knows why I am here."

She had to ask. "Why are you here, Nate?"

"I am here to bring you back to Brandanlyn. It is where you belong. It is where you have always belonged."

Dulcey shook her head. As strong as these feelings for him were becoming, she knew it was best they part now before it became too painful, no unbearable.

"I want you there as my wife, Dulcey. I do not plan on leaving here until you agree." It was not exactly how he planned on this but he needed her to know, he was very serious. More so now, than ever before. They were meant to be together. He knew it, he thought he always knew it, from the moment when he first woke up here days ago and saw her.

Dulcey gazed at Nate with such a longing, aching need. Before her sat everything she had so longed for, dreamed of and firmly believed was unattainable. Lord James had made it possible with his revelation of her birthright. But could she?

She closed her eyes. Nate still held her hands in his. She took a deep breath and opened her mind, her heart, opened herself to the influences of the spirits, the forces around her. She drew on the forces that surrounded Nate, to see his future. She took another deep breath and let it out slowly. Her vison was hazy but she could see his future. She was Nate's future, just as he was hers. The forces decreed it so. She had learned years ago they were reliable. She knew this is where her destiny lay. She could no longer stand in the way of the inevitable.

She opened her eyes. Nate was watching her closely. The love she saw shining in his eyes, she knew what she needed to do. He was her destiny, just as she was his. She was fighting a losing battle, a battle if she was honest with herself, she had lost the moment Nate walked through that door from the snow storm. The forces had just told her, she was his future, just as he was hers. Accepting that fact, allowed the forces to begin to clear, to show her, his future, her future, how intertwined they were.

Dulcey let go of the fear and allowed his love to flow to her like a raging river washing over her. She smiled and let the peace of her forces guide her, knowing there was only one decision she could make. "Yes."

Nate let out a deep breath of relief. He had not realized he had been holding his breathe until that moment. He smiled and rose to his feet pulling her to her feet as well before him. "Yes, what?" He had to be sure.

"Yes, I will be your wife," she said as she stared into his eyes. The relief of having made the decision, left her open to an array of feelings that bombarded her from every direction. The mists that had surrounded her, clouding the forces for the last few days, evaporated like the rising sun dispersed the mists over the moors. His love was her sun, warming her from the inside out.

"I was prepared to be more persuasive." His lips claimed hers. She tasted like sweet honey. He pulled her tightly against him till he could feel every part of her. He urged her lips apart till his tongue met hers. When she met his tentatively at first then more boldly, he knew it would not stop with just a kiss. She would be his tonight. He wanted her as he had never wanted a woman before. She was a part of his heart. He wanted her to be a part of his body. He needed to make her his, to bury himself deep within her till nothing mattered but their joining.

He trailed kisses across her cheeks and tasted the salt from her tears. No, he would turn them to tears of joy. He raised his head for a moment, looked deep into her eyes and said, "I will stop if you tell me to, though it will be the hardest thing I have ever done. I do so want to make love to you. To make you completely, totally mine. To show you the delights between a man and a woman. But if you need the blessing of the church, I will------."

Dulcey placed her fingers across his lips. The love she saw shining brightly in his eyes she knew, "I have the blessings of fate and the forces about me. They have decreed, we are the two halves that make a whole. I need nothing else to tell me, I am yours and you are mine. I want to be whole with you, now and forever." Dulcey knew she wanted him with an ache deep down within her. She wanted to know all there was between a man and a woman. All the delights he promised her. She wanted, no, she needed with every fiber of her being to become a part of him.

Nate smiled and took a step backwards.

Dulcey looked at him confused for a moment.

His fingers began to slowly unlace the front of her dress. "I plan on unwrapping you, my love, slowly. I want to savor every part of you I unveil to my eyes." He pushed her dress from her shoulders till it fell at her feet. He placed a kiss at the top of each mound of her breast that showed above her chemise.

Dulcey stood perfectly still, afraid if she moved, she would collapse in his arms. She felt her nipples tightened and that place deep within tighten and ache with such a need.

Nate's eyes devoured her. She was more beautiful than he imagined. He slowly untied the ribbon that held her chemise and pushed it from her shoulders until her breast were bare. He bent to push it down passed her hips but stopped for a moment, to pay homage to each nipple with his tongue. He heard Dulcey's sudden intake of breath and smiled.

She stood there in the firelight with nothing but her stockings and garters on. He knelt down before her, undid the garter then slowly rolled down one stocking placing a kiss at the top of her inner thigh. He felt her quiver. He placed his hand on her hip to steady her as he removed the stocking from her foot. She placed her hands on his shoulders. He began his assault on her other leg, placing another kiss on that inner thigh. He heard the soft moan that escaped Dulcey's lips and her hands tightened on his shoulders. With the second stocking removed, she stood before him naked. Never had he seen such a beautiful sight. He placed her discarded clothes on the chair by the table.

His kissed one thigh leaving a trail with his tongue and then the other one. His fingers parted her till he found the bud and lightly rubbed it, only to replace his fingers with his tongue softly flicking back and forth.

Dulcey moaned deep within her throat. She clung to his shoulders feeling that any moment her legs would give completely out from under her. Her whole body tingled with such a burning sensation and a need for more. When she felt his tongue at the bud of her womanhood, she didn't know how much longer her legs would hold her.

Nate sensed her inability to stand for much longer, gently pushed her back till the back of her knees hit the edge of the bed. She fell backwards her legs open to him. Once again, he licked and sucked at the bud. He tasted her juices and had never tasted anything sweeter. One hand held her open to his tongue while his other hand found her breast, teasing the nipple, gently rolling it between his thumb and forefinger, knowing it would send her close to the edge. He increased the pressure. His body pulsed with the need for her, but he was determined to savor every precious moment of instructing her in the ways of passion.

Dulcey felt like her body was sensitive to everything about her, the coolness of the air against her heated body. The heat in her body raged within her till she thought she would burst like the embers in the fireplace. Just when she thought she could not survive a moment longer, she did burst like the embers shooting into every direction at once. She thought her heart would beat out of her chest. Mary had never said it was this intense.

Nate felt her release. Oh, how sweet she tasted. After he had tasted his fill, he lifted her legs onto the bed so she lay in the bed. He watched her slowly open her eyes, a look of contentment on her face. He sat at her side and touched her cheek. She covered his hands with hers. He brought her hand to his lips and kissed her palm.

For that brief moment, she felt like she was floating, but his lips and tongue on her palm immediately sent quivers deep within her making her ache for something more. She smiled up at him and licked her bottom lip. She wanted to feel his skin, to feel it against hers.

She reached up and undid his cravat and began undoing the buttons of his waistcoat. "My lord, I do believe you have too much clothes on." All she could think of was seeing all of him, no needing all of him.

Nate chuckled. "I can remedy that situation quickly." He removed his jacket, waistcoat, and shirt and placed them on top of the pile of her clothes on the chair. He quickly pulled off his boots and removed his pants.

Dulcey smiled.

Nate saw her smile and raised an eyebrow in question.

"Abby and I had more trouble than that, the other day. You were of no help."

Nate smiled. "It's easier when they're not wet." He stood in just his linen drawers, his manhood making it tent out. "I have been haunted by dreams of your body under mine. It has felt so real."

"I have been." When she saw the question in his eyes, she explained. "That first night, you were feverish. I gave you your medicine and you pulled me down on top of you, kissed me then turned so I lay under you. And then you fainted."

As she explained, Dulcey reached out and untied the ribbon of his drawers and pushed it down. She took in a shaky breath at the sight of his erection. She raised her eyes to meet his. It was larger than what she had believed.

Nate sat down on the side of the bed. "I do not plan to faint tonight, my love."

"Mary says it hurts the first time."

Nate nodded. "I promise you I will be gentle, but it will hurt only for a moment." He lay beside her and gathered her in his arms. He kissed her softly, teasingly and felt her relax. He began a deliberate assault on her senses. He trailed kisses down her neck, tasting the area where he could feel her heartbeat. He paid homage to one nipple and then the other. He slipped one hand to open her legs and rubbed the bud of her womanhood. It was still sensitive from his earlier ardor. He could feel her response.

The fear Dulcey first felt when she saw his erection quickly vanished. The feel of his skin against hers, his lips and tongue tracing circles around her nipples made her move under him. She moaned in need.

Nate eased the tip of his manhood against her opening. He could feel the wetness. It took every ounce of his control. He wanted her so much. Slowly, he pushed forward.

Dulcey felt him and let her body take control. She wanted him, she wanted to be joined to him. She raised her hips pushing against him just as he pushed forward. She felt him enter her in one swift thrust. The pain was sharp but brief. The feel of him deep within her was what she wanted, what she had ached for.

Her sudden intake of breath and the resistance he felt as he entered her halted him. He lay still, allowing her to adjust to him. He licked her bottom lip as his hand teased a nipple. He felt her slowly move under him. He began to slowly withdraw and thrust, meeting her movements. He allowed her to set the rhythm.

Dulcey felt him move in and out of her. She met his every thrust, wanting more and more of him. The tightening of her insides was almost unbearable, yet at the same time, it grew stronger. She wanted more. She grabbed his buttocks to hold him tightly against her. She met his strong thrust and her world about her, exploded into a myriad of stars of every color. And then she was floating amongst the stars. She felt his last strong thrust and then his quiver within her, as he emptied his seed deep within her. She felt complete.

Nate rested on his elbows, not allowing his full weight against her. His breathing was ragged. When she grabbed his buttocks and held him tight, he nearly lost it. But he managed to hold on enough to send her over the edge before he came. Never had it felt so good, so intense. He kissed her lips lightly and her eyes fluttered open.

"Mary never said it was so intense."

Nate rolled to his side, "Who is this Mary?" pulling Dulcey to lie at his side.

Dulcey smiled. "Mary works at the tavern in the village and she explained how it happens between a man and a woman. But she never said anything about how strong the feelings are. I can see now why she likes it so."

Nate laughed. "You, my love are adorable," and he kissed the tip of her nose. "So I take it my love, you like it?"

Dulcey smiled, turned and kissed him, teasing his tongue with hers. "If it is like this every time, then yes, I like it. I like it very much." Just having his skin against hers, feeling his body next her, knowing all the things he could make her feel, made her hunger again for him. How could that be when only moments ago she felt so satisfied, so satiated.

She laid her head on his chest. The light brown splattering of hair on his chest felt soft under her cheek. His nipple was just inches away. She turned her head slightly and traced it with her tongue. She felt his sudden intake of breath and smiled. His were just as sensitive as hers. Interesting. She did it again only spent more time on it.

Nate took a handful of her hair and gently pulled till her face was turned to his. "Be careful what you start, my lady." How could his body be responding to her again so soon? But responding it was.

Dulcey licked her lips and looked at him. Her hand lowered and felt him responding to her touch. She liked the feel of it, as it grew larger in her hand. She also liked the fact, she could affect him as he did her.

Nate groaned. She lowered her lips to his nipple again and began her assault, as he had done to hers just moments earlier.

She felt him stiffen in her hand. He placed his hand over hers and instructed her how to move her hand up and down along his shaft. She liked the feel of him in her hand, full hard.

Nate pulled her to face him and kissed her deeply. He wanted her again. He felt her move closer to him. Never letting go of her lips, he grabbed her hips in his hands and pulled her on top of him.

She broke from his kiss and stared at him, her hands on his chest to steady her. He raised her hips until she straddle him. Slowly, he lowered her onto his waiting shaft and watched as her eyes widened in surprise.

"This way too?" Dulcey asked curious. She felt him wiggle under her, sending different sensations through her. She closed her eyes and moaned.

"Sit up, my love."

She sat up as he instructed her. She felt all of him within her, filling her more than before, if that was possible. He moved under her, raising her hips till she felt herself go up and down on him. When she felt his lips on her nipples, first one than the other, she thought she would just melt on top of him. Her arms could barely hold her up but she refused to let herself fall. She wanted that sweet release she knew would come. She moaned as she climbed higher and higher. It was there just out of reach. She grabbed hold of it and it burst within her. Her arms could no longer hold her. She collapsed on top of him floating down from the highest precipice. She felt his shudder. His heartbeat pounding in her ear, his breath rasping as well. Was it Nate's or was it hers echoing in her ears? She didn't know, she didn't care.

Nate held her close to his chest, his hands gently rubbing her back, a feeling of contentment the likes he had never known. Marriage to Dulcey would be everything he wanted marriage to be. He felt her breathing become even.

"Dulcey?" he said softly. He smiled. He reached and pulled the covers over them as he moved Dulcey to his side. She murmured. "Sleep, my love." Nate closed his eyes and let sleep take hold of him, as well.

Chapter 12

There is room in the smallest cottage
For a happy loving pair.

　　　　　　　Friedrick Schiller

Dulcey woke slowly and stretched. She felt muscles she never knew existed. She was also naked under the covers. Memories came flooding to her mind and she smiled. The contentment that surrounded her was like the warm quilt that covered her naked body. She turned her head and watched as Nate went about setting the table with food Cook had sent with him. He wore just his pants, bare footed and bare chested, a grand example of the male specimen. He was hers.

She remembered everything from earlier. He had asked her to marry him. He was to be her husband. No, he was her husband, in every way, except for the blessings of the church. That would come in time. She had seen it so.

He had made her his, as the forces had showed her. She blushed but smiled, remembering how delicious those feelings were of being his. With Nate as her husband, she had the rest of her life to enjoy these feelings. The forces around her were clear and bright, the mists were gone.

Nate turned and found Dulcey awake and watching him. The smile on her face and the love reflected in her eyes made his heart sing. "Get up woman. I am half starved to death. It seems this fairy princess I know has taken all my strength. I need nourishment if I'm to keep her satisfied."

Dulcey laughed and swung her legs off the bed and stood up. The admiration she saw in Nate's eyes made her ache for him again. But he was right. She needed nourishment, as well.

"There's some water in the pitcher by the fireplace to wash up," he told her.

Dulcey nodded. She did feel sticky. She walked to the pitcher feeling Nate's eyes watching her every movement. She washed with the warm water in short time. She grabbed Nate's shirt and put it on. She liked the smell of him on his shirt surrounding her.

Nate pulled her toward him and kissed her passionately. Dulcey returned his passion. Reluctantly, Nate pulled away from her. Married to Dulcey would be enjoyable, very enjoyable.

"Later, my love. We have the rest of our lives to enjoy each other. Right at this moment, I need food or I shall just fade away unto nothing." He pulled out the chair for her.

Dulcey sat down. "Yes, let's eat. I can't have you fading away, just when I found out all the things you can do."

Nate laughed, "Not all, my love," as he began filling his plate with chicken, ham, cheese, greens, potatoes, and sliced a piece from the loaf of bread. Nate sat down. "Shall I fix your plate?"

Dulcey shook her head. She gazed at the food on the table. Nate was indeed right. Cook had sent enough food for two weeks. Dulcey piled her plate high with food. Suddenly she realized she was hungry, starving like Nate.

She bit into a piece of chicken. It was delicious. Food had never tasted so good.

"Some wine Dulcey?"

She nodded and watched as Nate poured her wine. She took a long drink.

They both ate in silence, neither needed to talk. The comfort of each other's company was all they needed at the moment. They finished eating and Dulcey helped Nate store their food for later.

Nate stood at the window. "Dulcey come look at this."

Dulcey stood beside him and gazed out of the window. Nate pulled her in front of him and wrapped his arms around her. The full moon was just beginning to rise in the night time sky, a big cream colored orb shedding its luster onto the snow making it glisten like a thousand points of lights.

"My fairy princess, the king has granted your wish. You are to marry your human" said Nate remembering the story Dulcey had been telling Abby.

Dulcey nodded, not trusting her voice. When she had begun the story of the fairy and the prince for Abby, she wanted to end it with a happily ever after. But she had begun to realize, she was talking about her and Nate. She had doubted the happily ever after.

"Abby?"

"You'll be able to tell Abby more of your stories. She made me promise I would bring you back."

Dulcey smiled. "She has come to mean a great deal to me. I've come to love her as my own." Abby had come to dwell in a special place in her heart.

"I know. She's come to mean a lot to me, as well. You have been good for her. She needs a woman in her life to love her. Heaven knows, my mother is not that person."

Dulcey sighed. The Countess. Surely, she was against all of this. She hated the thought of having to deal with the Countess on a daily basis. It would be daunting. But to have Nate's love every day, she would deal with the Countess.

Nate could feel the worry from Dulcey. He knew, she was remembering the ugly statements his mother had made about her. He needed to reassure her.

"I am not certain if mother will be there when we return. I have strongly suggested she go back to London or

Shefley Hall. I've had a long talk with her. You will not have to deal with her. She knows my decision. Please understand my mother likes very few people, if any. I now realize how miserable she made my brother, Grayson and his wife, Carolyn. I have informed her, I will not put up with any of her condescending melodramatics. She did not like what I had to say. She has been given a choice. When we get back to Brandanlyn, I will know her decision."

"But Nate, she is your mother," argued Dulcey. She who had never had a mother, felt that a mother mattered. But she also thought mothers loved their children and she had not seen any signs of love from the Countess.

Nate nodded. "Yes, she is but I am not blind to her shortcomings. My brother and I were raised by a tutor and then sent off to school. She was not a part of our lives growing up. I do not want that for Abby."

Dulcey smiled. "I don't want that for Abby either. I missed growing up with a mother. I had Grammy Digby to care and love me, also Lord James. I want Abby to have that love."

"So do I," replied Nate. His hands had found their way to her breast and had begun teasing her nipples through the fabric of his shirt till they budded hard between his fingertips. He could feel his shaft hardening against her buttocks, buttocks he had learned to watch sway with her hips. Remembering the way her hips swayed, how he liked watching them, made him even harder. He smiled.

Dulcey leaned back against him savoring the feel of his hands. A low moan escaped her lips as she felt those feelings begin again. She felt him open his shirt till he freed her breast to his hands. The cool air that came in through the cracks around the window felt good against her warm skin. His fingers found its way to that place between her legs and played homage to the bud of her womanhood. She felt his lips on the back of her neck as his shirt slipped off her shoulders, kissing, nipping the side of her neck, her shoulder.

She tried to turn, but he stayed her. "Nay, love," he whispered in her ear. "Place your hands on the window sill."

She did as she was told but she so much wanted to touch him. She felt his shaft poking her from behind. She felt one of his hands on her buttocks, his other hand at her front pull her back. She felt his shaft and then he entered her from behind with a quick thrust. She gasped from the suddenness of it, but as he began to move and his hand began rubbing her bud, she desperately needed to hold onto the window sill in front of her. She arched her buttocks to meet his every thrust trying to feel every part of him. She felt his other hand come around her and hold her breast teasing the nipple, rolling it between his finger and thumb. When he tugged on it, she soared to the heavens and moaned and pleaded, "Please!"

Nate smiled and increased his assault. "Please, what my love?"

She didn't answer him, just moaned. The feelings he was creating in her were the same, yet different. Each new position he showed her, brought about different sensations. Each thrust brought her closer and closer to the edge. He pulled her tight against him time and time again. The crescendo built within her with each thrust. She cried out as she burst into million pieces of light like the stars that studded the night time sky then slowly, she drifted back down to earth.

He felt her come. Her spams tightened about him. With several hard thrust he emptied his seed deep in her, as he groaned with pleasure.

Dulcey held on to the sill in front of her for all her support. She felt him scoop her up in his arms and deposit her on the bed. His shirt was halfway down her arms. Her gazed traveled over him and came to rest on his limp shaft that showed from the front opening of his pants. She gazed back up to his eyes. When he raised one eyebrow in question, she replied, "It seems lack of clothing is not necessary. Different positions, too. Interesting."

Nate threw back his head and laughed. "Oh, my love. And yes, there are many positions. I shall enjoy showing you each and every one of them." He removed his pants.

Dulcey bit her bottom lip, smiled and replied. "I think, I shall like being instructed by you very much."

"Minx," he replied as he joined her in bed and claimed her lips. Yes, the thought of instructing her in all the many things he had learned along the way, was a very pleasant future to look forward to. He would enjoy every minute of it. So would Dulcey. He smiled with anticipated pleasure.

For the next two days, he did exactly that. Dulcey proved to be the adept pupil learning everything he showed her. A very eager pupil indeed. It was a time of discovery of each other.

Chapter 13

We've been through a lot already,
And have many more hurdles to cross,
But I can't wait to cross them together.
                    Jennifer Smith

Nate stopped at the top of the rise. Brandanlyn stood in the distance. How had he come to love this place? Maybe, because he had come to love the woman he held in his arms who was so intertwined in this place.

"It is beautiful, is it not?" asked Dulcey. She stared at the three story red brick manor house that had been her home for half of her lifetime. Now, it would truly be her home. Her's and Nate's and Abby's. She shifted on Nate's lap atop Max.

Nate groaned. "My love, if you continue to rub that sweet arse of yours against me again, I promise you, I will dismount from this horse and take my pleasure with you right here on top of this hill and be damned, if there is anyone wandering about."

Dulcey turned to Nate, swishing her arse temptingly against him again. "Promise, my lord," she replied saucily.

Nate groaned again, "I think I have unleashed an insatiable monster."

"I have heard no complaints the past two days," she replied, as she batted her eye lashes at him.

Nate laughed, then groaned as Dulcey swished against him again. "If you don't behave, I'll drop you here and let you walk the rest of the way." He slapped her arse rather forcefully.

"Oww! That hurt." Dulcey gave him a disdainful look.

"I do not plan on walking in and have the whole staff able to see my discomfort," replied Nate haughtily.

Dulcey laughed then sobered up. As wonderful as the past two days had been, she knew it was time to join the real world again. It had been amazing having Nate's undivided attention, to learn all he had taught her about loving but now there would be people and things that would need their attention. She sighed and leaned her head against his chest.

Nate kissed the top of her head. "I know. The cottage will always be our refuge, my love."

Dulcey nodded. Nate had promised her earlier, the cottage would always be their place, their place to escape from the outside world.

At the steps to the front door Nate dismounted and eased Dulcey down from Max. Evers had the front door open. One of the footmen took the reins from Nate's hands.

Nate squeezed her hand and placed it through his arm as he walked through the open door.

"Good afternoon, Evers."

"Good afternoon, my lord, my lady. Welcome back."

Dulcey smiled. "Good afternoon Evers. Has lunch been served yet?"

Before Evers could answer, a screech sounded from the top of the stairs. "Dulcey!" A small whirlwind ran down the stairs and straight into Dulcey's arms. "You've come back." Abby hugged her tightly. She had been so afraid the last two days Uncle Nate would not persuade her. Grandmother had told her several times not to expect Dulcey to come back. But she had. She was here. She knew Uncle Nate would keep his promise. He always did.

Dulcey hugged her back. It felt good to be so welcomed.

"And what about me, Poppet?" asked Nate, glad to see Abby welcome Dulcey as she did. This was his family, the loves of his life.

"Oh, Uncle Nate, I missed you, too."

Nate knelt down to Abby's level. "You know how I promised you I would bring Dulcey back."

Abby nodded.

"Well, I have asked Dulcey to marry me and she has said yes. So now, she will be staying with us for forever."

Abby's eyes widened and smiled, "You promise?" She looked from Nate to Dulcey who nodded.

"Yes, I promise."

"When?" asked Abby.

Dulcey looked at Nate. They had not talked about when. There had been more important things to talk about or rather do. "Yes, when?"

"I have sent for a special license and should receive it in a couple of days or so. As soon as I get it, we will marry," explained Nate.

"Can I come to the wedding?" asked Abby.

"Of course," said Nate and Dulcey in unison.

"I will need someone to hold my flowers," stated Dulcey.

"Flowers. Can we have a party, too?"

Nate looked to Dulcey. "I think a party is a grand idea. We can invite all the locals and I can meet everyone." Nate looked to Dulcey and then to Evers. "What do you think?"

"Twelfth night is in about a week," suggested Evers.

Nate nodded. "Yes, twelfth night. Great idea, Evers. Do you think the house can be ready by then? I mean can it be done?"

Evers smiled. Lord James would be so pleased. Of course, it could be done. The staff would do everything in their power to make it happen. "Of course, my lord."

Nate looked at Dulcey. "Twelfth night, Dulcey?"

Dulcey nodded. The sooner the better, she thought.

"Good. Now, let's hope the special license is delivered in time," stated Nate. If he knew Worth, he would do all in his power to get it to him, but would it be in time.

Abby clapped her hands. "Yea, Uncle Nate's gonna marry Dulcey." She began to dance around Nate and Dulcey.

"What is going on here?" asked the Countess.

No one had heard her come down the stairs. They had been so involved in the plans for the wedding.

"You have decided to stay, it appears," said Nate, rather hoping she had taken his advice and gone back to London.

"Grandmother, Uncle Nate and Dulcey are getting married," peeped in Abby.

The Countess eyes narrowed and her lips pursed. "You have decided to go through with this after all."

Nate shook his head. "Yes, mother. I told you of my plans before I left. Dulcey and I will marry on Twelfth night. That will give the staff here, time to get everything ready and Worth to send the special license I requested he obtain for me."

"That's too short a period of time to make all the necessary preparations," replied the Countess. Maybe, she could delay this wedding until she could come up with a plan to stop it from even happening.

"Evers has assured us, it can be done. I have instructed him to begin preparations. Mr. Kinley said Reverend Treadwell is the vicar here. Let's invite him to dinner tomorrow night and talk with him."

Dulcey smiled. "Reverend Treadwell, I am certain will be most pleased. I will write to him shortly and have it delivered."

"I shall be happy to see to it, Lady Dulcey. Shall I have lunch served or tea?" asked Evers.

Dulcey looked to Nate who looked back at her. "Lunch." They said in unison and laughed.

"Can I have lunch, too?" asked Abby. She wanted to stay with them. She had missed them.

"Of course," answered Dulcey as she took Abby's hand and walked to the dining room. She left Nate to tend to his mother. She had felt the negative force that surrounded the Countess. She was able to see it clearly now. This was a woman to avoid. She would try to disrupt their lives. Of this, she was certain. She would take extra care around her. She would not trust her.

"We will have to look at your clothes after lunch. We will need to decide on what you will wear." Dulcey told Abby as they walked into the dining room.

"Can I wear my yellow dress? I never wored it," asked Abby.

"Wore it," corrected the Countess. "The yellow one will not do at all."

Dulcey looked to Nate. The Countess had followed them into the dining room.

"Mother," stated Nate. She would not ruin this for Abby or Dulcey.

The countess looked at him in all innocence. "Yes, Nathaniel?"

Nate was not fooled by her sudden acquiesce.

"All of the decisions concerning this wedding will be made by Dulcey, Mother. And if you want to wear your yellow dress, Abby, and Dulcey says it will do, then you will wear it," stated Nate looking as his mother, daring her to argue with him.

Abby smiled. "You will like my yellow dress. It's pretty."

Dulcey smiled. "Very well, as soon as we finish eating, you and I will go upstairs and take a look at it. If it is as pretty as you say it is, I think it just might do."

They ate lunch and made plans for the wedding. Several times during the meal, Nate reached over and touched Dulcey's hand. She always looked back at him and smiled. She loved the connection she had with this man. She marveled how it fulfilled her. He was the part of her she had been missing.

Lady Shefley watched these silent exchanges and seethed with anger. How could her son put their family name is such jeopardy by marrying this woman, this witch woman. She had to be such, for she had put some sort of spell on her son to make him lose all sense of propriety. She had to put a stop to this. How? She did not know.

Dulcey watched the countess. She could feel nothing had changed. This woman was an enemy. The forces about her warned her, the Countess would never accept her. She would have to be careful around her. She would try to be tolerant for Nate. She was his mother. But even that would not save her, if she harmed Abby.

After lunch, Abby and Dulcey went upstairs to look at Abby's yellow dress. The countess stayed behind to talk with Nathaniel.

"Nathaniel, have you truly thought this decision through? The repercussions from this marriage could be long lasting. Again, I beg of you, think of how this will all affect Abigail, perhaps not now, but in the future. Her opportunities for a good marriage will be greatly reduced." Surely he could see that. The rumors would destroy her opportunity for a good match.

"I am thinking of Abby," explained Nate. "Abby needs mothering. Someone who will love her. Dulcey already does. I have no plans on going back to London in the near future. It may be years. I have found I have liked it here at Brandanlyn and plan on remaining here. I know Shefley Hall is the seat for our family and I will visit from time to time. But I feel more at home here at Brandanlyn, than I ever felt at Shefley Hall. As far as Abby's future is concerned, by the time Abby makes her debut, we will be an old couple."

Lady Shefley frowned. He refused to listen. "Nathaniel."

Before she could continue, Nate interrupted. "Besides it is too late, Mother. Dulcey could very well be carrying the heir as we speak. Do not think over the last two days, I haven't made certain this marriage will take place. Just think Mother, if that information got to the *ton,* that your son compromised the new Lady Fergers, just as she found out who she was. How could you face all those gossip mongers when they would be talking about how nefarious your son was? And that it was all your idea. That would surely overshadow any talk of her being a witch, would it not? " He smiled at the stricken look on his mother's face.

"You would not dare, Nathaniel. That would ruin this family and our good name. We could never show our faces in London again." He would not do such a thing. When she said we, she truly meant, she would never be able to show her face in London again. She was appalled that he would even consider such a thing. To put such a thing to be bandied about would be disastrous for all involved. No, he would not dare.

Nathaniel smiled. For the first time, he had shut his mother up. He knew it was her biggest fear, that she would be the object of the *ton*'s gossip. He would use it to his advantage.

"I think I'll go upstairs to see if Dulcey and Abby have decided on a dress. Oh, and mother, we don't need your assistance. I believe we can handle this," said Nate as he walked out the dining room leaving his mother speechless.

Nate found Dulcey in Abby's room with Miss Franny. Several dresses were scattered about the room. Abby was in her undershift.

"Uncle Nate, we decided, we like the yellow one best. I tried all of these on but we like the yellow one," explained Abby, as she held up the yellow dress.

Nate looked it over very carefully. He knew nothing about little girls' dresses. But it did look very pretty. If Dulcey said it would do, then who was he to argue.

"Looks very pretty to me," replied Nate, looking at Dulcey for direction. When Dulcey nodded, he added, "Yes, very pretty. I think you did well in choosing that one, Poppet."

Abby nodded. "This is my dress. Now, we need to choose Dulcey's dress."

"Let's save that for tomorrow, Abby. I need to look for something special. And I need to write a note to Reverend Treadwell, to invite him for dinner tomorrow. We will need to talk with him about our wedding plans," explained Dulcey.

"Can I talk to Reverend Teadwell, too?" asked Abby.

"Reverend Treadwell, Abby. And yes, you can. Maybe, he can tell us what you will need to do, because I'm not sure."

Abby nodded.

"Come Abby, let me dress you back into your clothes," said Miss Franny, holding out Abby's dress for her.

At the door, Abby asked, "Will you still come tell me a story about the fairies before I go to bed?"

Dulcey smiled. "Of course, Poppet. Always."

Abby nodded and let Miss Franny dress her as Dulcey and Nate walked out.

Out in the hall, Nate grabbed Dulcey and brought her to him. "Will you tell me a bedtime story?"

Dulcey smiled. "Every night, Nate, I promise."

Nate slowly kissed her. He had her back at Brandanlyn. Wedding plans were in the making. All was right with his world. Out of the corner of his eye he saw his mother's maid slip into his mother's room. But the taste of Dulcey's lips and his body's response, he forgot all about it.

When at last he tore his lips away, Dulcey was breathless and aching with need for him but, "I think I need to stay in my rooms tonight." When he looked like he was about to argue, she continued, "Abby and your mother." It was the hardest thing she ever had to do, to deny him what she wanted, just as much as he did.

Nate sighed deeply. She was right. It would only mean a few nights. A few nights, too many. After the last two days at the cottage, this would be the hardest thing he had ever done, but he realized, she was right.

He leaned his forehead against hers. "Yes, you are right. But I don't have to like it, my love. I have enjoyed waking up to you in my arms."

Dulcey smiled. "So have I. It will only be for a few nights." She cupped his face in her hands and kissed him lightly on the lips. Anything more and she would have given in to him. "Good night, my soon to be husband."

Nate watched her turn and walk away towards her rooms. Damn, how he liked watching her walk, the sway of her hips nearly undid his resolve. It would be a long several days and nights. He turned and reluctantly went to his rooms.

~~~~~~~~~~~~~~~~

Reverend Treadwell was a portly man with very thin gray hair. His wife was as thin as he was portly. She wore her gray hair braided in a crown around her head. Both had the lightest blue eyes and smiles that made them well liked by the patrons of the church. Lord James had liked them. Dulcey had met with them many times, at church services and here dining with Lord James, no Uncle James, Dulcey corrected. She had had many a philosophical discussion with the good Reverend concerning her abilities.

Reverend Treadwell took Dulcey's hand in his. "Mr. Kinley told me what Lord Fergers had done. I always knew you had to be family. There was something about you that always reminded me of him. You and he had some of the same mannerisms."

"Yes, my dear, Isaiah has always said that. I am so happy for you that you are his family and now to be marrying the new baron," said Mrs. Treadwell. "Lord James would be so happy, I know he would be."

Dulcey smiled. "Reverend and Mrs. Treadwell, this is Lord Beckham, the Earl of Shefley," introduced Dulcey as Nate joined her. "Nathaniel, this is Reverend Isaiah Treadwell and his wife, Esther."

"Very pleased to meet you both. Mr. Kinley spoke highly of you. I truly hope you can help us with our wedding. I have a request in for a special license with the Archbishop. I am hoping it will be delivered within the next few days," explained Nate. He wanted to get them on his side before his mother had a chance to say something that would influence them in some way.

"Of course, Lord Beckham," said Mrs. Treadwell. "Oh, a wedding will be just the thing for everyone about. Everyone has been most anxious to meet the new baron and to have him marry our Miss Dulcey, will be much cause for celebration. I hope you know how much everyone about here cares deeply for our Miss Dulcey. Oh, I must get used to calling you, Lady Dulcey, my dear. Forgive me, my dear, if it takes me some time."

Lady Shefley came down the stairs just in time to hear Mrs. Treadwell words. She would get no help here. Had this woman bewitched everyone here?

Nate saw his mother. He had hoped she would not join them, but he should have known better. "Mother, this is the Reverend Isaiah Treadwell and his wife, Esther. Reverend and Mrs. Treadwell, my mother, Lady Beckham, the Countess Shefley."

Lady Shefley acknowledged the introductions just as Evers announced dinner.

Nate offered Dulcey his arm. "Shall we?"

The reverend offered Lady Shefley his arm. She hesitated a moment but maybe, just maybe, she could talk with him and convince him how wrong this marriage was.

Nate had Dulcey on his right, his mother on his left, with Mrs. Treadwell next to his mother, and the reverend at Dulcey's side.

Dinner talk consisted of talk about the wedding.

Lady Shefley tried to deter the talk, saying it should not be entered into so quickly, but Mrs. Treadwell appeared to be a romantic and thought this was the best thing. They were definitely not going to be of any help to her in stopping this fiasco from taking place.

Nate watched how well Dulcey got along with the reverend and his wife. Her manners were impeccable. But then he had seen that from the beginning. How could his mother ever think Dulcey could not hold her own in London was beyond him? It was not something they were considering anytime soon, anyway. If Dulcey did not want to go to London, he was more than content with that.

Lady Shefley could no longer be quiet. She had to ask. The reverend was a man of the cloth. Surely, he had something to say about her status. Since he lived in the area, he knew she was a witch.

"Reverend Treadwell, since you have known Dulcey for such a long time, what is your opinion on these claims she is a witch?" Lady Shefley asked innocently.

Nate wanted to reach across the table and shake her. His eyes narrowed threateningly at her. How dare she do this?

The Reverend looked at the Countess, confused for a moment. "Lady Dulcey has never been considered a witch," stated Isaiah emphatically.

Mrs. Treadwell asked. "Do you mean, Lady Dulcey's healing ways or her gift of seeing into one's future? Yes, we all know about that. I can't see how that would make Lady Dulcey a witch. I think it makes Lady Dulcey, very special." She had always thought so. She knew Lady Dulcey had doubts about her gift but she and Isaiah had firmly believed Lady Dulcey was a special child of the Lord.

"Yes," agreed Reverend Treadwell. "Our Lady Dulcey is very special. I have counseled her many times how this was a gift from God. She has always used her gift for good. There was nothing wrong or evil about it. It has worried her for many a year, but I have assured her time and time again, she is a special child of God for he would have not blessed her so."

"But some have called her a witch," continued Lady Shefley. "Her parents were burned because of it."

Both the Reverend and his wife gasped. "Is this true, Lady Dulcey?" asked the Reverend.

Dulcey hung her head. Why had the Countess brought this up? Now, the Treadwells would know her dark secret from her past. "I'm afraid Lady Shefley speaks the truth. Lord James explained it all to me in his letter."

Reverend Treadwell placed his hand over hers on the table. "Oh, my poor dear, how terrible to learn such news!"

Mrs. Treadwell asked, "Oh, my dear, I heartily agree. How terrible! What happened? Surely they must have misunderstood what happened."

Dulcey looked up to see Lady Shefley smiling smugly. She was determined to have everyone know her past. She would do or say anything to accomplish her downfall. Dulcey could feel it, like hundreds of tiny arrows being shot at her. She was afraid it would never end.

"It seems the new vicar's wife died and the vicar blamed my mother. He called her a witch and burned their house down. My father was able to get me out but when he went in for my mother, the house collapsed," explained Dulcey.

She could not look at anyone, including Nate. The forces said Nate was safe, but what if her forces were wrong. She had not been able to trust them of late.

"Oh, my poor dear, no wonder you have questioned your gift. You are no witch. I have watched you grow. You are a special child of God whom he has given very special gifts. All of us are given special gifts by the good Lord. How we use those given gifts for good or bad is up to us. My dear, you have always used your gifts for good. I will not consider any other explanations. I don't care what some people say. You, my dear have a good and kind heart." stated the Reverend firmly.

"Yes, my dear, I so heartily agree. That poor vicar must have been so distraught with the death of his wife, he did not understand what he was saying or doing. You must not allow that one incident to color your gift. Everyone here knows you have always done good, my dear," stated Mrs. Treadwell. She could now understand Dulcey's reluctance to admit to these special gifts of hers.

Lady Shefley wanted to scream in vexation. Didn't these simple country folk understand what kind of havoc this knowledge would cause, if it became common knowledge in London? Her son's life would be ruined. This woman was a witch, no matter what these stupid country people said or believed. Dulcey, no doubt, had them under a spell as well.

Nate watched his mother's plans to discredit Dulcey amongst her friends totally fall apart. He could see how vexed his mother was.

He smiled and turned to the good reverend. "I, too, have told Dulcey this several times. I am so glad to hear that you so agree with me. Her gifts are special, just as she is."

"You are most correct, my lord. Our Lady Dulcey is a most special lady as are her gifts," said Reverend.

Before any more could be said, Abby burst in followed closely by Miss Franny. "Are you talking about the wedding yet, 'cause I'm going to wear my yellow dress. Dulcey said so. She said you would tell me what I'm supposed to do."

"Abigail Beckham where are your manners. You do not interrupt!" admonished Lady Shefley.

Abigail stopped dead in her tracks and looked down at the floor.

"Who is the lovely young child?" asked Mrs. Treadwell. She glanced at Lady Shefley and thought poor child.

Dulcey looked at the Countess. Why did this woman always berate this child? "Abby, come here. This is the Reverend Treadwell and his wife Mrs. Treadwell. This is Abigail Beckham, Nate's niece and ward."

Abby came to Dulcey's side and stood between Nate and Dulcey but looked tentatively at her grandmother. She looked to Dulcey. "I just wanted to hear about the wedding."

Nate laughed. "She has been so excited since we have told her about the wedding." He gave his mother a look that warned her not to say anything more.

"Of course," replied Reverend Treadwell. He had two daughters but they were grown and married. He remembered how excited little girls got about weddings. "You said your dress was yellow. Yellow is a very pretty color, is it not Esther?"

"Oh, yes, yellow is a very good color for a wedding, especially for a flower girl, my dear. You do know the flower girl is very important to a wedding, a very important help to the bride," explained Mrs. Treadwell.

Abby eyes grew big with awe and excitement. She looked to Dulcey.

"Yes, Poppet. I told you I needed your help," said Dulcey with a smile.

She looked to her Uncle Nate who smiled and nodded. "What am I supposed to do?" she asked.

"You are a very important person. You will walk in front of Lady Dulcey and scatter flower petals on the floor before her,' explained Mrs. Treadwell.

Abby smiled. "I can do that."

"Yes, Abby, you can, that is why I asked you to do this for me," said Dulcey.

"And you will stand on the altar at Lady Dulcey's side while she marries Lord Beckham," explained Mrs. Treadwell again. "You can hold her flowers during the ceremony."

"I can do that, too," answered Abby nodding.

Such a pleasant child, thought Esther Treadwell. She could see how attached the child and Dulcey were to each other. She smiled. She had always thought Dulcey would make a wonderful mother. She was happy Dulcey would now be able to experience such joy. And this child would have such a kind and loving person in her life.

"Well, my dear, have Lady Dulcey bring you the church on Sunday for service and afterwards, I can show you exactly how to do it," suggested Mrs. Treadwell.

Abby looked at Dulcey for an answer.

Dulcey in turned looked at Nate. "I think that is an excellent idea," said Nate. He, too, was wondering, what he would have to do. He had not attended very many weddings himself. He had avoided them for the most part.

"Good, then we shall see all of you at church on Sunday," stated Reverend Treadwell.

"I think it's time for bed, Poppet," said Nate. He could see his mother getting irritated and he did not want a scene. "Now you know what your duties are for the wedding."

Abby nodded. "But Dulcey hasn't told me my story about the fairies. Dulcey knows the fairies. They teached her about her medicines." Abby suddenly put her hands over her lips, her eyes wide. "It's supposed to be a secret."

The Reverend tried very hard not to laugh. This child reminded him very much of his own Elizabeth. "It's very important to keep secrets. But this secret is safe with us. I have thought for a very long time Lady Dulcey has had some help. Fairies can be very big help."

"Do you believe in fairies? Grandmother doesn't," said Abby matter of factly, looking at her grandmother.

Nate could see his mother was uncomfortable with the question. He smiled.

Reverend Treadwell looked at the Countess. "With some people it is hard for them to believe. For some people like us, it is hard not to believe."

Lady Shefley had had enough of this talk. "It is your bedtime Abigail. Miss Bennett, please take Abigail back to the nursery."

"But Dulcey needs to tell me my story. She promised," cried Abby.

"Then by all means, she must keep her promise," stated the Reverend.

"How about we all retire to the drawing room Reverend and Mrs. Treadwell? Dulcey can join us after her story," suggested Nate.

"Excellent idea, my lord. Good evening to you, Miss Abby," replied Reverend Treadwell.

"Yes, my dear, go hear your story about fairies. Pleasant dreams," said Mrs. Treadwell with a smile.

Dulcey rose. "I shan't be long," she told her quests. She took Abby's small hand in hers.

"Take your time, my dear," said the Reverend, as he and Nate rose.

Dulcey smiled. She and Franny escorted Abby upstairs. Dulcey made her story a little shorter than usual, in order to join the guests downstairs.

Dulcey walked into the drawing room to a strained atmosphere. She could see the Reverend and Mrs. Treadwell appeared agitated and the Countess appeared smug. Nate looked like he wanted to shake his mother.

"Lord Beckham, it has been a most interesting evening. We look forward to seeing you at services this Sunday," stated Reverend Treadwell as he rose from his seat on the green brocade sofa. He offered his hand to his wife and assisted her to her feet.

"Yes, Lord Beckham. It will be our pleasure to assist you and Lady Dulcey with all the preparations for your wedding. We look forward to it. It has been a pleasure to meet you, Lord Beckham, Lady Shefley," replied Mrs. Treadwell with a smile.

Nate rose to accompany them out. "The pleasure has been ours. We look forward to Sunday. We appreciate all your help with the wedding ceremony."

Dulcey waited at the door as they joined her. "Yes, thank you, so very much, Reverend and Mrs. Treadwell."

Dulcey took Nate's arm as they escorted the Treadwells to the door.

At the door, Mrs. Treadwell kissed Dulcey on the cheek and whispered in her ear, "Patience dear. She will come around." She looked back to the drawing room.

Dulcey nodded and smiled. She stood with Nate at the door and watched as the Reverend and Mrs. Treadwell's carriage drove away. At the bottom of the stairs, Dulcey sighed and leaned her head against Nate's shoulder. The mental strain of having to deal with Lady Shefley was taking its toll. "It seemed rather strained when I came back from telling Abby her bedtime story."

Nate put his arm around her. "Nothing more than Mother being her usual autocratic self. I believe the good reverend and his wife were not impressed," he said with a smile.

Lady Shefley walked out of the drawing room. Nate stood at the bottom of the steps with his arm around Dulcey, her head on his shoulder. She ached with every being in her body to tear them apart.

"Good night, Nathaniel," she said as she walked passed them and up the stairs.

Nate went to say something, but Dulcey put her hand on his arm and stopped him. She knew his mother had deliberately snubbed her. It was not worth the effort. She had come to the understanding and acceptance that Nate's mother would never accept her.

"Come let me escort you to your room, my love," said Nate. He would allow his mother to stay for the wedding but after the ceremony, he would send her back to Shefley Hall. He would not put Dulcey through any more of his mother's censure.

Lady Shefley waited at the top of the stairs.

Nate raised an eyebrow. "Mother?"

"I would like to speak with you Nathaniel," she whined.

Nate shook his head. "Not tonight, Mother. I am rather tired." He was tired, tired of dealing with her. Yes, he would send her back to Shefley Hall, as soon as the wedding was over. He had had enough of this. "Good night Mother." Nate turned and continue walking down the hall to Dulcey' room.

Lady Shefley turned, furious with her son and that witch at his side and strode to her room. She had never been so angry in all of her life, until this moment.

Dulcey walked quietly at Nate's side. She wasn't sure how much more she could take of Nate's mother's constant harping. She made everything so difficult. She had hoped his mother would come to accept her but it seemed, it was not to be. She saw her and Nate, living a good life but she wondered how, with his mother acting as she did.

At the door of her room, Nate pulled her into his arms. He had needed the feel of her body against his, all evening. He allowed the stress of the evening to slowly ebb from his body and let her body calm him. He knew, he had promised her to wait till after the wedding but damn, it was proving to be the hardest thing he had ever done, no not do, because he so desperately wanted to make love to her again.

Dulcey looked up. She saw all the love and longing in his eyes. It was nearly her undoing. She so desperately wanted to feel him next to her, to be a part of him again, because it was the only time she truly felt whole. But she knew this was not her cottage, where nothing mattered there but them. They were here at Brandanlyn and everything they did was under scrutiny. She did not want gossip bandied about for Nate and Abby's sake.

Nate thought, he may not be able to lie with her tonight, but he would get his fill of the taste of her lips. Slowly, he lowered his head and claimed her lips, softly, tasting her sweetness, pulling her closer, till he could feel her softness against him. His kiss deepened, his tongue met hers in open invitation. He could feel his response to her warm body. He could also feel her response to him was as desperate as his was.

Dulcey opened herself to him. Her hands entwined in his hair, holding his head so his kiss wouldn't end. She knew she had asked him to wait till after the wedding, but it was proving to be harder than she first thought. She eased her hold on his head and reluctantly pulled away. Her heart was beating so hard against her chest, her breathing shallow.

Nate looked into Dulcey's eyes. The love he saw shining in them made his heart swell. What had he done to deserve the love of this woman? Nothing. But fate had put them together and no one would take her away from him. He rested his forehead against hers, holding her hands against his chest.

"This has proven to be harder than I first thought," said Nate softly.

Dulcey sighed with longing. "I know, my love. But it is for the best, I think."

Nate smiled. "Perhaps you are right, but I don't have to like it."

Dulcey very slowly opened the door to her room, still holding his hand, slowly pulled away from him, till finally their fingertips just barely touched. For a moment, she stopped, "Good night, my heart." She continued on into her room and watched Nate pull her door closed. She sighed with such longing. Her wedding day could not come soon enough. Her body ached for him.

Nate turned and walked slowly away, after closing her door. That special license he had requested had better be delivered in time, for he was uncertain how much longer he would wait. He passed in front of his mother's room. He could hear some conversation, his mother's voice, from behind her door. No doubt, she was talking with her maid,

Leta. He would tell her soon, she was leaving whether she wanted to or not.

It was going to be another night of tossing, turning and dreaming of Dulcey. Soon, she would be sharing his bed.

Chapter 14

Friends show their love in time of trouble
Not in happiness.

Euripides

Evers opened the door to the richly dressed gentlemen he saw gallop up moments earlier. A large gray stallion stood near the steps.

"Ah, my good man, my card. Please inform Lord Shefley, Lord Colin Hallwell, the Duke of Worthingston is here as requested." Worth pulled his gloves off and placed them in his hat. "Also, could you have someone see to my horse. My carriage should be here in the morning."

Evers took his hat and gloves. "Very well, your Grace. I will see to it all. Would you care to wait in the green drawing room? Would you like some refreshment while I get Lord Shefley?"

Nate walked down the stairs and there in the hall was Worth talking to Evers. "Ah, Worth, so very glad to see you. I thought you would have just sent the special license. I did not expect you to deliver it yourself." He took Worth's out reached hand.

"What Beck? You would think I would not self delivery this. My best friend's younger brother sends me a request for a special marriage license. Of course, I am curious as to who has managed to capture this ne'er-do-well." He laughed.

Nate laughed, too. It seemed like it had been ages since he had been called Beck. It was the nickname Grayson and Worth had given him as a child. It wasn't only because it was his name but because as a younger brother, he had followed them like a shadow. They had said he was always at their beck and call, whenever they needed something they did not want to do.

"I am glad you are here. It means a lot to me that you came. Shall we retire to my study? I have an excellent bottle of brandy. The old baron left an excellent cellar." Nate said as he escorted Worth to the study.

"I think this may be an interesting story. Brandy should be just the thing to warm me after this long ride and will definitely make the listening easier."

Nate closed the door behind him, pointed to a chair for Worth. At the side board, he poured two generous glasses of brandy, handed one to Worth and sat down in the empty chair.

Worth took a sip and raised his eyebrows. "Excellent brandy, indeed. All right, my friend, you have my undivided attention. Tell me this story of yours." Worth leaned back and listened.

Nate began and told Worth, Dulcey's story, from the moment he met her to the reading of Lord Fergers' letters. The only thing he left out was the two days at the cottage.

Worth rubbed his chin with his forefinger, deep in thought. "A witch you say." He did not believe in witches or any of those types of things. He was a realist. He believed in the here and now and the tangible that could be seen or touched.

"That is what some people may say. She does see things about people before they happen. Most people about here come to her because she knows about herbs and medicinal brews and things. From everything Simmons has found out, she has helped nearly everyone about here, in one way or the other. She is very well liked," explained Nate. "Abby believes she talks to the fairies."

Worth smiled. "How is our Poppet?" He had a soft spot for his niece.

Nate smiled. "Very well. Abby has come to love her, but most important Dulcey loves Abby. Wait till you see them together. You will see for yourself. I have never seen her so happy since Grayson and Caroline died."

Worth nodded. "I was told your mother accompanied you here. How has she been with all of this?" He was not a fan of the Countess. Caroline had complained to him too many times about her. She had made Caroline's life miserable up to the day she died.

Nate let out a breath of frustration. "You, above all, know how mother is. She is determined that Dulcey is not good enough for our family. Our reputation will be ruined, if I marry her."

"Yes, I do know your mother. Nothing is good enough for your mother, including a duke's daughter. I do believe the stress your mother put on Caroline caused her to lose the baby which ultimately caused her death. I firmly believe it to be so," stated Worth with contempt. The Countess could be a formidable woman when she was crossed. Nate had every right to be concerned.

Nate nodded. He hadn't been around when that had happened. Occasionally, he had worked for the war department. He had been on a special assignment and had only heard about it when Grayson died several weeks later. He had often wondered how it had all gone about. Mother's story had never added up.

"Yes, well I have threatened to ship her back to Shefley Hall to the Dowager House with grandmother. She has said she will behave but I do not trust her. I have Simmons watching her. But I will not let her upset Dulcey. I had hoped she had left when I went after Dulcey. But since she hasn't, I have decided after the wedding, she will leave for Shefley Hall or the townhouse in London. I have had enough of her interference. It is my wedding gift to Dulcey."

"I agree, that will be for the best," Worth nodded. "I brought a small valise with me. Bennings and the carriage with the rest of my things should get here perhaps later tonight but most probably tomorrow morning."

"I'm sure Evers had had a room prepared for you by now."

"And when am I to meet this fairy of yours and Abby's?" asked Worth, curious, now more so, since hearing her story. He would not call her a witch for he believed they did not exist. Neither did fairies but Abby did, so he would play along for her sake.

"Why don't you go upstairs, freshen up. I'll send Simmons to you. Come down for tea. I'll have Abby and Dulcey waiting for you."

"Very well. But forget Simmons. Though Bennings would never admit it, I can do for myself. He firmly believes, I am helpless babe without him." Worth chuckled.

Nate smiled. He and Worth had worked together a couple of times. Worth was a master of disguises. Bennings would have had apoplexy, if he had seen some of how Worth had dressed for some of his work.

Worth pulled an envelope out of his breast pocket. "Before I forget, I do believe this is what you requested of me." He handed it to Nate.

Nate took it, opened it and smiled. "Yes. I was beginning to think it was not going to get here in time for Twelfth Night."

"Twelfth Night?"

"I have plans on marrying Dulcey on Twelfth Night. Invitations have been sent out to the locals. You will be staying Worth? I will need someone to stand with me if you would?" asked Nate. Worth was as close to a brother he now had with Grayson gone.

Worth took his out held hand. "Of course. Why do you think I am here?" He smiled, knowing his best friend, Grayson, would not want it any other way. In many ways, he felt like Beck was his younger brother. It was one of the many things, he and Grayson had shared over the years.

Worth raised his glass that had one last sip. "To Grayson."

Nate raised his. "To Caroline."

They clinked glasses and downed their last sip.

Nate and Worth walked out of the study. Evers was in the hall to meet them. "Your Grace, I have had your room prepared. Your valise has been brought to it."

"Thank you, Evers."

Evers called one of the footmen over to escort the duke to his room. Halfway up the stairs, Worth met with the countess coming down. He stared haughtily down his narrow pointed nose at her. He agreed with Beck, she was not to be trusted.

Lady Shefley looked him in the eye for a moment then dropped her gaze and murmured, "Your Grace." Damn, she thought. Worth had come after all. She had hoped he would send the license by courier. She had even thought about intercepting it.

She had never gotten along with the duke. He blamed her for Caroline's death. Why she had no idea? Caroline was too sensitive. She was often overly upset about something or other. How could he blame her for Caroline's miscarriage and subsequent death?

Worth barely gave her a nod. He was on Dulcey's side just for the mere fact that the Countess did not like her. He smiled at the thought of getting under the Countess's skin. He would enjoy this visit.

Nate watched his mother come down the stairs and the silent exchange between Worth and his mother. It would be good to have Worth, here on his side.

"I see his grace is here," stated the Countess as she faced her son.

"Yes, mother. He personally brought the special license from the Archbishop. My marriage to Dulcey will take place on Twelfth Night as planned." Nate watched the distaste cross her face.

"So you say, Nathaniel," replied his mother.

"Yes, Mother, I do. Worth will be joining us for tea. So will be Abby. I'm going upstairs to tell Abby and Dulcey and escort them down."

"I will await everyone in the drawing room," she said as she continued walking to the drawing room. She wanted to scream but she knew she could not.

~~~~~~~~~~~~~~

Nate knocked softly on Dulcey's room and walked in. Dulcey was sitting at her writing desk. He never got tired of looking at her. Now in a few days' time they would be wed, thanks to Worth bringing the special license.

Dulcey looked up and smiled. She still found it hard to believe this man would soon be her husband in the eyes of the church and the court. He was already a part of her body and soul. It seemed like a lifetime ago she had resigned herself to living a life alone. Now she had a future of a life filled with love. She felt so lucky.

"I've come to escort you and Abby downstairs for tea. We have a guest," he informed Dulcey as he helped her to her feet and into his arms.

Nate claimed her lips. It had been hard not to visit her in the middle of the night. But he had promised her. His body screamed with the want and need of her. Having tasted her sweetness, he wanted her again and again. Just a few more days, he told himself.

When Nate raised his head to gaze into her eyes, Dulcey whispered, "I have missed you." She could see the longing in his eyes and she wanted him to know, he was not alone.

Nate sighed. "Soon, my love, Worth delivered the special license himself. I think you will like Worth. He was my brother's best friend. Also my brother was married to his sister. I have known him for forever." He needed to think of something besides the need to take her to bed and bury himself deep within her as he had done in the cottage. This waiting was beginning to be a great strain on him. Just a couple of more days, he told himself.

"Shall we get Abby and go downstairs before I take you to bed right here and now. I envy that bed."

Dulcey smiled, took his hand and pulled him to the door. "Come, Nate, before I succumb to your charms."

Nate laughed softly. "I'd rather you succumb to my body, my love."

Dulcey laughed, too, and pulled at his hand harder till he began to walk by her side.

"All right, you win," he said as he followed her out of her room.

Down the hall to Abby's room they walked. Dulcey looked down the hall, the forces around her trembled. She looked harder but she could not see anything or anyone. "Where's your mother?" asked Dulcey. She had been avoiding the Countess as much as possible. Her rooms were further down the hall.

"Mother awaits us downstairs," answered Nate, wondering why Dulcey was asking. "Why?"

Dulcey shook her head. "It was nothing," she replied for the feelings were gone.

Nate opened the door. Abby was having tea with her dolls. "Poppet, how about you join us downstairs for tea? Someone you know has come for a visit."

"Uncle Nate, Dulcey who is it?" she asked, her eyes wide. "Someone for the wedding?"

Nate smiled. "Yes, someone for the wedding. He brought us a special present."

"A present? Did he bring one for me, too?" She liked presents.

"That I don't know but I would not be surprised if he did," answered Nate.

"Who is it? Tell me please." She begged.

"Let's go down and find out," suggested Nate. He looked to Miss Franny. "You are invited too."

Franny smiled. "Thank you, my lord but I have some correspondence to write to my mother. Otherwise, she will be worried about me." She appreciated that since Lady Dulcey had come, they had included her in many of the family functions but she had not written her family since just before Christmas. If she didn't write regularly, her mother would be worried.

"If you finish sooner than you think, please join us," requested Dulcey. She had come to like Franny.

Miss Franny nodded and watched them walk out of the door, Abby begging Lord Beckham to tell her who their visitor was.

Abby walked into the drawing room looking all about but the only person there was Grandmother sitting in her chair. She turned, "I don't see anybody here except Grandmother?"

Nate laughed. "Be patient little one. He is upstairs cleaning up. I promise you he will be down shortly."

"I'm sure his Grace could have visited Abigail upstairs in the nursery, just as well," suggested the Countess. It was not proper to have this child attending so many of the adult functions.

"Mother, I hoping to surprise Abby," chided Nate.

Abby looked from Uncle Nate to her Grandmother. What were they talking about?

"Hello, Poppet," said Worth as he quietly walked in.

"Uncle Colin," cried Abby as she ran to Worth's open arms.

Dulcey watched as the Duke of Worthingston gathered Abby in his arms. He was taller than Nate, a little heavier than Nate as well, but it appeared to be all muscle. His hair was light brown with streaks of gold. He wore it brushed back from his face, a face that supported a square stubborn jaw, a long narrow nose above thin narrow lips. His clear brown eyes held flecks of gold and at the moment twinkled with joy as he held Abby in his arms.

Dulcey smiled. He cared about Abby, just as Nate did. That was good for Abby.

"Uncle Nate said you brought him a present. Did you bring one for me, too?" she asked.

"Abigail, you do not ask for presents. It is not proper for a young lady to ask for presents," admonished Lady Shefley.

Worth could feel the joy leave Abby's small body in his arms. It took every bit of his control not to turn and give the Countess the tongue lashing he was known for. Instead, he turned and looked at the Countess with narrowed eyes.

"Mother, Abby is but a child. I beg you to remember that," said Nate. Why did she continue with this type of behavior?

Worth raised Abby's chin till she looked him in the eye. "Yes, Poppet, I would not come to see you without a present but I am afraid you will have to wait for it. I packed it in my carriage and my carriage will not arrive until tomorrow," he explained.

"Can you tell me what it is?" she asked. Uncle Colin had brought her a present, too.

"Now, it wouldn't be a surprise then would it?" replied Worth.

Abby pouted for a minute then she caught sight of Dulcey. "Uncle Nate's getting married. I'm going to be in the wedding. I'm going to be Dulcey's flower girl." she explained as he put her down beside him.

"I'll tell you a secret," said Worth. Abby looked at him. "I'm going to be Uncle Nate's best man."

Abby nodded but had to ask, "What are you going to do? I'm going to put rose petals for Dulcey to walk on and then I'm going to hold her flowers."

"You, Poppet, have a very important part in this wedding. All I have to do is stand next to your Uncle Nate," replied Worth, happy to see Abby excited about the wedding.

Abby frowned. "That's all." Poor Uncle Colin, he didn't have a very important job at all.

Nate laughed. "My love, this is the man who was so kind as to procure for us the special license and was good enough to bring it to us himself. This is Colin Hallwell, Duke of Worthingston."

Dulcey curtsied as Lord Fergers had instructed her to when being presented to a duke. "Your grace."

Worth smiled as he looked into the greenest eyes he had ever seen. She did have that pixie look about her. No wonder, Abby called her a fairy. He saw the look on Nate's face as he looked at her, but most important he saw, how Dulcey looked at Nate. The love shone bright from both of them. But as important as that was, he had watched from the door the look on Abby's face as she looked at her fairy. He could see the love between the two. That was very important to him.

Worth took her hand in his and brought it to his lips and just brushed the top of her hand. "Family and friends do not observe the formality, my dear. Please I am Colin or Worth."

Dulcey smiled as he took her hand. She could feel so many swirls of the forces around him. This man exuded power. It surrounded him but Dulcey could see through it to man underneath. Here was a man capable of strong loving. "Lord Worth."

Worth smiled. "No, just Worth, my dear."

Dulcey returned his smile. Here before her stood an ally. From the feelings, she could feel from Lady Shefley, she and Worth did not get along. It would be nice to have a duke of the realm on their side.

Evers was at the door, "Shall I serve tea now, Lady Dulcey?"

Dulcey looked up and smiled, "Yes, please, Evers."

"Very well," replied Evers as he pushed the tea cart in. He brought it to Dulcey's side.

Dulcey sat on the green brocade sofa. Nate joined her. Worth took the big gold winged chair at the side of the sofa. Abby sat on his lap. The countess sat across from them separated as though off on her own.

Worth observed as Dulcey poured tea and her interaction with Abby. Nate was right. He could see the loving relationship between the two of them.

Worth accepted his cup of tea and waited till everyone had their cup when he asked Abby, "What's this about fairies? Nate tells me-----"

"Uncle Nate, it's a secret. Dulcey talks to the fairies. They teached her about the medicines."

"Taught Abigail, not teached," corrected Lady Shefley tersely. Here they were talking about fairies again. Did Worth know this Dulcey woman was a witch?

Abigail gave her grandmother a disgruntled look. "Do you believe in fairies?" asked Abby. "Uncle Nate and Dulcey does. But grandmother says they are not real."

"What do you believe Abby?" asked Worth. He had noticed the worrisome look that crossed Dulcey face. Was she afraid he would judge her? He smiled.

"I believe in fairies. They helped Dulcey find me and make Uncle Nate better," explained Abby.

"Then, Poppet, I believe, because if they help Dulcey with all of that, they must be real." Worth looked to Lady Shefley. He could tell she did not like this conversation and smiled.

"They are, cause, look Uncle Colin, Dulcey gave me this necklace. The fairies catched the moonbeams and put them in the necklace," explained Abby, as she pulled the pendant away from her dress to show him.

Worth took the small pendant in his fingers. It was rather old looking. Something, no doubt, Dulcey must have had. For her to give it to Abby, said much to him. "Moonbeams. Then this is a special necklace indeed." He looked to Dulcey who smiled. Yes, she was going to be good for Abby.

Nate grabbed Dulcey hand that lay on the couch between them and held it. He rubbed the palm of her hand with his fingers. It sent shivers to that part deep inside of her. Dulcey looked up to him and smiled. Nate could feel her response. He was pleased Worth had accepted Dulcey. He had had such a difficult time from his mother. It was such a relief to have someone supporting his relationship with Dulcey.

~~~~~~~~~~~~~~~

Supper proved to be a delightful affair since the Countess had sent her regards saying she would not be coming down due to a migraine.

Worth sat at her left. Dulcey found herself between him and Nate. He entertained her with stories of the escapades, he and Grayson often found themselves in and how often Nate accompanied them, rather tagged along. Dulcey could not help but laugh. She was learning a whole different side of her husband to be.

Nate tried to halt some of the stories but to no avail, so began adding to them from is point of view.

"Do you remember that time when Grayson brought you to that brothel in--------" started Worth.

Nate shook his head. "Don't you dare tell that story Worth," warned Nate.

Dulcey looked from one to the other. Worth had that look of pure mischief about him. Nate had a look of desperation on his face. She could almost swear there was a touch of blush to his cheeks. What was this about, she wondered.

Worth held up his hands in surrender, then turned, leaned over to Dulcey and touched her hand. "Ask him, my dear, about Bristol," stated Worth, with a conspiratorial wink.

Dulcey smiled at him and then closed her eyes. The forces about him were strong. They showed her a path for him. He was a powerful man very used to getting his way. Of being in control of all things about him, but he was about to meet his match. His life was about to change and he was going to be embroiled in a merry chase. She opened her eyes and looked from Worth to Nate and back again.

"You were gone for a long moment, my love," stated Nate. He had never seen her go off like that. No, yes he had. Just before they left that first time from her cottage, she had gotten that look, that far away look.

Dulcey smiled and looked from one to the other. "I am sorry. Your forces were strong Worth, when you touched my hand."

Worth shrugged slightly, but was curious. "And you saw something?"

Dulcey smiled. "I saw something or I should say someone in your near future."

"A special someone," asked Nate, curious.

Dulcey nodded.

Worth laughed. "All this talk of love and weddings has you seeing such things as that for everyone."

Dulcey laughed softly. He wasn't the first to not believe her. "She is going to give you a merry chase, your grace. But eventually you will get her attention. Hair of red comes across."

Worth looked at her through narrowed eyes, then shook his head and laughed heartily. "Should be interesting and when will all of this happen?" he asked. He thought back on any acquaintances but none with red hair stood out. He would play along with her fortune telling. Others may believe in such things. He was a realist and did not.

"I'm not sure, but I would think soon because the force was strong," explained Dulcey. She smiled. She would enjoy when the time came and she would be able to remind him of this conversation in the future.

Worth looked to Nate who shrugged. "This is new to me, as well," he replied.

Dulcey smiled. "Gentlemen, excuse me. I will leave you to your drinks. I believe our Abby will be most upset, if I do not go upstairs and tell her a bedtime story. I have promised her." She rose as did Nate and Worth. She turned to Worth, "Good night, your grace. I am so very glad that you have come."

Worth nodded. "Good night, Dulcey. I am most pleased to be here."

Dulcey stopped at Nate's side. He touched her cheek with his hand then leaned down and kissed her tenderly. "Good night, my love."

Worth watched the exchange and envied his friend. To have a woman look at him like that was a dream, but not one for him. He knew he had to marry to ensure the continuation of the family with an heir but he had resigned himself, in all likelihood it would be a marriage of convenience. He would not have a love match such as this. Then he remembered her words just moments earlier. "Hair of red." He smiled. If only what she said came true but he knew better.

Nate watched Dulcey walk away. He would never tire of watching her walk, of watching the sway of her hips. He could feel himself responding. Soon, he told himself. He turned to Worth with a smile.

"You're a lucky man, my friend. She is a special young woman," said Worth.

Nate nodded. "I heartily agree." Then he added with a chuckle, "Seems you're about to find yours, too."

Worth laughed. "We shall see. We shall see."

Chapter 15

And now fair maid, I'll marry wi' thee,…
The Riddling Knight
Traditional English

The days to the wedding sped by. The atmosphere in the house changed with the Duke's arrival. The Countess for the most part was quiet, at least when the Duke was present. Yet, Dulcey could feel the forces about her influenced by the Countess's malice. Dulcey felt there were eyes in the hall, watching her, constantly watching. The forces about her told her so, but who it was, was not clear. It was time such as these, she sometimes wished her power was not a hit or miss thing. At times such as these, Dulcey had decided long ago, it did her no good, to force the seeing. No matter how desperately she wanted to see, it was best to allow it to show itself.

They all attended church services. Dulcey introduced Nate and Worth to all of the locals who it seemed filled the church, curious in meeting the new Baron especially after having gotten invitations to the wedding breakfast for the Twelfth Ninth celebration. After services, the Reverend Treadwell and his wife went over the wedding ceremony. Abby took her part in the wedding very seriously.

~~~~~~~~~~~~~~~~

The morning of the wedding shone brightly. The temperature had warmed to nearly spring like. Peggy had brought her breakfast earlier, but Dulcey had been too nervous to eat very much. After a quick bath with Peggy's help, she had dressed. She had chosen a dress of cream colored silk with roses embroidered in a slightly darker hue along the bottom with tiny vines and leaves of dark hunter green. Embroidered roses embellished the puffed tops of the long slender sleeves, as well as the fitted bodice. The back of the dress lengthened to a short train, the embroidered roses hemmed it and ascended up the middle.

Peggy had braided her hair and wrapped around her head like a coronet with soft tendrils allowed loose to frame her face. A ring of small cream colored flowers adorned the top of her head with several long ribbons of cream hung from the back. A string of perfectly matched cream colored pearls hung about her neck, a gift from Lord---- Uncle James for her sixteenth birthday.

Dulcey stared at herself in the long mirror. The young woman who stared back at her was beautiful. The colors that surrounded her were colors of joy and happiness. She smiled at her reflection. She turned to Peggy.

Peggy had tears in her eyes. "Oh, my lady, you look just like an angel, you do. Lord James would be so proud."

For a moment, Dulcey eyes teared. Yes, he would have loved this, she thought. She had felt his presence, ever since she had awakened earlier. Her hand went automatically to the pearls around her neck. She smiled.

Abby burst into the room with Franny close on her heels. Both stopped, as Dulcey turned to face them. Abby's eyes were big round orbs, her mouth hung open. "Oh, Dulcey you look like a fairy princess."

Franny stopped in awe, too. "Miss Abby is correct, Lady Dulcey. You do look like a fairy princess."

Dulcey smiled and looked Abby over. "Poppet, you look like the perfect flower girl. You do know, I couldn't do this without you."

"Everybody'd gone to the church. It's just us left," informed Abby matter of factly.

"Then I suppose it is time for us to leave," replied Dulcey as she grabbed hold of the small posey of roses from her bed. The roses in the conservatory had bloomed as though they knew they would be needed for the wedding.

Dulcey and Abby walked down the stairs. Franny and Peggy followed.

Evers stood at the bottom of the stairs, a lump in his throat. He offered his hand to aide her down the last few stairs. "You carriage awaits, my lady. You look beautiful, my lady." His voice crackled with emotion. He had been the only one to know of Dulcey's history from the beginning. Lord James had entrusted him with that secret from the day he brought her back from Wales. He had been entrusted with the job of making certain every visitor who came to Brandanlyn was not after doing harm to the child. That small child had turned into a very beautiful lady, both on the inside as well as the outside.

Dulcey smiled. Evers had always been there. He was a trusted friend as well as servant. She allowed him to drape the softest wool cloak of darkest green about her shoulders. She wanted to say something but the words caught in her throat making speech impossible.

Evers nodded. "Everything is ready for your return as the new Countess."

Dulcey nodded. Evers had not allowed her to see the grand ballroom, the staff had prepared for her wedding breakfast. He had explained, the staff had wished to surprise her. It was to be their wedding present to her and Nate.

He escorted her to the waiting carriage. It was a black shiny coach with the Shefley crest emblazed on its side. Dulcey found the interior to be opulent. The softest of benches alighted the inside covered in brown velvet. Abby followed as did Miss Franny.

Dulcey thought she would be nervous but she was not. A peace settled upon her. She was marrying the part of her soul, the part that made her whole, the part she never realized had been missing until she met Nate. The forces about her were calm and gentle. Dulcey listened to Abby prattle on about the wedding and her part. The ride to the church seemed to take forever yet, at the same time, Dulcey suddenly found herself outside the church.

Several of the townsfolk were waiting for her outside the church. Abby and Miss Franny disembarked. With the help of Mr. Kinley, Dulcey alighted from the carriage. Many of the people curtsied as she passed them. She smiled at the respect they gave her. She saw Mary out to the side. When she rose from her curtsy, she gave Dulcey a broad smile and big wink. Dulcey smiled back at her.

Mrs. Treadwell awaited them at the door of the church. She led Dulcey off to the side. Mr. Kinley assisted her with her cloak while Mrs. Treadwell gave Abby her instructions again. Abby gave Dulcey a look, smiled, turned and began her walk down the aisle dropping rose petals on the floor.

Mr. Kinley offered her his arm. "My dear?"

She nodded. She had asked him to walk with her. It only seemed like the right thing to do. As they stepped on the aisle, Dulcey saw the church was filled. Her eyes were immediately drawn to the altar where Nate stood next to Worth waiting. He was dressed in a dark chocolate brown coat. His pants and waistcoat were cream colored to match her dress.

Dulcey's breath caught in her throat for a moment. This handsome man at the altar, in moments from now, would become her husband, for all of eternity. She smiled with joy bursting in her heart. She felt Lord James' presence in the church walking beside her as much as Mr. Kinley was at her side.

~~~~~~~~~~~~~~~~~

Nate stood at the altar not nervous but impatient for the ceremony to take place. In his heart and soul, Dulcey was already his wife. This would only make it official to the rest of the world. He watched Abby walk down the aisle, dropping her rose petals and smiled. Abby took her place, just as she had rehearsed. He pulled edge of his waistcoat for what seemed to be the hundredth time. The hush of the church alerted him and he looked up.

There stood Dulcey on Mr. Kinley's arm at the end of the aisle. A beam of sunlight streamed through one of the stained glass windows directly on her. He would have sworn in that moment his heart stopped beating and when it began beating again it wanted to burst out his chest. His chest tightened, his lungs could not be appeased. She looked like one of those fairy princesses she described to Abby in her bedtime stories.

This beautiful fairy woman walking down the aisle was about to become his wife. She would be his for forever. With that thought, his breathing eased and so did his heartbeat. Nate took her hand brought it to his lips and kissed it. He assisted her up the two steps and together they faced Reverend Treadwell.

The smile Nate gave her, the love she saw ablaze in his eyes, Dulcey knew her entire life had been getting to this moment. Nate was the part of her that had been missing. Nate was the part of her that made her whole.

Reverend Treadwell stared at the couple standing before him. As solemn a ceremony this was, it was also a moment of celebration. He began, "Dearly beloved, we are gathered together here in the sight of God, and in the face of this congregation to join together this man and this

woman in holy matrimony, which is an honorable estate----
----."

Dulcey looked at Nate listening as Reverend Treadwell said the words that would legally bind them to each other.

Nate heard Reverend Treadwell state, "Therefore, if any man can show any just cause, why they may not lawfully be joined together, let him now speak, or else hereafter forever hold his peace." He was about to turn and look at his mother, but out of the corner of his eye, he saw Worth look in his mother's direction. He had never known anyone to disregard that look. If anything, one cowered before that look. He smiled. Yes, he was glad Worth had come. He gave Dulcey's hand a squeeze.

Dulcey wanted to look at the Countess but she would not give her the satisfaction of her knowing she was a thorn in their side at this time. The Countess was quiet and did not say a word, much to every ones amazement.

"Lord Nathaniel William Hollins Beckham, Baron of Chesterton, Earl of Shefley wilt thou have this woman to thy wedded wife, to live together after God's ordinance in the holy estate of matrimony? Wilt thou love her, comfort her, honour, and keep her in sickness and in health; and forsaking all other, keep thee only unto her, so long as ye both shall live?"

Nate looked at Dulcey. With a strong voice he replied, "I will." He would do that and more. She was already his, the very heart of him.

Reverend Treadwell turned to Dulcey. "Lady Dulcey Elizabeth Langely Fergers, wilt thou have this man to be thy wedded husband, to live together after God's ordinance in the holy estate of matrimony? Wilt thou obey him, and serve him, love, honour and keep him in sickness and in health; and forsaking all other, keep thee only unto him, so long as ye both shall live?"

Dulcey looked to Nate and smiled and said with a clear voice, "I will."

Reverend Treadwell looked up and asked, "Who giveth this woman to be married to this man?"

Mr. Percy Kinley stood up with pride, took Dulcey's right hand in his, squeezed it softly and presented it to Reverend Treadwell. "I do."

Dulcey smiled with tears in her eyes. Mr. Kinley had been so pleased when she had asked, if he would give her hand in marriage to Nate.

Reverend Treadwell took Dulcey's right hand and placed it Nate's right hand. "Please repeat after me."

Nate looked at the reverend and began in a firm voice. "I, Nathaniel William Hollins Beckham, Baron of Chesterton, Earl of Shefley take thee, Lady Dulcey Elizabeth Langely Fergers to my wedded wife, to have and to hold from this day forward, for better or worse, for richer, for poorer, in sickness and in health, to love and to cherish, till death us do part, according to God's holy ordinance; and thereto I plight thee my troth."

Dulcey let go of Nate's hand reluctantly just as the Reverend had instructed her to.

Reverend Treadwell nodded and Dulcey took Nate's right hand in hers. She took a deep breath and repeated as the reverend instructed her to. "I, Dulcey Elizabeth Langely Fergers take thee, Lord Nathaniel William Hollins Beckham, Baron of Chesterfield, Earl of Shefley to my wedded husband, to have and to hold from this day forward, for better for worse, for richer for poorer, in sickness and in health, to love, to cherish, and to obey, till death us do part, according to God's holy ordinance, and thereto I give thee my troth."

Nate dropped Dulcey's hand and took the wedding ring, Mr. Kinley had given him. He had not told Dulcey about it. He placed it on the book the Reverend read from.

Reverend Treadwell took the ring, looked at it for a moment, then gave it back to Lord Beckham. "Please place this ring on the finger of her left hand and repeat after me."

Nate took Dulcey's hand and said, "With this ring I thee wed, with my body I thee worship, and with all my worldly goods I thee endow: in the name of the Father, and the Son, and the Holy Ghost. Amen." He placed the ring on her finger.

Dulcey smiled when Nate said "with my body I thee worship." She remembered the cottage and the worshipping he had done there. She looked down at her hand and the ring he placed on her finger. It was old looking and very different than what she would have expected, a crisscross woven of silver.

Nate smiled, and whispered, "Your mothers."

Dulcey looked at him in shock and then smiled with such love in her heart that Nate would give her mother's ring. Where, how had he gotten it?

"Please kneel."

Reverend Treadwell led everyone in prayer. He joined Nathaniel and Dulcey's right hands together again. He looked up to the people that filled his church.

"Those whom God hath joined together let no man put asunder."

He paused and then added, "Forasmuch as Lord Nathaniel William Hollins Beckham, Baron of Chesterton, Earl of Shefley and Lady Dulcey Elizabeth Langely Fergers have consented together in holy wedlock, and have witnessed the same before God and this company, and thereto have given and pledged their troth either to other, and have declared the same by giving and receiving of a ring, and by joining of hands; I pronounce that they be man and wife together, in the name of the Father, and of the Son, and of the Holy Ghost. Amen."

Reverend Treadwell said his prayer over them and the church book of registry was signed. Reverend

Treadwell smiled and said, "My lord, you may kiss your bride."

Nate leaned over and gently kissed her lips. A peace the likes he had never known settled over him. Dulcey was now legally his wife. Nothing and no one could come between them.

Dulcey returned his kiss. The forces around her celebrated this union leaving her feeling one with all the world about her. It was a most glorious feeling. She walked proudly at his side as he escorted her out the church to the waiting carriage. Nate helped her into the carriage and sat next to her. A quick tap on the roof and they were off.

Nate pulled Dulcey onto his lap and kissed her properly, his tongue met hers in a dance of mutual enjoyment. Long moments later, Nate raised his head.

Dulcey pushed his hand away from her breast though she felt it deep inside of her. She had missed his touch.

Nate raised his eyebrow in question. "We are married, my love. I did wait till we were married, like I promised."

Dulcey laughed. "It is not that I don't want to continue with this but we do have our wedding breakfast to attend. I would like to attend in some semblance of decorum."

Nate laughed. "I have my decorum on. I wish I did not."

Dulcey shook her head. "We have the rest of our lives, my husband." She liked the sound of that, my husband.

Nate relaxed. "Very well, my lady, I will wait till tonight. But no longer."

Dulcey cupped his face in her hands. "I promise you will not be sorry you waited," she promised.

"I'll hold you to that promise, my love," replied Nate with anticipation. These past few days had been difficult, not being able to touch and love her like he had at the cottage. But that would end tonight. He smiled with anticipation.

She looked at the ring on her hand and remembered what Nate had said during the wedding ceremony and asked, "Is it true? Is this my mother's ring?" She examined the silver crisscross woven ring that adorned her left hand. It appeared old.

Nate nodded, "Yes, I thought you would like it."

"How? Where did you get it?"

"It seems it survived the fire. Your uncle gave it to Mr. Kinley for safe keeping and he gave it to me. He thought you would like it. I thought so, too." He watched her face closely. There were tears in her eyes, but a smile on her face, a smile of serenity and peace.

"Thank you. It is perfect," Dulcey replied. She felt like her mother and father had been a part of her wedding and now she knew why. The forces around the ring had embraced her like a loving wrap. It filled her heart with joy.

Dulcey cuddled in his lap and sighed. She was glad the wedding ceremony was over but the wedding breakfast was next. All the surrounding gentry and most of the town's people would be there. She wondered if they would treat her different now that she was the lady of the manor. She hoped not. Many of them, she considered her friends.

"What's troubling you? I can feel you are worried?"

She confided her fears to him.

"Adding lady to your name will not change you. They know you and they know that as well. Everyone I have talked with could not be happier for you."

Dulcey nodded.

"When you see the grand ballroom, you will understand."

"Evers has refused to let me anywhere near it. What has he done?" asked Dulcey. It had been a big secret the past couple of days. Evers had been adamant, she not go anywhere near the grand room. She had watched the staff go in and out, smile and nod at her. She was anxious to see what had been done.

Nate smiled smugly. "It is a surprise. A surprise, I am certain you will like."

"A hint, please?" Dulcey begged.

"And get on Evers bad side. Never, my love. I have promised. My lips are sealed," replied Nate as he closed his lips tightly.

Dulcey smiled and kissed his closed lips, licking them with the tip of her tongue. She felt him smile, his lips open and his tongue met hers.

The carriage came to a halt and Dulcey glanced out of the window to see the steps of Brandanlyn.

Nate pulled away. "Ah, we are home and now, you will be able to see for yourself."

Dulcey sighed then smiled. "Yes, lets." She scooted over to the other seat as Nate opened the door. Dulcey took his offered hand and allowed him to help her down.

Evers awaited them at the open door. "Welcome, Lord and Lady Beckham."

Dulcey smiled. "Thank you, Evers. Is all ready?" She knew it would be.

Evers smiled. "Of course, my lady. Follow me, as there are many of the guests have already arrived." Dulcey noticed Evers left Thomas at the door to greet the rest of the guests that followed. A glance over her shoulder saw Worth, Abby and Nate's mother coming through the door.

Evers stood at the closed doors to grand ballroom. With a grand flourish, he opened the doors. Dulcey stepped through the doors with Nate at her side. She stopped after several steps through the door. The grand ball room had been turned into enchanted fairy woodland with trees and flowers.

Dulcey stopped and placed her hand over her heart. Her breath was caught in her chest. Her eyes glanced from the trees, the flowers to the butterflies and the small fairies scattered throughout. This was the middle of winter with a snowstorm but a couple of weeks ago. How had Evers brought this about? To have done this for her touched her heart with such love.

She turned to Nate, then to Evers at his side. She was speechless. She tried to say something but the words would not come out.

Abby stood beside her and pulled on her arm. "Do you like it Aunt Dulcey? I telled them it had to be like the stories you tell me. Maybe the real fairies would come," explained Abby

Dulcey looked down at Abby. "It was a very good idea, Abby." She turned to stand in front of Evers. "Oh, Evers, I don't know how to tell you, how much this means to me." She placed her hands over her lips to stop them from trembling; the tears in her eyes blurred her vision. She took a deep breath and placed her hand back over her heart. "I am so touched by this. Thank you. Please thank everyone for me. This is the best wedding present I could have ever had. It is beautiful."

Nate watched Evers puff up with pride. He noticed the brightness in his eyes. He knew Evers had worried maybe Dulcey would not like it, no matter how much Nate had assured him he was certain, she would love it.

"It has been our pleasure, my lady. We are glad that you like what we did."

Dulcey smiled. "I love it. I have no idea how you did it, but it is so beautiful, so very beautiful. Thank you." She overwhelmed with such feelings of elation. The forces about her were ablaze with the colors of joy and love.

"Come love, we have guests to greet. I do believe everyone about is here," stated Nate, as he began to walk further into the room.

Dulcey followed where Nate led. She was amazed and so touched because everywhere she looked, she was truly amazed, how much work they had done to make the grand ball room look as it did. There were small round tables scattered throughout, where all those invited sat.

Nate led her to the long table set at the end of the hall. It was set up like the medieval feast she and Lord James had done several years ago, because she had been studying the time. That Evers remembered how they had both loved it, to have incorporated into the wedding breakfast was overwhelming and so lovingly thoughtful. It made Dulcey feel like the fairy princess of Abby's stories.

She looked at Nate as he escorted her to the seat of honor. "Evers?" she asked.

Nate nodded. "He thought since you and Lord James had enjoyed it so much and so often talked about it, you might feel like Lord James was here with you."

Dulcey nodded, trying desperately to hold back the tears of joy. She never once imagined her heart could hold so much joy. Surely, it would burst. She watched as Nate sat beside her. Abby sat at her other side with Worth at her side. Nate's mother was at his other side.

The lavish feast was enjoyed by everyone. What was supposed to be a wedding breakfast was instead a feast of such magnitude. There were platters of ham and eggs, beef and poultry, with bowls of currents and fruits of plums, peaches and berries of every kind. Breads and pastries accompanied by pots of honey and fruit marmalade were in abundance. Guests served themselves and since it was also a celebration of Twelfth Night everyone mingled together.

The centerpiece of the celebration, the Twelfth Night cake stood on its own table, an elaborate white sugar confection decorated with images of fairies and pink roses. A large bowl of wassail complimented the feast as was custom for Twelfth Night.

She looked out onto the ballroom to see so many friends and neighbors mingling about. The hum of voices and the sounds of laughter filled the grand ball room. It sounded like bees in a busy hive. Dulcey smiled. Lord, Uncle James would be so pleased.

Dulcey ate bites of everything placed in front of her yet she could not remember any of it. Abby kept asking her questions about everything and everyone. She enjoyed explaining all of it to Abby. Abby was having a grand time which made it all the more enjoyable.

Worth stood up and raised his glass. Evers had the staff quieten everyone.

"Friends, as the best man for my good friend Lord Nathaniel Beckham, I raise my glass and wish he and his new bride, the Lady Dulcey, a happy, prosperous and fruitful marriage." He raised his glass in Nate and Dulcey's direction, "To Lord and Lady Beckham!"

The hall echoed with "Lord and Lady Beckham." Worth downed his glass.

Nate tapped Dulcey's glass and each drank in response to Worth's toast. As Dulcey looked over the rim of her glass in Nate's direction, she noticed his mother put her glass back down on the table. Dulcey shrugged it aside. She was not about to let the Countess put a damper on her wedding. After all, she would be gone in a couple of days. Nate had told her it was part of her wedding present.

Dulcey stood up. "I wish to mingle and talk with everyone. Will you come with me?"

Nate stood up, grabbed her hand and brought it to his lips. "I will follow you anywhere you lead me, my love."

Dulcey smiled and took his offered arm. She was going to enjoy introducing her husband to the people that had been a part of her life.

Chapter 16

What's here? A cup closed in my true love's hand.
Poison,.......

William Shakespeare

Dulcey grabbed the last flute of champagne on the tray and turned to Nate several feet away. She returned his silent toast. The love and promise reflecting in his eyes made her heart sing. Never had she been so happy. She raised the glass to her lips and the liquid touched her lips.

The colors of the forces about her changed to darkness, to black. A vision appeared, a hand adding drops to the glass. She knew that vial. She knew that face. Her eyes widened in disbelief and horror. The glass slipped from her hands to crash to the floor and shatter into pieces.

She looked desperately to Nate but already she could feel herself slipping away. She had to tell him but all she could do was whisper, "Poison," before its affects took over her body. The last thing her mind cried was Nate's name.

Nate watched. The happy smile on his face turned to shock, as he watched the glass slip from Dulcey's hands. Fear and desperation replaced the joy on her face. He rushed to her side in time to catch her as she collapsed in his arms and heard her whisper.

"No!" he screamed like a man tormented to hell as he held her tight.

Worth was at his side in a second demanding, "What? What has happened.?"

Nate fell to the floor with Dulcey in his lap and began rocking back and forth holding her tightly, his face an image of pure anguish. No! No! his mind cried. No, this could not be happening.

Worth put his hand on Nate's shoulders. "Tell me."

Nate looked up to him lost, adrift in a sea of pain. He held his life, his heart in his arms. Dulcey was his life, was his heart. "She's been poisoned. She whispered poison." He held her tighter. It felt like his heart was being ripped out of his chest.

Dr. Mead knelt down beside him and grabbed Dulcey wrist. He could feel a faint pulse. "She's alive, my lord."

Nate looked at him in disbelief and then hope. Oh, please let it be so, he prayed. He couldn't think, he could only feel.

"Let's get her up to her room. I need to examine her more closely," ordered Dr. Meade.

Worth and Dr. Mead helped him up. He refused to let Dulcey go. Dulcey was alive. "Please, Worth see to --------." He couldn't finish the sentence.

"Of course. See to Lady Dulcey," replied Worth, as he watched his dear friend leave with his new bride in his arms. Damn how could this be happening? Who could have done such a thing?

Slowly, he turned to everyone and commanded in pure ducal manner, "No one leaves this house until I have talked with everyone." He slowly looked over every person in attendance, eyeing each of them as a possible murderer. He was going to find out who did this dastardly deed, if he had to torture every person here.

His eyes came to rest on the Countess for a moment. Why did he look for her first? She had just left the head table just moments before and was standing next to the Reverend. She had been nowhere close to Dulcey. Yet still, he considered her.

A tall thin man with balding hair approached him. "Your Grace, I am George Burrows, the local magistrate. How can I help?"

He eyed the magistrate and pushed the Countess to the back of his mind for the moment. She had been nowhere near Dulcey. Worth nodded. He took him aside. "We need to talk to everyone. It appears Lady Dulcey has been poisoned. I believe it was someone in this room and I intend to find out who it is?"

Mr. Burrows nodded. He was of the same frame of mind. But he could think of no one from the area who would wish Lady Dulcey harm. He looked carefully over everyone in attendance. He could see no one here looking the least bit suspicious. He knew everyone here from the town and surrounding area. There was no one here who held the least bit of animosity against Lady Dulcey. She had helped each and every one of them at some time or another. All he saw was concern on their faces.

"Evers, would you see to it that everyone remains here as we talk with each and every one separately in Lord Beckham study," instructed the Duke. In the few days he was here, he had come to know Evers was the pulse of this place. Nothing ever happened here without his knowledge except this, damn it.

"Of course, your Grace," replied Evers. No one would leave until the Duke said so. He nodded to Thomas and Henry who stationed themselves at the two outer doors.

"Well, Mr. Barrows let us begin."

~~~~~~~~~~~~~~~~~

Nate carried Dulcey in his arms, following where Dr. Meade and Peggy led. She felt so lifeless in his arms. Every beat of his heart hurt as though someone had it in a tight grip. Her face lay against his chest, much too pale. He couldn't think. All he could do was feel this pain consuming him.

He laid her carefully on her bed. Peggy had turned the covers down. Dr. Meade removed some vials from his bag and began mixing.

"We need to make her empty her stomach, in hopes, we can get her to get rid of the poison," explained Dr. Meade. "Hold her head up, my lord. We need to get this down her."

Nate nodded as he held her head as the doctor poured the liquid into her mouth. It appeared to Nate that most of it was running down her chin. "Swallow, love. Please, swallow. Dr. Meade is here. He says you need to swallow this. We need to get this down you." He pleaded.

Dr. Meade continued to pour. He hoped some of it was getting down. It was the recipe Grammy Digby had instructed him with. Oh, how he wished she was here.

Dulcey began to cough and empty the content of her stomach. Peggy had the basin ready.

"Hold her head up and to the side my lord. We don't want her to swallow it back again," instructed Dr. Meade.

Nate held her as the doctor instructed, wiping her face with the cool cloth Peggy handed him. When at last it seemed, she had emptied all within her stomach, she collapsed in his arms again. Nate raised his eyes to the doctor in question.

Dr. Meade felt her pulse. It was not as weak as it was at first, not as strong as he would have liked it to be but it was an improvement. Her breathing appeared less shallow.

"All we can do now, my lord, is hope and pray we were able to get enough of the poison out of her. Now is the hard part, waiting. I just wish I knew what type of poison was used. I would have a better idea of what more I need to do."

Nate nodded unable to trust his voice. He could not lose Dulcey. No, he could not even bear the thought of it.

It felt like there was this iron fist in his chest squeezing his heart. Every beat of his heart hurt, every breath was difficult. This was not happening. It had to be a bad dream. He was bound to wake up soon and all of this would not have happened. He felt so lost.

"My lord," said Peggy, "let me change her into her night shift and get her out of her wedding dress. She'll be more comfortable."

Nate nodded again and began undoing the buttons. He had teased her earlier about enjoying undoing every button. It seemed like a lifetime ago. His hands shook.

Peggy put her hand on his. "I can do this, my lord."

"No, I will help," replied Nate as he continued with the buttons. He needed to be doing something.

Together, he and Peggy removed her bridal dress and chemise. Carefully, they put her nightdress on. Nate concentrated on the task and tried desperately not let anything enter his mind except getting Dulcey comfortable. But now with that done, he looked to Dr. Meade.

"I wish I could tell you more, but I just don't know. She is resting. We have done all we can at the moment. I know this is not what you wish to hear, my lord. All we can do now is wait and pray." Dr. Meade wished he could tell him more. This was something Dulcey would have handled. She knew more about these things.

Nate pushed his hands through his hair in frustration. "Who would do this?" asked Nate.

"I can't imagine anyone in the area wanting to do harm to Lady Dulcey. She is very well liked," explained Dr. Meade. He was at a loss. It did not make sense to him either.

"Dr. Meade, is right, my lord. Lady Dulcey has helped everyone about," said Peggy. She shook her head in confusion.

"Have there been any strangers in the area?" asked Nate. All he could think of was the story Lord James had written concerning Dulcey parents' death. Could it be possible that vicar had finally found her?

Both shook their heads and answered, "No."

"Why?" asked Dr. Meade.

Nate went on to explain what Lord James had written concerning the death of Dulcey's parents.

Dr. Meade shook his head. "No, my lord. There have been no strangers here in the area that I know of. The only new people are you, my lord, and your mother and your staff."

Nate shook his head. Perhaps, it was someone nobody noticed.

"Perhaps, Lord Beckham you, would like to go downstairs and talk with his grace. He may have found something out by now," suggested Dr. Meade.

Nate shook his head. "No, I am not leaving Dulcey's side till she wakes up. I trust Worth implicitly. No, I am not leaving. I trust no one else to protect her." But then, he had not been able to protect her before. He had not known there was a threat, he told himself. Now he did. No one would get to her except through him.

"Please, Dr. Meade, go downstairs and talk with his grace. Let me know, as soon as he has found anything. Thank you for your help, Peggy. I may need it again."

"Of course, my lord. I am my lady's maid. I will stay here with you, my lord. I can go back and forth for you," suggested Peggy. She was like his lordship. She was hesitant to leave Lady Dulcey's side.

Nate nodded. Yes, that would help.

~~~~~~~~~~~~~~

The Duke of Worthingston and Mr. Barrows began slowly questioning the guests one at a time. Worth put Simmons, Bennings and Evers in charge of making sure no one left till they were cleared. The more Worth questioned, the more he grew to realize how many of these people Dulcey had helped in some manner and how much, so many of them cared about her. It was like looking for the needle in a haystack.

Evers stopped the Duke. "Your Grace, I think you should talk with Mary, Mary Stewart."

"Who is this Mary?" asked the Duke.

"Mary works at the tavern in the village. She knows Lady Dulcey. She says she may have seen something. She doesn't know if it's important."

"Then bring her to me, Evers. If she knows something I need to talk with her," demanded Worth. It had been over two hours and he was losing patience. He had discovered nothing.

Mary followed Evers into the study. She made a small curtsey. "Yer, grace."

Worth looked her over. He had seen many a tavern maid in his life. Mary stood before him, bright red hair with warm brown eyes, big breasted and big hips as typical as any he had ever met. He was certain she knew how to please a man in the bed. Hair of red, he thought, then shook his head. Maybe Dulcey had gotten this red hair mixed up with what would happen to her.

"You've told Evers you may know something," questioned Worth.

Mary nodded. "Don't know how important it is, yer grace? But I've been rememberin' somethin'. It didn't sit right with me. There was this woman, she was prowlin' by the glasses. Kind of 'minded me of the big tom in the kitchen. I watched her but when she saw me watchin' she walked away. Ain't never seen her before. Didn't see her again. Does that help ye, yer grace, cause Miss, Lady Dulcey she's always been kind to me, she has," she explained hoping this was of some help.

Worth nodded. "Describe her to me, Mary."

Mary blew out a breath. "I believe she be one of us."

Worth looked at her in question.

"Not nobility like yer grace. One of the servants. Her clothes be dark, her hair gray, pulled back, dark tiny eyes, big hawk nose----"

"That's Leta, the Countess's maid," interrupted Evers. "She's been saying some cruel things about Lady Dulcey since she's been here, same things we've heard the Countess say. I warned her several of times about it. She stopped coming downstairs. She's been staying in her room or the Countess's since Lord Beckham brought Lady Dulcey back."

Worth narrowed his eyes in anger. The Countess! Why was he not surprised? He firmly believed, she was in a way responsible for Caroline's miscarriage that led to her death. Now, possibly this. Yes, this needed further investigation.

"Evers, bring her to me. Mary, I would like you to stay, please. Can you sit in this chair?" He turned the chair so the back faced the door. The maid would not see Mary when she came in. "Once I have begun to talk to her, I will come and stand next to chair. I need you to peek around the chair and tap me, if she is the one you saw."

Mary nodded, "Of course, yer grace." She sat down in the chair just as Evers brought Leta in.

Leta glanced about her nervously. She knew she would be questioned but Lady Shefley said not to worry. She was worried. What if-----

Worth studied her through narrowed eyes. She met them only for a moment then looked quickly away. How devoted was she to the Countess, he wondered.

"You are Leta, the Countess's maid?" he asked.

"Yes, your Grace."

"I'll ask you, like I have everyone else. Where were you when Lady Dulcey collapsed?"

Leta continued to look down at her feet. She could answer that question. "I was near the Countess."

Worth walked over to the chair Mary sat in and stood beside it, hiding Mary from view.

"And where exactly was that?" he asked.

Leta continued to stare at her feet. She had gone straight to the Countess's side. "We were by the fireplace by the vicar."

Mary had peeked around the chair and tapped the Duke on the side of his leg. She smiled. From that small tap, she could feel the hard muscle of his leg. Ah, she wouldn't mind getting to know the Duke a lot better.

"You weren't by the table that held the glasses at any time tonight?" Worth questioned.

"No, your grace. I stayed by the Countess's side all night. She was not feeling well."

Worth nodded. "So you were never by the glasses of champagne at any time?"

"No, your grace." She shifted nervously on her feet.

Mr. Barrows watched her and didn't like her nervousness. He felt she was hiding something.

"So if Miss Stewart here said, she saw you by the glasses, moments before Lady Dulcey took her glass, she would be lying," stated Worth as he offered Mary his hand and aided her to her feet and face Leta.

Leta looked up and met Mary's eyes. Her eyes widened with fear. She was certain---

"Do you still say that you were never at the table with the glasses?" asked Worth

"I----I may have. I don't remember," she answered with a stutter. "The Countess will tell you, I was at her side."

"Evers, would you have the Countess come in here as well. We need to straighten this out, who was where."

Lady Shefley entered the study. She did not care for this room. This was where that letter was read. How her son could believe that letter and as such, marry this witch woman was beyond her. And now this. Hadn't she told him time and time again, he was putting them in danger. But no, he would not listen to her. That woman had bewitched him. Of that, she was certain.

She did not care that Worth was in charge of the interrogation. She and Worth did not see things in the same way. Why was he wanting to speak with her? She had not poisoned Dulcey but she would not be opposed to the possibility of Dulcey's demise.

Leta, her maid, was in the room. Leta was getting old but she had been with her since she was a child and knew her likes and dislikes. She could not dismiss her. Leta was devoted to her.

"What is Leta doing here?" she demanded. She looked at Worth directly. She then noticed another woman in the room. Who was this woman? Some servant from the looks of her.

"Leta was seen by the glasses just prior to Lady Dulcey's collapse. She says she has been by your side." He watched the Countess's face closely. He also watched Leta's face as well.

The Countess let out a breath of annoyance. "Leta was by my side once I left the table."

"She did not get you a glass of champagne?"

The Countess shrugged. "No, I do not drink champagne."

"So, if Miss Stewart saw Leta by the glasses, she would not be getting a glass for you?" asked Worth watching Leta's reaction closely.

The Countess pursed her lips in displeasure. "Who is this Miss Stewart, you speak of?"

"Miss Stewart, this is the Dowager Countess of Shefley. Did you or did you not see her maid, Leta near the table where Lady Dulcey took her glass of champagne?"

Mary looked at the Countess and then at Leta. If they were behind the poisoning of Lady Dulcey, she was not about to back down. "Yes, yer grace. I saw this woman at that table."

Leta shifted under Mary's gaze.

Worth noticed the shift.

"Again, who is this woman that accuses my maid?" demanded the Countess. She eyed the woman. She was not a servant of Brandanlyn. She must be a servant from somewhere about here. She should have not been a part of this, attending this wedding. But then, this Dulcey woman associated with all this low class of people.

Worth ignored the Countess. "Are you certain, Miss Stewart?"

Mary nodded, "Aye, yer grace. She be there and then she be gone."

"What do you say now Leta?" addressed Worth. He did not like the way Leta shifted when confronted by Mary. He had seen that nervousness before, when working for the war department. It usually meant guilt.

Leta looked nervously to the Countess. The Countess would protect her.

"You have not answered my question, Leta? Were you at the table? Were you the one that poisoned Lady Dulcey? I need your answer," commanded Worth. He was tired of this game.

"You will stop this at once Worthingston. You will not berate my maid in this manner. I don't know this woman who accuses her so. It could possibly be her and she wants you to think otherwise." The Countess had had enough of this.

Worth narrowed his eyes. "No, perhaps Leta is doing this under your direction. It is no secret that you do not like Lady Dulcey. Perhaps you are behind this," accused Worth.

Lady Shefley blew out a breath in anger. "Do not be absurd. She is a witch. Her parents were burned. I tried to tell Nathaniel that we were all in danger. This just proves it."

Magistrate Barrows replied angrily. "Lady Dulcey is well loved in this area. No one believes she is a witch. We will not stand for this story to be bandied about. We care for her. It appears you do not. So perhaps his Grace may be on to something."

Lady Shefley bristled in indignation. "I beg your pardon. Who are you to accuse me? I am the Countess Shefley. I will not be talked to in this manner." She turned to walk out but Magistrate Barrows put himself between the Countess and the door.

"We have not finished questioning you or your maid," stated Worth in no uncertain terms. He felt like there was more here than either woman was telling.

"I will not be interrogated any further." She looked daggers at first Barrows and then turned to Worthingston. "I am leaving now!"

"No, Countess, you are not. I am determined to get to the bottom of this and I am beginning to think you are involved somehow. You will not leave until I find out whether you are or not." All the memories, of all the complaints Carolyn had told him, came to mind. He had no qualms believing this woman was capable of such a thing. He was going to find out, if they had to stay here all night.

The Countess narrowed her eyes. The Duke was not about to hold her prisoner and question her like she was some low class servant. How dare he? Duke or not, she was not going to allow him to continue questioning her or Leta because of what this woman said, whoever this woman was.

"This will end now. Leta and I are going to walk out of that door and I am going to my room," she stated as she nodded to Leta for her to follow her. She turned to face Barrows again and gave him a dismissal look through narrowed eyes.

"You bloody hell will not," growled the Duke. Everyone in the room stopped and looked at him in shock. He had not meant to let his anger get the better of him, but he couldn't get Carolyn out of his head. Here the Countess was doing the same thing. He knew she was behind it. He felt it. This time she was not going to get away with it.

The Countess stared at the Duke in wide eyed shock.

Leta began shaking. "You must not talk to the Countess in that manner," she whispered.

"Worth you will not use that type of language in my presence," admonished the Countess.

"Then I suggest Countess, you tell me exactly why you did this?" asked Worth. He still thought she had done this. Now, he was determined to prove it.

"I do not know how to make you understand, I did not poison that witch. Someone else must have, but it was not me," she argued. She was getting extremely irritated with all of this.

"No, Countess. I do not believe you. You hate Dulcey just as you hated Carolyn. You will not stop until you have Dulcey dead, as well. If you confess now, I will stop this interrogation and you can leave." He had no intention of letting her go.

Lady Shefley put her hand on her heart. She had used this ruse before. "I am not a well person. This is highly upsetting to me. I need to go to my room and lie down."

Worth shook his head. He had seen her act before. He was not about to be fooled by it. "Well, you tell me the truth Countess and I will be glad to allow you to go upstairs."

Lady Shefley patted her chest again for emphasis. "I am not well, Worth and this is most upsetting. I must go to my room and rest."

"No, you will not. Not until I get to the bottom of this."

"I did it. Leave my lady alone. She has been upset enough because of that witch woman. She needed to be gone," whispered Leta as she came to the Countess's side to assist her. "She is not well and you are making her worse. She needs to rest. Has she not been upset enough worrying that she would be burned by that witch woman?"

All eyes in the room looked to Leta. The Countess stared at Leta in disbelief. "What?" she asked.

Leta looked at the Countess as though why was she asking that question. "Because she upset you. You said over and over again, she needed to go. I could not let her continue to upset you. It is what you wanted. You said so. I have always made certain you have always gotten what you wanted, Countess. It is my job to make certain it is done. It is what I have done for you all of my life," explained Leta calmly, as though it was the most natural thing for her to do.

Countess looked to Worth and said, "As you can see, it was not me."

Worth shook his head. "You did this Leta? The Countess put you up to this?" She had to be behind it.

Leta looked at him strangely, then stated calmly. "No. I did this for the Countess. That witch upset the Countess. The Countess said over and over again, how we were all going to burn because of that witch woman. I had to protect the Countess. I could not let the Countess burn. So that woman had to go." She turned to the Countess. "You are safe now, m'lady." She turned back to the Duke. "Now may I take the Countess upstairs, she needs her rest."

Worth looked at Barrows who raised his shoulders in question. He didn't understand this calmness with Leta, as though she did not understand what she had done. "Leta, do you understand what you have done?"

Leta cocked her head in confusion as she looked at him. "Of course, your grace. I was protecting the Countess. That is my job." She turned to the Countess, "We can go upstairs now, m'lady and you may rest. You do not need to fear that witch woman any longer, now."

"Leta, tell him I did not instruct in any of this." Worth needed to know, she was not behind this but she was not against what Leta had done. After all, Leta's intent was to protect her. At least Leta understood why that witch woman was going to harm them. Look at what she had caused Leta to do. That should be example enough for everyone to see.

Worth looked at the Countess in incredulity. All she could think of was making certain she was not blamed in any of this and yet, she was the very reason, Leta did what she did. It was beyond his comprehension someone could be so self-centered.

"Leta, what poison did you use?" asked Worth. Knowing would help Dr. Meade. Perhaps there was still time. No, there had to be time.

"Why nightshade, your grace? I am not familiar with it. Did I use enough? It simply would not do for her to live and continue to upset the Countess. The Countess could not abide it."

Worth stared at Leta as though she had lost her mind. And then it dawned on him, she was indeed mad. Her devotion to the Countess had made her that way. And the Countess did not, could not, see what she had done by all her harping and complaining. No, she had not poisoned Dulcey herself. No, the likes of her would never dirty her hands. But she would lead someone like Leta to do it for her. He shuddered at the thought of those two.

"Evers, please escort, the Countess and her maid to the Countess's room. They are to stay there under guard, until I speak with Lord Beckham concerning all that we have just learned." He looked at the Countess for argument but found none.

"You will explain all of this to Nathaniel, will you not Worth? That it was Leta and not me." asked the Countess.

"Rest assured Countess I will inform Nate of all of this. Now be so kind as to go."

He watched as Mr. Barrows moved from the door and allowed Evers, Lady Shefley and Leta to leave.

"I'll be leavin' too, yer grace," said Mary.

Worth looked at her in surprise. He had forgotten she was still in the room with them. "Yes, by all means, but a word with you first. What has been said in this room must remain here until a decision has been made about how to deal with all of this."

Mary nodded. "Fer Lady Dulcey's sake, I'll not say a word, yer grace. I'll be a prayin' for m'lady." She curtsied and left through the door Mr. Barrows held open for her.

Worth walked over to the sideboard, pulled out a bottle of whiskey and filled two glasses nearly to the top. He handed one to Mr. Barrows and downed his in one long gulp. It burned all the way down. He desperately felt the need to get the taste of the Countess's duplicity and self-importance out of his mouth.

Mr. Barrows sipped his. "How shall we handle this, your grace?"

"At the moment, I am uncertain as how to proceed. It appears Leta has gone mad. She is obsessed with the need to protect the Countess. I need to go to Lord Beckham with this." He shook his head. How does one tell one's friend, his mother's maid has just poisoned his new bride? All because she believed, she was doing his mother's bidding. "If you can see to it the guests are sent on their way while I speak with Lord Beckham. Once that is done have Evers escort you upstairs."

Chapter 17

Why dost thou wrong her that did n'er wrong thee?
When did she cross thee with a bitter word?

Talk not to me, I will go sit and weep
Till I can find occasion of revenge.
William Shakespeare

Worth met Dr. Mead in the hall outside of Lady Dulcey's room and informed him of all he had learned.

"I hope this helps," said Worth.

Dr. Mead nodded. "Yes, it has. I know what more needs to be done. His lordship is at her bedside. He refuses to leave."

Worth passed a hand over his face in weariness and sadness. As much as he disliked the Countess for the hell she had put Caroline through and he was more certain now more than ever she was responsible for Carolyn's death indirectly, just as she was here, she was not his mother. Nate would need to deal with that fact. It would not be easy.

He knocked softly then entered quietly. Dulcey lay in her bed pale but alive. Nate sat at her bedside, her hand in his gently rubbing it with his fingers. This was a far cry from the handsome man he stood beside on the altar of the church just hours ago. This man before him, his hair disheveled, no doubt from numerous times of having passed his hand through it, his jacket and cravat off and draped over the back of the wing chair he sat in, looked like he had been to hell but had not made it back yet.

Nate looked up when he realized Worth had entered the room. He had not heard him enter. The only thing he was interested in hearing was Dulcey's next breath. The look on Worth's face did not bode well.

He placed Dulcey's hand on the coverlet. He nodded to Peggy and she came to her bedside. He motioned his head to the small sitting room that was part of Dulcey's room. He walked to the window and stared out unaware of the scenery before him. He turned to Worth when he joined his side.

"Please tell me you know who did this to Dulcey," asked Nate.

Worth nodded. "I'm not sure you are going to like what I have found out," answered Worth.

"Nothing you can tell me will make the least difference. Someone poisoned my bride and finding out who did this is my main concern at the moment besides praying that my bride survives. So Worth tell me, who did this?"

Worth gazed at his friend who looked harried, yet angry. He knew he could no longer delay. "We questioned nearly everyone with no luck, until one. Miss Mary Stewart thought she saw someone. When questioned, Leta, your mother's maid, admitted to the deed."

Nate looked at him momentarily stunned. "Leta?"

"Yes," answered Worth, then went on to explain. "It appears she heard your mother become so upset with the fact that Dulcey was a witch. She was afraid for your mother. Afraid someone would try to burn Dulcey and your mother would burn, too. Your mother kept harping on that fact and how upset she was that you were marrying Dulcey. That something needed to be done to stop this marriage from taking place."

Nate took a moment to allow the information to sink in. His mother's maid. Leta, his mother's maid. He closed his eyes in torment and anger. His mother and her constant complaints. "Did the Countess know about this?" asked Nate. At the moment, he could not call her mother.

Worth let out a sigh. "I am not sure. It does not appear as though she had any knowledge of it directly. Of course, she has denied it. Something happened with Leta, she was very nervous at first and then when we, I accused your mother, she changed."

Nate looked at him confused. "What do you mean changed?"

Worth shook his head. "I'm not sure. It was like the life went out of her. Like she became a shell of who she was, no emotion. The only thing she cared about was your mother, pleasing your mother was the only thing that mattered. It was strange. She did not understand the seriousness of what she had done. Everything was about protecting your mother." He tried to explain, but he wasn't sure exactly what had transpired with the Countess's maid. He believed her to be mad, unbalanced, for only someone who was mad would act like that.

Nate nodded slightly. "Do you believe if the Countess had not constantly harped about Dulcey, Leta would have not believed the Countess was in danger?"

"I believe her mind is not right and that she is completely devoted to your mother. The Countess's constant complaints contributed to her doing this. I am sorry, Beck. I know she is your mother. She may not have been directly involved, may not have used the poison herself, but I believe she precipitated this. Leta does not understand her involvement in this. Because Leta did this, your mother believes she has had no part in it. She is the most selfish person I have ever come across." Worth remembered some of his conversations with Carolyn when she had said as much. At the time, he thought she had exaggerated but looking back, he regretted not having listened to Carolyn more.

Nate closed his eyes and clenched his fists at his side. He should have shipped her home days ago as he threatened to. He was filled with guilt for not having done so. Part of this was his fault as well, for not having sent her home. Damn her, he thought.

"If I had shipped her home as I threatened to days ago, this would not have happened. I am to blame in that part. I should have known," stated Nate with self-loathing. His hand was in this, too. How could he claim to love Dulcey yet to have put her in such danger? He could never forgive himself for having allowed this to happen. He would spend the rest of his life making this up to her. If she lived that little voice in his head said. No, she had to live. He could not, would not think, otherwise.

"You mustn't blame yourself, Beck. If anyone, I should have known how she could be after listening to Carolyn. But it is neither of our faults. The fault lies in your mother. And that leads us the crux of it all. What is to be done now?" asked Worth. He knew what he wanted to do, but locking someone in a dungeon somewhere was bound to be against the law. Newgate prison perhaps, but then the stigma of it, for there was bound to be someone of the *ton* to find out.

Nate gazed out the window watching as dusk fell. Tonight was his wedding night. How he had looked forward to lying with Dulcey again. It had been difficult the last few days, not being able to love her as he had at the cottage. It had only increased his appetite for her. Now, he stood wondering, if he would ever again hold her in his arms and taste again that sweet love she gave so willingly. She had become a part of him, a part of him he now realized he could not do without. The thought that she may be dying, froze his soul to its very core.

Worth stood by Nate's side waiting, watching. He had never experienced the connection he had witnessed between Nate and Dulcey. He had envied his friend but had been happy for him to have found such a love. He knew it to be rare and to be treasured. To have it taken way so soon and by one's own mother, he, Worth had no idea what he would do. Yes, he did, but it was not his decision to make.

"So you believe, Leta is no longer in her right mind."

"Yes. But because of her devotion to your mother, I still think, believe, she may still be a danger to Dulcey. I don't think she would harm anyone else, but her obsession with Dulcey puts Dulcey still in danger, in my opinion. Yet, should any of this get out and the gossip mongers get hold of it, it could be detrimental to the family." Worth thought of Abby. This could affect her if not now, then when she was older.

"You're thinking of Abby?" asked Nate. She had been on his mind, as well. Peggy had informed him earlier, Miss Franny had explained to Abby, Dulcey had gotten sick but Abby still wanted to see her. Here was another life his mother had tried to damage with her constant harping.

"Yes," answered Worth. "For the good of the Shefley name, we need to keep this as quiet as possible. For Abby's sake, for Dulcey's sake, as well."

Nate nodded. "As much as I would like to throw them into Newgate prison or ship them off to the nether ends of the earth and never deal with them ever again, I know that is not the solution." Nate wiped a hand over his face in frustration and let out a deep sigh. He wanted to send her to the some far corner of the earth. Somewhere so far she would never be able to touch their lives ever again. Suddenly, it came to mind. He knew of a place, a place he knew his mother would hate and would be the nether ends of the world, as far as his mother was concerned.

"We do own a property up near the Scottish border just past Newcastle. I have been to it once, several years ago. It is isolated and very far from London. Mother would hate it. Very rustic, if I remember right." He was beginning to truly enjoy the idea of sending his mother there. A just deserve, as far as he was concerned.

Worth smiled. He knew the Countess loved the London scene, the constant gossip among the *ton*. She thrived on it. This she would an unbearable punishment to her. "That could very well be the answer to the problem. She will hate the idea."

"Exactly. I want her miserable! As miserable, as she has made all of us, all her life," seethed Nate. He turned to Worth. "Another favor of you, Worth?"

"Anything, Beck."

"I need you to inform my mother of my decision and to see to her escort there. Once there, make certain she is never allowed to leave unless under my direction. At the moment, I can never in my lifetime see that happening." He did not want to have anything more to do with his mother. He was afraid of what he would do to her, if he did see her in the frame of mind he was in. He was furious with her and could not be held responsible, if he encountered her.

"I would be most pleased to see to that chore for you. You do know, I hold no regard for your mother," stated Worth. He wanted Beck to understand, he had strong feelings against his mother, as well.

Nate nodded. "Yes, that is why I know I can trust you to do it. She cannot manipulate you into doing her bidding. I don't care how you do it. I just want her out of this house as soon as possible."

"I will see to it myself, Beck. You take care of Dulcey. I firmly believe she will survive this and you and she will have your happiness." He had to believe it to be so.

Nate took a deep breath. "I have to believe that. I cannot bear to think otherwise. I cannot lose her." He turned and gazed lovingly at Dulcey lying in her bed. No, he could not lose her.

Worth put his hand on his friend's shoulder. "You will not. Now let me see to this problem of yours. Rest assured I will take care of it."

Nate followed Worth to the door just as Dr. Meade entered.

"I have something else to give her, m'lord. This should counteract any of the nightshade that remains in her system," explained Dr. Meade.

"I will come back before we leave to make certain all is well," said Worth.

Nate nodded and went to Dulcey's side to assist Dr. Meade. He prayed the good doctor knew what he was about. It seemed the good doctor had learned much from Dulcey and her grandmother. He had to put his faith in that.

~~~~~~~~~~~~~~~~

Nate was certain he didn't want to see his mother. He could see nothing good coming from meeting with her. He was so angry. He wanted to shake her till he made her feel the fear that gripped his soul. Dulcey was alive, but no thanks to her. When Worth had explained to him, how she had been involved, he wanted to scream. And now her insistence, she had to talk with him before she left. No, he had nothing to say to her.

But then on second thought, he wasn't going to pass up the chance to make her understand what she had done. He stepped out of Dulcey's room. He left Peggy at her bedside. He would take a few minutes to make his mother understand exactly how he felt, how badly she had hurt him, how badly she had hurt Dulcey

As she came walking to him, her head held high like she hadn't been responsible for any of this. All he saw was a manipulative bitter woman, who would never be happy and would never let anybody else be happy. He had to convince himself, he was looking at his mother, the woman who had given him birth. At the moment, he couldn't see that woman. All he could see was the woman, the cause of why his wife lay beyond the door behind him, fighting for her life. A life that was meant to be lived with him and Abby. His hands itched to take her and shake her.

"Nathaniel, I had to see you, to explain to you," the countess began. She had to make her son understand. It had all been a grave misunderstanding. Leta was sick and didn't know what she had done. She had to make him understand, she had nothing to do with any of this. Yes, she did not like this Dulcey woman. Yes, she thought this Dulcey woman was not the right woman for her son or for their family. No matter, what the letter the Baron wrote, it would not undo the fact, this woman was a witch.

"There is no explanation you can give me Mother that will make any of this right. Your maid tried to murder my wife because you were upset with her. Your constant harping that my wife was a witch, that we were all in danger, drove your maid to protect you. I believe, I have the facts, do I not?" His words were terse. He was having a most difficult time in controlling what he really wanted to do to her.

"Nathaniel, please-----" she began again. The anger she saw in his eyes frightened her. But it wasn't only anger, it was disgust, it was outright loathing. She could feel it like a blast of frigid air hitting her full on. He was just upset at the moment.

"You are to pack your bags, Mother. Worth and several men from here will escort you and Leta to Northcutt Hall. You and Leta will be under constant surveillance and should either of you move off the property, I will have charges brought against both of you." He could no longer bear the sight of her. He turned to go. She put her hand on his arm to stop him.

Her touch nearly pushed him over the edge. "Take your hand off of me, Mother."

"Nathaniel, please I never meant for any of this to happen, believe me," pleaded the countess. "Northcutt Hall, if I remember correctly is in the middle of nowhere. It is like you are banishing me to a life of seclusion. I was not directly responsible for any of this. This is much too harsh, Nathaniel. I will go back to Shefley Hall instead. All my things are there, Nathaniel. It is my home, and I will not allow you to turn me out of my own home. " No, Nathaniel must listen to reason. He had always been a biddable boy. Surely this was a decision he had made under duress.

"I will see to it your things are packed and shipped to you. Northcutt Hall is your home now and under the circumstances, I can send you wherever the hell I want to."

"Nathaniel, do not use that foul language with me. I am not responsible for any of this. I see no reason why I should be punished such as this. Please, be reasonable about this." He could not be doing this, he simply could not.

She was lucky it was only foul language he was using. "The fact, that you were not directly responsible for this, does not matter to me, Mother. Directly or indirectly, it happened and I can never forgive you for that. You destroyed Caroline and Grayson and now you have tried to destroy my life because of your arrogance. I will not allow you anywhere where you can destroy someone else. You had better pray all the way to Northcutt Hall that Dulcey survives this because heaven help you, if she doesn't." Nate shuddered because he could not think along those lines. "Good bye, Mother," Nate turned and walked back into Dulcey's room and closed the door in his mother's face. He could no longer abide the sight of her or be in her presence. Peggy still sat at Ducley's side just as he had left moments before.

~~~~~~~~~~~~~~~~

Lady Shefley sighed deeply and turned and walked back to her room. Simmons followed her. Nathaniel was upset. Once he got over the shock of all of this, he would change his mind. He would not hold to this imprisonment. He was just upset. He would calm down in a few months. After all, none of this was of her doing. Leta had acted on her own accord. It was not her fault that Leta was so devoted to her. No, she firmly believed in time, Nathaniel would see that. Till then she would bid her time. She firmly believed he would eventually see the truth. She had not been behind any of this.

She shuddered at the thought of Northcutt Hall. She had never been there but she did know it was rather out of the way. Very far from London. She would just have to keep up her correspondence with some of her old friends until this ridiculousness was over with. Nathaniel could not stay angry with her for very long. He would come to his senses. She was his mother, after all.

She turned and walked back down the hall to her room where Leta awaited her, hopeful her packing was complete, though she did not understand why Worth wanted to leave now. She hated traveling in the night, but Worth was being adamant. Talking to Worth had been impossible. He blamed her for Caroline's death. He had to have colored Nathaniel's opinion in all of this. She did not like Worth and did not understand why he was escorting her. She truly wished now, she had been more persuasive when Nathaniel had insisted they come here all those weeks ago. Then they never would have met this witch woman.

Chapter 18

The sweetest of all sounds is that of the voice
Of the woman we love.

Jean de la Bruyere

It was morning, the sun shone brightly through the windows, but nothing had changed. Dulcey lay still as she had throughout the night. Peggy had brought him a breakfast tray but it lay untouched on the chest by the door. Several times through the night he had dosed off only to dream in the predawn hours he had lost her. He sat by the side of her bed and held her hand against his cheek. He brought it to his lips and kissed her palm. He loved the response it brought forth from her. But at the moment, there was no response. He hung his head.

No, he could not, would not give up. She never would.

He leaned over and whispered. "My love, please come back to me. You are my love. You are my life. You have made me whole. I did not know I was not, until I met you. Perhaps, you are a witch, for you have truly bewitched me. But I think I agree more with what you told Abby. You are a fairy princess, my fairy princess. Abby misses you. Please, my love, she has lost so much. She cannot lose you. Neither can I. Oh, my fairy princess, come back to me."

But there was no response. Just the steady sound of her breathing. He took comfort in that. She was still alive. As long as there was still breath, there was life within her, there was hope.

A soft tap on the door interrupted his thoughts. Peggy had left moments ago. It would not be her returning so soon, besides Peggy did not knock. Nate opened the door. Abby stood in the hall just outside of the door. She looked up at Nate with those big blue eyes of hers and the most woe be gone look on her face. He should have taken a few moments to reassure Abby.

"Where's Miss Franny?" he asked softly.

"I accidently spilled my milk," explained Abby, as though that explained everything.

Nate smiled. He saw Miss Franny hurrying down the hall and raised his hand to halt her.

"Are you worried about Dulcey?" asked Nate.

Abby bit her bottom lip and nodded her head.

"She's still sleeping," answered Nate.

"Can I see her Uncle Nate? I promise, I won't make any noise to wake her up. I'll be very quiet, I promise," Abby pleaded. She was scared.

Nate smiled. He knew how worried she was. She didn't understand it all. He wished he didn't, but he did.

"Just for a moment. Dulcey needs her rest."

Abby nodded.

"All right then. Be very quiet," instructed Nate as he took her small hand in his and lead her back into the room. Miss Franny waited outside in the hall.

Slowly, he walked over to Dulcey's bedside, watching Abby carefully. He stopped.

Abby looked up to Nate and asked softly, "She's sleeping?"

Nate nodded.

"Who's gonna make Dulcey better? She talks to the fairies and they tell her. Have the fairies come to make her better?" she whispered. She didn't understand.

Nate sighed. How did he explain it to Abby when he didn't understand himself?

"This is what I know. Dulcey knows how to help people with her medicines."

"The fairies teached her. She told me so Uncle Nate when you were sick," explained Abby.

"Yes, Poppet, I know. And she has taught Dr. Meade, who is taking care of her now."

Abby nodded. "Can I talk to her? Will she hear me?"

"I've been talking to her. I believe she hears us. She's resting, getting better."

Abby nodded again. "You rested too, Uncle Nate and got better."

Nate smiled and nodded. That just a little over a fortnight ago. It seemed more like a lifetime ago.

Abby leaned over to Dulcey. "Uncle Nate said you're gonna get better. I told the moon last night, to tell the fairies, they needed to come and give you their medicine." She took off her moonstone necklace and put it on Dulcey chest. "This will bring the fairies to you. And when you're better you can give it back to me." She leaned over and gave Dulcey a kiss on the cheek. She turned to Nate and said, "Now, the fairies will come for sure and make her all better."

Nate could only nod. The tears in his eyes and the lump in his throat made speaking impossible for him. He took her hand and escorted her to the door where Miss Franny awaited her. At the door, Abby turned and hugged Nate then followed Miss Franny down the hall assured she had called the fairies to take care of Dulcey now.

Nate turned and walked back to Dulcey's side. The moonstone necklace Dulcey had given Abby still lay on her chest. He rubbed the moonstone between his fingers.

"Any fairies out there? Abby believes you are. Please, do your magic and bring my Dulcey back to us. She is very important to us. She is our fairy princess." He placed the moonstone necklace back on her chest and laid his head on the bed beside her and let the tears flow.

Dulcey slowly opened her eyes. Her body ached. She didn't understand why. She sighed. She was lying in her bed. Why her bed? She remembered her wedding. The ceremony was beautiful. Nate had looked so handsome standing at the altar waiting for her. So many of the town's people had filled the church, but the breakfast that followed afterwards was fit for the king. Evers and the staff had decorated the grand ball room with such love and had truly out done themselves. She smiled as she remembered. She had felt like the fairy princess she had told Abby about in her nightly stories.

She turned her head. Nate was asleep sitting in the dark green winged chair at her bedside, her hand clasped in his. Why was he sitting there?

Why was he---- and suddenly she remembered--- the glass of champagne----the vision. She jerked her hand in response to the vision.

Nate immediately awakened and found himself staring into those beautiful pixie green eyes of Dulcey's. That they stared back at him filled his heart with joy. She was awake. She was alive. He let out a deep sigh of relief and smiled. "Hello, my love." He brought her hand to his lips and kissed the palm.

It sent shivers through every part of her. She remembered those feelings. Dulcey smiled back. "Hello, my husband." She whispered back.

"Have I told you how beautiful you are and how much I love you?" He finally felt like he could breathe again. The weight in his chest was gone.

Dulcey smiled and nodded, then turned serious. Nate looked tired, his hair disheveled like he had run his hands through it over and over again. His cravat was missing. He looked haggard. The stubble of his beard shadowed his face. Something was amiss. "I think, I need to have a long talk with Simmons. You, my husband look like hell."

Nate chuckled. She was concerned about him, about how he looked. "That's because I have been in hell these past two days. Simmons has tried, believe me, my love."

Dulcey looked puzzled. "Why?"

"Do you remember anything? Anything of what happened at our wedding breakfast?"

Dulcey nodded and looked away. Yes, she did remember. That memory is what had made her jerk her hand out of his.

How did she tell him, his mother had tried to poison her? This was his mother. It was so clear. She saw Leta, his mother's maid place two drops in her glass. She saw it as clear as if Leta did it right in front of her eyes. The champagne barely touched her lips when she saw the vision.

"You saw who poisoned you?" asked Nate. He had to know, if she knew.

Dulcey nodded. "Leta." She looked to Nate for his reaction and found none. "You know?"

Nate nodded. "Worth found out. She says Mother was not aware of her plans. Mother says she knew nothing of it. I tend to believe them. Why, I'm not sure."

"Did Leta say why?" Dulcey asked, curious. She had had no dealings with Leta. Why would she do this, if not for his mother's sake?

"Yes. Leta has been with my mother since mother was a young girl," explained Nate. "She has always been devoted to my mother. I believe she has no family. Mother is everything to her."

Dulcey nodded her head in understanding.

Nate continued. "Mother kept going on and on about you, how you were a witch. She even asked the servants about you because my mother asked her to. But none of them would tell her anything. So all she had to go on was what mother said. She hated seeing my mother in such distress. Mother mentioned on several occasions how everything would go back to normal, if you were to suddenly disappear. If you were no longer here, all could go back to normal. With you out of the way, she thought mother would have nothing to worry about again. It seemed, she became obsessed with the idea. Mother's harping on the fact that you were a witch and all of us were going to burn because of it, frightened her. She feared Mother would burn. I'm afraid in her old age, she has become unbalanced. She believed you were a danger to us all. "

Dulcey sighed. She should have seen it. Actually, she had to a certain extent but she had not paid attention to it as she should have. The wedding, marrying Nate had been more important and all the good had overshadowed the bad.

"What has happened to her?" Dulcey did not want her harmed, even though Leta had tried to kill her. She felt sorry for the poor woman. To be so devoted to a person such as the Countess, must have made for a miserable existence.

Nate looked away for a moment, hesitant, but decided it was best to tell Dulcey the truth. "Mother was insistent. Worth and I decided to allow her to stay with mother. I informed Mother, I could no longer trust her or Leta. Mother and Leta have been banished to Northcutt Hall near the Scottish border. It is one of the properties that belong to Shefley name. She is to be as far away from all of us as I could possibly send her.

Worth and I both thought this was the best solution for all involved. We did not want this information getting about, especially in London. I had to consider Abby, as well. I have left detail instructions that her behavior and Leta's is to be monitored. I am to get monthly reports until further notice."

Nate looked at Dulcey for understanding. As much as he wanted to kill them both when he was first told, he knew he could not, after all this was his mother.

"I hope you can understand why I did it this way?"

Dulcey nodded. How could she not. It was an uncomfortable situation. "Nate, she is your mother. Yes, I understand. How is Abby with all of this?"

Poor Abby, she thought. To be frightened by her collapse and then to have her grandmother sent away. Poor child must be so confused.

Nate smiled. Her first concern was with Abby. That was so like Dulcey.

"Abby has been especially worried about you. She has escaped from Miss Franny several times over the last couple of days to come here to sit and talk to you. At first we tried to stop her, but Dr. Meade thought it would do you good to hear her voice. She will be most pleased to see you awake as will everyone about. We have all been worried."

"I will be glad to see Abby and reassure her that I am recovering. I'm certain she has missed our nightly stories." She seemed to remember Abby's voice and Nate's calling her.

"She has not once mentioned your stories, but she did give your moonstone necklace back to you, temporarily, till you woke up. She believed it would help the fairies find you and make you well," replied Nate. No matter what Nate or Dr. Meade had told her, she had continually showed up at Dulcey's side determined the fairies would come and make Dulcey well.

Dulcey smiled. "She must have truly been frightened."

Nate brought her hand to his lips again. "Yes. So was I. I was so afraid I was going to lose you." How did he explain to her, the terror that gripped his soul when he thought he had lost her? Now looking at her smiling face, everything had changed in that heartbeat.

Dulcey smiled. She sensed his fear. "You were never going to lose me. I was here all this time." She needed to reassure him, she was here. She had never left him, even though he may have thought she did.

Nate wanted to tell her how worried he had been, how worried everyone had been but now that she was awake and talking, he could not bear to tell how serious it had been. Let her believe as she must.

Dulcey continued, "While I was asleep, mother, father and Lord James came to visit with me. I stood with them at the edge of the bed, looking at me lying in the bed. They told me they loved me but I could not stay with them. I needed to come back to you."

Nate raised an eyebrow. "Your mother, your father?" The poison must have made her hallucinate.

Dulcey nodded. "Yes. Lord James, as well. I think Grammy was nearby, too." She could tell from the look on his face, he did not believe her. But they had come to her in a vision. They felt as real to her as he did. She wondered if he would ever understand the forces that surrounded her and brought her visions. Maybe one day, in time.

"They told me, I needed to come back to you. You needed me. They said, we would see our children's children?" Dulcey smiled at the thought. She would have Nate's children. She liked the thought of that.

"Our children's children?" asked Nate. That meant he and Dulcey would have children and they would be together for a long time. That he would gladly believe.

"Yes, our children's children. That is why I needed to come back to you," explained Dulcey. She wanted him to know, all they had told her. She wanted him looking toward the future.

"Then I'm glad they gave you back to me." Nate would believe anything she told him at the moment. She was back with him and that was all that mattered.

Dulcey sighed. She was tired. "Will you come to bed and hold me, Nate? I'm sure my bed is more comfortable than that chair."

Nate smiled. "An invitation by a beautiful woman to join her in her bed. How can I refuse? Of course, my love."

Dulcey smiled. He had said almost the same thing when he was ill back at the cottage. He wouldn't remember but she did. He was meant to be with her.

Nate blew out the candle at the bedside, crawled into bed beside her and wrapped her safely in his arms. It felt so good to have her in his arms again. It felt like his heart had come home to where it was meant to be.

Dulcey snuggled so she lay spooned against him. It felt so good to have his arms about her. She remembered the time at the cottage, the feel of his body against hers. She longed for those feelings again but she knew she would have to wait a few more days.

"I love you, Nathaniel Beckham," said Dulcey but she could feel herself falling asleep, knowing she was safe and secure in Nate's arms.

As Nate closed his eyes, he glanced at the foot of the bed thinking of what Dulcey had told him. There stood a two men with a woman between them floating just passed the edge of the bed. He quickly opened his eyes only to see darkness there.

Nate smiled and just in case, he whispered, "Thank you for sending her back to me."

"Umm?" murmured Dulcey almost asleep.

"Nothing, my love," answered Nate as he cradled her closer to him and kissed the top of her head. How good it felt to have her in his arms. He finally felt whole again. The other half of his heart lay cradled in his arms. Dulcey was going to be all right. Hadn't they said, they would see their children's children. Nate closed his eyes with a smile on his face, Dulcey safely in his arms. Tomorrow, he

241

would see about the pleasure of the beginning of those children they just talked about. Yes, he would.

Epilogue

Christmas Eve one year later.

As you give love, you will have love.
                    Lord Alfred Tennyson

Nate walked out of his study and down the hall in time to watch Evers direct several of the footmen as they brought the yule log in. He raised his eyebrows in surprise.

"Did we get one large enough Evers?" asked Nate

Evers smiled. "Lady Dulcey ordered that we get biggest one that would fit in the fireplace, my lord."

Nate laughed. That sounded very much like what Dulcey wanted. He stopped and sniffed. He looked at Evers in question, then smiled. "Gingerbread planks?"

"Lady Dulcey, Miss Abby and Miss Franny are in the kitchen."

Nate shook his head. So much for his attempt to have Dulcey take it easy today and let the staff handle everything that needed to be done. He should have known better. She would not listen to his advice. "I'll be in the kitchen, Evers."

"Of course, my lord," nodded Evers with a smile.

Nate walked into the kitchen. The sweet smell of gingerbread planks cooking permeated the air. Abby had flour in her hair as usual. Miss Franny was helping stamp the planks. Dulcey was across the kitchen deep in conversation with Cook.

Dulcey looked up when she felt Nate's presence and smiled as she watched him walk over to her. It still surprised her at times that this man before her was her husband.

Nate nodded to Cook as she walked away. Lightly, he kissed Dulcey's lips. "I thought you agreed to take it easy with the Christmas preparations and rest."

Dulcey smiled back at him. "I am. I rested all morning," but reached behind her and rubbed her lower back.

Nate stood behind her and had her lean back against him. Nate rubbed her overgrown belly that carried his child. He raised an eyebrow in question at her answer.

"I'm just over seeing the gingerbread planks. It is tradition," stated Dulcey. "Cook, Abby and Franny are doing all the work. I promise."

Abby walked up to Nate munching on a gingerbread plank, "It's tradition, Uncle Nate."

Nate raised his hands in surrender. "Very well, who am I to mess with tradition?" He took a piece of gingerbread plank from Abby's hand and popped it in his mouth. He smiled. There was something to be said about tradition. These gingerbread planks were delicious.

"Am I getting another present tomorrow, Uncle Nate?" asked Abby as she looked at the small pug puppy asleep in the basket on the chair. Uncle Nate and Aunt Dulcey had given her the puppy as her present a few days ago. It was going to be the best Christmas ever.

"I don't know, Poppet, maybe," replied Nate.

Abby nodded. "I like Honey. She is the bestest present ever."

Nate smiled. It had been Dulcey's idea to get Abby a puppy. She thought if Abby had something of her own to take care of, it would be easier for Abby, when the new baby came at the end of January.

"I think there might be another present or two for you tomorrow, Poppet," answered Dulcey.

"I do know that a present came in from Uncle Colin," said Nate.

"Can I open Uncle Colin's one now?" asked Abby.

"No, not until tomorrow. Then you can open all of them," explained Nate. He looked at Abby, remembering last Christmas and the snowstorm. Abby had blossomed under Dulcey's care. No longer was she the shy little girl.

Abby nodded and walked back to the gingerbread planks on the table grabbing another one to eat. He could not correct her. They were so good. They were hard to resist.

"Miss Franny can you take over with Abby, while I take Dulcey upstairs to rest and put her feet up like she is supposed to?" asked Nate looking at Dulcey as though daring her to argue with him.

Dulcey smiled. Nate was so overly protective of her and the baby.

"Of course, my lord. Abby and I will bring tea upstairs when it's time."

Abby nodded her mouth still filled with gingerbread.

Nate took Dulcey's arm and guided her up the stairs to her sitting room. He made her lie on the chaise and then placed a wrap about her legs. "Now you are to rest until tea time. I plan on sitting right here to make sure that you do."

"You are a tyrant," teased Dulcey.

Nate smiled. "No, just a mere mortal in love with his fairy princess." He leaned over and lightly kissed her lips. He sat down in his chair bedside the chaise.

Dulcey just smiled at him. It was the same routine every afternoon. "Did I hear you tell Abby, Worth sent her a Christmas present?" asked Dulcey.

They had gotten sporadic correspondence from Worth over the last few months. It had appeared Worth had met his red head and she had indeed led him on a very merry chase from Scotland to London and back to Scotland again.

"Yes, and that reminds me. He sent a letter with it." Nate removed the letter from his coat pocket and gave it to her to read. "He mentions you in it. Said to tell you, yes, he is now a believer. It has been a merry chase but it is at its end. He said they will stop for a visit on their way back to Stonebrooke."

Dulcey laughed. "I shall be very pleased to meet this woman who has led our Worth on his merry chase. So he believes me now. And what about you, my love?"

"Me?" asked Nate. "My love, I have always believed you."

Dulcey laughed again. "Only some of the time. But you will when the babe comes, when our son comes."

When Dulcey had informed him she was with child, she had also informed him, she was carrying their son. He had not believed her at first. She had laughed at his non-belief. But when everyone did not question her when she said she carried his son, he had been told she was the one, all the ladies came to, when they wanted to know whether they were giving birth to a boy or a girl. Slowly, he had begun to believe.

"Then how fares our lil James today?" asked Nate.

She had been so thrilled when he suggested they name the babe, James, if it was a boy. It was the only name that seemed suitable. Since she appeared so certain it was a boy, the last month or so, he had begun to call him James.

Dulcey sighed. "He is doing fine. He moves often." She rubbed her swollen belly. "He will be here soon. Our first born."

Nate placed his hand over hers. He felt the babe move beneath his touch. It amazed him every time. He looked at Dulcey and smiled. The love he felt in his heart knew no bounds. Here before him sat the woman he loved with all of his heart, the woman who was the very heart of him, the woman who carried his child.

He smiled. "Yes, and we shall see our children's children, you and I, my love. That I do believe."

The End

ABOUT THIS AUTHOR

This writer has written all of her life. As an only child for the first fifteen years of her life, she learned story telling could keep her and her friends entertained. But it was only near the end of her nursing career and retirement was on the horizon that she picked up her writing again and began to devote her time and energy onto this new adventure. And an adventure it has been.

She is an avid reader mostly romance novels with historical and regency being her favorites. Her greatest influences were/are Kathleen Woodiwiss, Laurie McBain, and Johanna Lindsey. They made her believe in romance during a dark time in her life. She nearly gave up after her first endeavor, but with the support and help of her family, friends and fellow authors, she trudges on. Besides writing has become that lost love once found again and one does not let go of. There are too many stories that were begun and never finished in all those years to let go now.

Born in the city of New Orleans, she grew up along the bayous of South Louisiana. Though she has traveled extensively, she will always call south Louisiana home. She now lives with her husband of nearly 33 years in their home on two wooded acres or on their houseboat on the banks of Bayou Terrebonne. Her three daughters and their families live nearby but her son and his family live in Texas. When not writing, most of her time is occupied by her 13 grandchildren. She and her husband have always loved to travel and now that they are both retired have and plan on doing more once their Airstream camper has been restored. Accompanying them on their travels are the three pugs---Kahlua, Maggie and Lillie, her writing compatriots.

www.ingramcontent.com/pod-product-compliance
Lightning Source LLC
Chambersburg PA
CBHW071145170626
46809CB00002B/778